J.H. MONCRIEFF

THE RESTORATION

This is a **FLAME TREE PRESS** book

Text copyright © 2021 J.H. Moncrieff

FLAME TREE PRESS
6 Melbray Mews, London, SW6 3NS, UK
flametreepress.com

US sales, distribution and warehouse:
Simon & Schuster
simonandschuster.biz

UK distribution and warehouse:
Marston Book Services Ltd
marston.co.uk

Publisher's Note: This is a work of fiction. Names, characters, places, and
incidents are a product of the author's imagination. Locales and public names
are sometimes used for atmospheric purposes. Any resemblance to actual
people, living or dead, or to businesses, companies, events, institutions, or
locales is completely coincidental.

Thanks to the Flame Tree Press team, including:
Taylor Bentley, Frances Bodiam, Federica Ciaravella, Don D'Auria,
Chris Herbert, Josie Karani, Molly Rosevear, Mike Spender,
Cat Taylor, Maria Tissot, Nick Wells, Gillian Whitaker.

The cover is created by Flame Tree Studio with
thanks to Nik Keevil and Shutterstock.com.
The font families used are Avenir and Bembo.

Flame Tree Press is an imprint of Flame Tree Publishing Ltd
flametreepublishing.com

A copy of the CIP data for this book is available from the British Library
and the Library of Congress.

HB ISBN: 978-1-78758-705-2
US PB ISBN: 978-1-78758-703-8
UK PB ISBN: 978-1-78758-704-5
ebook ISBN: 978-1-78758-706-9

Printed and bound in Great Britain by Clays Ltd, Elcograf S.p.A.

J.H. MONCRIEFF

THE
RESTORATION

FLAME TREE PRESS
London & New York

For Thomas McLeod,
with thanks and gratitude

PROLOGUE

It was love at first sight.

Terri thought she'd done a decent job of concealing her reaction, but she must have been fooling herself, because Miss Vandermere turned to her and smiled.

"It's gorgeous, isn't it?"

It was. Gorgeous, and a whole lot of work. The older woman hadn't been kidding about that. The red-brick, three-storey house loomed over them, doing its best to appear imposing, and to an amateur, Terri bet it would look breathtaking. An amateur wouldn't notice the fine cracks along the stone foundation, the way the wraparound porch wasn't quite level, the cloudy windows, and that trim – the color was all wrong for the time period.

"When was the trim last painted?"

Vandermere frowned as she stared up at the mansion. "Dreadful, isn't it? That was the committee's contribution two summers ago. Wrangled a high school football team into doing it, and some of those fools nearly killed themselves, from what I understand. I *told* them the color wasn't right, not that anyone listens to me."

Terri was surprised. As the last living descendant, Vandermere *owned* Glenvale – didn't she? Best to find out now, before she'd undertaken a lot of work that wasn't sanctioned.

"But the estate belongs to you, doesn't it?"

Vandermere flapped her hand. "Well, yes and no. Since I hired the committee to run the museum, I agreed to give them a say in whatever happens to the house. I won't be around forever, and I have no real use for the place. No one wants an old lady hovering over them, interfering in their business. I've mostly tried to stay out of things, but hiring you – that was my decision."

"I'm sure they don't mind," Terri said because it seemed expected, not because she had any clue whether it was true or not. She was relieved she'd be dealing with Vandermere directly. Judging by her remark about the color of the house, the woman had good instincts. Terri had dealt with committees before – they were par for the course with old estates like this one – but it had never been her preference. As the cliché goes, it's impossible to please everyone.

When she craned her neck to see the roof, a flicker of movement caught her eye. In one of the attic rooms, a curtain twitched. She peered at the window high above them, using a hand to shield her eyes from the afternoon sun. "Is there someone in the house?"

"No, I shouldn't think so. We're closed for the summer, so it's the perfect time to start restoring her to her former glory." Vandermere's brow creased for a moment as she studied the structure. "I suppose Gertie could be hanging around. She loves the place. It's always difficult to convince her it's time to close up shop."

"Gertie?"

"She was the house manager. Organized the staff, managed the registration desk and greeted the public when they arrived for their tours, things like that," the woman said, taking a set of keys from her purse. The sight of the ornate iron keys thrilled Terri. She'd never get over her love affair with these old places – she was hooked. "Sadly, I had to lay her off. This economy has been hard on everyone. It was probably for the best. She's very efficient, but I don't think she ever quite warmed to me." She glanced up at the window. "We never did get her keys back, though. If someone's here, it must be her."

"Would she be in the attic?" Terri wasn't sure why she asked, but something had bothered her about that flutter of curtain. It struck her as furtive, *sneaky*.

"No, I shouldn't think so. Why do you ask?" Vandermere led the way up the wooden steps of the porch, which creaked under her stacked heels. Terri winced at the audible warning, picturing the rotting wood giving way and the lady of the house breaking her ankle. No coat of paint could hide that sound. She'd have to do something about the stairs before her daughter arrived in Pennsylvania.

"I saw the curtains move in one of the attic rooms. It looked like someone was watching us."

"Oh, the attic rooms are closed. The committee uses them for storage, but it's a bunch of old junk, mostly. You can barely get past the door." Vandermere's faded blue eyes studied her face. "It must have been the wind."

Right. Wind in a closed-up room.

"You know how old houses can be," she went on. "They're drafty."

"Yes, of course." Terri's initial excitement was tempered with concern now. Why was Vandermere lying? Was this 'Gertie' unhinged? Was the former house manager going to be a problem? Or was there something else wrong with the estate? The work required on the house was extensive, but the figure that had been quoted was staggering. Terri was surprised the job had remained available as long as it had, long enough for her to find out about it and snag it. Already, the paranoid side of her brain was working overtime. *Maybe there's a reason no one else wanted it. Maybe Gertie is the reason.*

"Are you an imaginative woman, Ms. Foxworth?"

The question startled her, and Terri was unsure how to answer. "How do you mean?"

The woman sighed. "There is something I didn't tell you on the phone."

Oh no. Here it comes. This is where I find out that my duties involve humoring a deranged ex-employee. "What is it?"

"You're not the first person I've hired for this job, I'm afraid."

"No?" Part of her was offended. What about all the wonderful things Vandermere had said about her work, about how she was the *only* one capable of restoring Glenvale to its former splendor? The other half was resigned. Sometimes having a paranoid mind was an advantage. It kept you from being shocked.

"There have been others." Seeing Terri's expression, which Terri could guess was a mixture of horror and dismay, the older woman amended, "Not *many* others, but a few. I didn't lie to you on the phone. I *do* think you're the only person for the job. I simply didn't think we could afford you."

Another lie. You didn't get this rich by being dumb, and even though Vandermere had inherited her fortune, she'd managed it well and increased it exponentially through wise investments and holdings. A woman like this would have done her research, just as Terri had. She would have known the going rate for this kind of job, and deliberately tripled it. But why? Was this Gertie that much of a problem? A heaviness settled on her shoulders. It wasn't the money; there would be other work. Well, not *just* the money. Dallas had been so excited about spending a year together in an old mansion, and Terri hated the thought of disappointing her daughter. Though she was ten, Dallas was already showing signs of adolescence. It was hard to get her excited about anything.

"What happened to them?" Terri asked, bracing herself. Whatever it was, it had to be bad to get them to walk away from that much money. Gertie must be a terror, maybe even homicidal. She shuddered at the idea of having her daughter around that kind of madness. Good thing she'd noticed the curtain. If she hadn't, would Vandermere have told her?

"They had too much imagination." The woman's nose wrinkled as if she'd smelled something foul, as if having an imagination was the worst possible crime. It was confusing, to say the least.

"It's...kind of a requirement for the job, Miss Vandermere. You have to be able to see these estates as they once were in order to restore them, and some of these places require more imagination than others. So far, Glenvale looks like it's in fairly decent shape, but I'm sure there have been some renovations made over the years that will need correcting."

She'd seen it a million times. Beautiful woodwork covered with layers of heavy paint, ornate grates hidden under linoleum, those lovely iron keys replaced by moderate plastic cards or, even worse, buzzer systems.

"I'm not referring to your vision for the house, Ms. Foxworth. That isn't the sort of imagination I'm talking about."

"I'm afraid I don't understand." What did imagination have to do with an insane house manager? Had the others imagined Gertie to be worse than she was? Glenvale was beginning to seem like more trouble than it was worth.

"You know how old houses are." The woman leaned against a column, brushing a strand of silvery hair away from her eyes. "They make strange noises. Things shift. Radiators clank. There are drafts."

Vandermere studied her face again, clearly trying to gauge her reaction. Terri decided to be direct. She didn't know any other way to be, and in this case, she had nothing to lose, because one foot was out the door. She was already deciding how to break the news to Dallas. "You were honest with me when we spoke on the phone." *Except for the 'you're the only one' bit.* "Please be honest with me now. What are you telling me?"

"They thought the house was haunted. Surely you see how ridiculous that is." Vandermere laughed, but it sounded forced. *Looked* forced. Not a hint of a smile touched her eyes. "All old homes have their quirks. You know that."

It wasn't a statement, but a question, a plea. *You won't abandon me like the others, will you?* Terri's instinct was to say no, of course she wouldn't. No ghost story was going to scare her away from paying for her daughter's first year of college. But still, it troubled her. Restoration experts tended to be creative, yes. However, like Vandermere said, they were familiar with old homes and their quirks. They knew them intimately. They weren't the type to leave a job because of a few drafts or radiators clanking. "Do *you* think Glenvale is haunted?"

Vandermere met her eyes without flinching. "No, I don't."

"That's good enough for me. I'd love to see the house."

Brightening, the woman strode to the door and unlocked it with a minimum amount of fumbling. She had to have been close to eighty, but her hands were steady. As Terri followed Vandermere inside, she wondered what she'd gotten herself into. It wasn't too late to say no, of course. Never too late until the first check was cashed and the first sledgehammer slung. But in another way, it was. She was already in love with the house and excited about the possibilities. Her fingers itched to lift that sagging porch to its rightful place and to get rid of that nasty blue paint. The estate spoke to her, whispering in her ear. Glenvale wanted to be returned to its natural ivory trim, or perhaps a nice, pale yellow. Its lines demanded elegance, nothing too garish. She *knew* this house. Everything was going to be fine.

But if black goo started dripping from the walls, she was getting the hell out of there, exorbitant fee be damned.

CHAPTER ONE

"I want this room."

"Really?" Terri attempted to see the space through her daughter's eyes. It was the smallest of the mansion's bedrooms, complete with bubbling, stained wallpaper, pockmarked floors, and a musty smell. "Are you sure? The other rooms are a lot nicer."

The girl nodded, her ponytail swinging. "Uh-huh. I like this one." She folded her arms, as if preparing herself for a fight, but Terri was hardly going to fight her on this.

"The other ones are bigger, but if you want this room, you can have it." Heaven knows she had no big plans for it yet. Certainly that horrible wallpaper would have to go, and the floors would need restoring, but she could leave it to the end. "Why do you like it so much?"

Dallas shrugged. "I dunno. I just do. It feels...friendly."

Terri took another look around, wondering how her daughter was getting a 'friendly' vibe. If anything, the room was bleak, especially compared to the others, with their colorful wall coverings and elaborate light sconces. Aside from the servants' quarters, it was the plainest room in the house. At least it didn't have the same hideous plaques on the wall. Imagine sleeping under *Thy Work Be Done* or *Prepare to Meet Thy God*. It made her wonder what kind of employers Vandermere's family had been. The rooms were a generous size, especially for servants' quarters, but those god-awful signs....

"That's odd," she said, almost to herself. It was difficult to tell if Dallas was ever truly listening to her, but so far, they'd been getting along well, and the girl appeared to be genuinely interested in the project. One could only hope it would continue. A long, winding road lay ahead.

"What is it, Mom?" Dallas followed her to the door, where Terri had spotted something unusual. One half of the knob was filigree metal, but the half facing into the room was white ceramic. "That's pretty, but why don't they match?"

"Good question." The white knob didn't make any sense. She consulted her notes again, confirming what she already knew. The room had once belonged to the son, Niles, who had died of complications from his diabetes when he was a teenager. "See this white knob? Typically, knobs like this were exclusively used in the servants' rooms."

"Why?" Dallas asked, twisting it back and forth. "Didn't other people like them?"

Clearly her ten-year-old would be getting a lesson in classism this year. "See how shiny it is? There's a reason for that. When the servants touched these knobs, their hands had to be spotless. If they weren't, they'd leave marks on the doorknob, and their employers would see they hadn't washed their hands well enough."

Dallas's brow wrinkled, a sign that a more challenging question was coming. "Couldn't the servants wipe off the marks before anyone saw them?"

"Maybe it was a test for them too, a warning to keep their hands clean. Back then people had just started to learn how germs could be passed from one person to another. If their servants had clean hands, it would help keep the family from getting sick. To the Victorians, cleanliness was akin to godliness. They were extremely fastidious people."

"But why is there a white knob on *this* door? This isn't a servants' room."

Terri stared at her. "What did you say?"

"This was a child's room. A boy. He wasn't a servant."

"That's right. This was the room of the Vandermeres' son. How did you know?" She hadn't told her daughter a child had died in here, in the room Dallas had chosen as her own. The last thing she needed was Dallas having nightmares or acquiring that dreaded 'imagination' Miss Vandermere loathed. Restoring Glenvale would most likely take several years, maybe longer. They'd both have to get comfortable in the house, no matter how old and odd it was.

Concerned by Vandermere's tales of fleeing workers and overactive imaginations, Terri had lived in the house for a full week on her own before telling her mom it was all right to bring Dallas over. That had given her enough time to shore up the front steps — no one would be falling through on her watch — and reassure herself that there was no black goo dripping from the walls, or disembodied voices urging her to *"Get out"*. In fact, nothing strange had happened at all. There wasn't a glimpse of the mysterious Gertie. Terri hadn't gone near the attic rooms, but hadn't seen a need to. If they were full of junk, she'd leave them be as long as possible. Often, some of the 'junk' stored in homes like this were antiques that could be restored and repositioned in their rightful places.

She adored houses like this: houses with character, houses that told a story. It was why she specialized in restoration work. But she'd never taken on such a huge job before, not since she'd had Dallas. They'd never had to live on site, and she hadn't been sure how her daughter would handle it.

Dallas shrugged. "I dunno. I just knew."

"Does it bother you that this was a boy's room?"

"Why would it bother me? Sometimes you say silly things, Mom."

Yes, she supposed she did. Still, she was relieved when her daughter agreed to check out the rest of the house with her. Terri didn't like Niles's room. Something about it gave her the creeps. Why on earth would the son's room have white doorknobs? He may have been sickly, but he was the family heir. Or, at least, he *had* been, until his untimely death. It had to have been a flawed restoration by someone who hadn't known what they were doing. Maybe one of the over-imaginative restorers had stuck around long enough to get something wrong.

Terri breathed easier once she'd closed the door.

⋆　　⋆　　⋆

Though most of the furniture had been left in place for her convenience – it was a matter of removing drop cloths if she wanted to use something – Terri opted to set up a small table in the manor's kitchen rather than eat meals in the formal dining room. The dining room was too grand for her tastes, too cold even in the heat of summer. She often wondered about the families who had commissioned these great old homes. Had they really enjoyed dining formally, or had they insisted upon grand dining rooms because they were expected? In that respect, she was glad times had changed.

Pizza was a special treat, designed to lull Dallas into an agreeable food coma, but Terri needn't have worried. Despite their differences, the child was her mother's daughter. Dallas had quickly fallen in love with the house too, perhaps too much. "Don't get too attached to it," Terri warned. "We're only here until my work is finished, and then we'll have to move somewhere else."

"I know that, Mom." Dallas rolled her eyes, and Terri got a glimpse of what she could expect when her daughter reached puberty. "This place isn't ours."

"For at least a year, it's as good as. I want you to feel comfortable here, but not so much it'll be hard for you to leave."

"When we leave, we'll move into another place like this, right?"

"Yes, that's right. It'll be time for another adventure." Or it could be an out-and-out disaster. In her line of work, she never knew what to expect. "Or maybe we'll rent an apartment for a while."

"What's that, Mom?" Dallas asked, pointing.

Terri wondered what Dallas had discovered this time. Her daughter was turning out to have a great eye, with a talent for finding unique details that rivaled Terri's own.

At first, it wasn't obvious what she was pointing at. The butler's pantry? The decorative wall tiles? The cast-iron stove?

"That thing on the wall that looks like a weird round keyhole."

She smiled, eager to share one of her favorite features of old

Victorian homes. "That's a speaking tube. It connects the kitchen with Lady Vandermere's bathroom. When the lady of the house was enjoying a bath but wanted her cook's attention, she'd blow into the tube, creating a whistling sound. The cook would hear the whistle and hurry over to the tube so they could talk, kind of like the intercom system we used to have at home."

"Cool! Does it still work?"

"It should."

"Can I try it?" Dallas was already half out of her chair.

For some reason, the idea of her daughter using the tube made Terri shiver, and she spoke more sharply than she'd meant to. "Not right now. Sit down."

Dallas looked stunned, and no wonder. It wasn't like Terri to snap at her, or to curb her enthusiasm for exploration. She couldn't understand what was wrong with her, but ever since they'd had the conversation in Niles's room, she'd felt anxious, jumpy. Her grandmother would have said that a goose had walked over her grave. Lack of imagination or not, the old saying wasn't exactly comforting.

"But *why*?" There was a whiny note to Dallas's voice that set Terri's teeth on edge. She could handle almost anything but whining.

Because I said so leapt to her lips, but she refused to be that kind of parent. That explanation, or lack thereof, had driven her crazy when she was Dallas's age. Not until she became a mother had she understood how tempting it was. "Because I'd like us to finish our dinner first. Takeout food is expensive, and I don't want it wasted."

At the mention of their finances, Dallas settled back in her chair, staring down at her plate. Terri regretted that her child was aware of her situation. It was her problem, not Dallas's, but it had been one way to quell the constant demand for *things*. Dallas may have been ten, but she had a desperate desire to keep up with the Joneses. Or in this case, the Tammys and Traceys.

Her daughter picked at her pizza, the happy mood ruined. Terri let several minutes of uncomfortable silence pass before she addressed it. "Why are you so upset? You'll have plenty of time to try it after dinner."

"But we'll go to another room after dinner."

"You'll have time to try it, I promise. We won't leave until you do. How's that?"

Dallas gave her a *don't-you-get-it-Mom?* look. "But then we won't be here when someone answers."

This time the goose-walking-over-grave feeling was accompanied by actual goosebumps. "Who's going to answer back? There's no one else here." She laughed, but it didn't sound sincere. She doubted it had fooled Dallas. Few things did.

Her daughter lowered her gaze again and shrugged, looking guilty. Icy fingers traced a path up Terri's spine.

"Dallas, have you seen someone in this house?" *Oh God, no, not the infamous Gertie.* Or perhaps a vagrant had managed to find his way in after the house had closed for the season, and had been doing his best to avoid her all week. That would explain the sensation she'd had of being watched.

"Not really." She still refused to meet Terri's eyes. Her daughter's reluctance was beginning to scare her. What if there *was* someone in the house? What if the 'ghosts' that had spooked the other restorers hadn't been ghosts at all?

"What do you mean, 'not really'? You've either seen someone or you haven't."

Now her daughter glared at her, her cheeks turning red. "Why are you getting so mad?"

"I'm not mad," Terri denied, though she realized she was angrier than the situation warranted. Again she wondered what was wrong with her. Landing this project was a big success for their little family – *if* they managed not to kill each other first. They should be celebrating, not at each other's throats. "But I want to know the truth. If there *is* someone in the house with us, you need to tell me. They could be dangerous."

Dallas glanced away. "He's not dangerous," she muttered, so quietly Terri almost didn't hear.

"*Who's* not dangerous?"

"The boy I told you about earlier."

Ignoring the feeling of freezing fingers along her back, Terri said, "I don't remember you mentioning a boy. Which boy?" *Please don't say it....*

"You know, the boy who stayed in my room before me. His name is Niles."

"That isn't funny, Dallas."

"I'm not *trying* to be funny. You asked me to tell you who's in the house, and I told you." She crossed her arms, narrowing her eyes.

"What does he look like?" While she hoped Dallas's imagination had been working overtime, maybe there was another explanation.

"He has dark, wavy hair. Sad eyes. His cheeks are bright red, almost like he's wearing makeup." Dallas lowered her voice. "He dresses funny. The collar on his shirt is stiff. It sticks straight up, like he's wearing a costume. Is he an actor, Mom?"

Terri coughed, trying to clear the lump that had formed in her throat when her daughter perfectly described Niles Vandermere. There was one possible solution. "Have you been reading about this house online, honey?"

"No. Why would anyone write about this old house?"

"The family who lived here was very important. You've heard of the Rockefellers, right?" At Dallas's nod, she continued. "They were kind of like that. They were quite wealthy. Howard Vandermere owned a law firm and became a powerful senator. He helped a lot of people, and there was talk about him becoming president one day. His wife, Elizabeth, was active in the community, and very well thought of."

But then Howard's son had succumbed to a terrible disease, and it destroyed him. He'd withdrawn from the public eye, turning into a recluse. No one appeared to know how the man himself had died, or what had happened to the rest of the family. Terri hadn't wanted to ask Miss Vandermere. It hadn't felt appropriate to pry.

One thing Vandermere *had* told her: there had been tours in the house not so long ago, with costumed actors playing the roles of various family members and servants. Maybe the boy her daughter had seen *was* an actor, a confused young man still playing the role of Niles even though the house had closed.

Seeing her daughter had finished eating, Terri wrapped the leftovers for their breakfast. They both loved cold pizza in the morning. "Where did you last see this boy?" she asked, striving to sound casual. As soon as she had a moment alone, she was going to call Henrietta Vandermere and report this so-called Niles for scaring the wits out of them. He wouldn't be employed in this house again, if she could help it. No wonder the other restorers had thought the place was haunted. Ghosts, her ass.

"He was in the hallway near my room. He says there's a game he likes, but that it's been packed away. Can we look for it?"

Chills raced up her spine again, but this time she focused on her anger. The nerve of this kid, hanging around where he wasn't wanted and playing tricks on her daughter. "Maybe later. I was going to do some work in the parlor for a bit. Want to help me?"

"Can I use the speaking tube first?"

Terri longed to say no, but she prided herself on not breaking promises, especially to her daughter. "Of course. Go ahead." She struggled not to show how unnerved she was. As much as she'd like to believe he was harmless, it wasn't normal for this boy to have stayed in the house after the tours ended and the rest of the employees went home. Someone must have told him the house was closing for the restoration. What if there was something seriously wrong with him? What if he *was* dangerous?

Don't court trouble. Another one of her grandmother's favorite expressions, and it remained true today. Dallas was a logical, older-than-her-years kid, but she was still a child, and probably as likely to have her imagination run away with her as any other kid.

Her daughter dashed over to the speaking tube like a racehorse who'd been cooped up for too long. She paused long enough to shoot Terri a wicked grin before blowing into the tube.

As the girl pulled back, staring at the contraption with a look of anticipation, Terri found she was holding her breath, praying no one would answer. *Great.* Now she was the one whose imagination was out of control. Tales of potentially disturbed boys aside, there was no one in the house aside from them. She hoped.

She let her daughter ride it out, not wanting to risk another skirmish. Minutes ticked by, feeling endless, but the kitchen remained silent. Finally Dallas gave up, looking disappointed. "I guess no one's there. We might as well go."

"Sorry, kiddo." Terri rested her hand on her daughter's head. "Maybe next time."

As they left the room, she could have sworn she heard a funny sound – a long, low echo, almost like a moan.

Air in the pipes, she told herself.

CHAPTER TWO

It took an hour before Dallas uttered those three little words every parent dreads.

"Mom, I'm bored."

Terri took a break from removing the wall covering. It broke her heart to do it, even though she'd managed to source a reasonable likeness from one of her favorite heritage-house suppliers. The replicas were never quite the same, no matter how expensive. But there was no way around it – the water damage had been extensive, and the old wall covering needed to be replaced. Still, it hurt. People didn't make things with that level of care anymore.

Wiping sweat and dust out of her eyes with a forearm, she regarded her daughter, who had an impressively large pile of the wall covering at her feet. She'd done a good job and had stayed with it surprisingly long, longer than Terri had thought she would. She had to remember that for Dallas, this was a holiday. Soon enough – too soon – the summer would be over, and she'd be back in school. A new school, if she decided she wanted to stay.

"It is boring, isn't it? You've done great, though, honey. I appreciate the help."

"Can I go look around?"

Her impulse was to say yes, of course she could, but then Terri remembered the boy in funny clothes. She hesitated, and before she could voice her misgivings, Dallas rushed to reassure her. "I won't go far. There's an old closet near my room and I want to see what's in it. Maybe I can find the game Niles was talking about."

Terri leaned back on her haunches, setting down her putty knife. "About that…." She took a deep breath. This was new territory for her. How was she supposed to explain this without terrifying her daughter? "Honey, he isn't really Niles. Niles was the Vandermere's son, and he died a long time ago. I think the boy you've seen used to *play* Niles for the tours they gave here, but he shouldn't be hanging around the house. If you see him, I want you to tell him to go home and come tell me right away, okay?"

Her mouth gaping a little, Dallas nodded. "I think he believes it, though. He really thinks he's Niles."

"That's why I want you to come tell me right away if you see him. He might be sick – okay?"

Sick covered all manner of ills, but from the time her daughter had been old enough to understand, it had meant a combination of *don't touch* and *stay away*. Terri hoped Dallas got that the deluded soul playing Niles was ill in a much more dangerous way, but she didn't want to scare her daughter.

"Okay."

"Promise?"

"I promise."

"Do you have your phone?"

Dallas pulled the small phone with its glittery pink case from her back pocket. Other parents complained about their children's attachment to such devices, but in moments like this, they were a godsend. The house was too large for Terri to hear Dallas if she cried out, and definitely big enough for the girl to get lost if she wasn't careful. "Good. Call me if you see him, and hurry right back here."

"I will, Mom."

"And if you decide to go any farther than the closet, give me a call."

"Okay." The novelty of a mentally ill boy wandering the house had given her more leeway than usual, but Terri could tell Dallas was growing impatient. Too much longer, and too many more directives, and her daughter would storm off and that would be that. The temper came from the girl's father, so she always reminded herself that it wasn't Dallas's fault. But it was hard not to resent that she still had to perpetually walk on eggshells long after the divorce.

"We're a team, right?" Attempting to coax a smile, Terri tried to hide how troubled she actually was. This fake Niles had unnerved her more than she wanted to admit. What if he didn't leave them alone? What if he terrorized them the entire summer? Her heart sped up at the thought of it, pounding in her chest with an intensity that was nearly painful.

Dallas nodded, ponytail bobbing. She wasn't the type of child to cheerfully parrot back her mother's suggestions, never had been. Terri would have to be satisfied with non-verbal gestures.

"Please be careful."

"*Mom....*"

"I know, I know." She raised her hands in surrender. "I'm being overprotective. Go ahead, go. Have fun."

Though she'd appeared to be exhausted a moment before, Dallas flew away from her like a bird escaping a cage.

"No running," Terri yelled after the rapidly retreating figure, but it was too late. Her daughter was gone. Rubbing her chest in a futile attempt to lower her heart rate, she was frustrated at the level of helplessness she felt. There was no way around it; she was going to have to call Vandermere in the morning. It was the last thing she wanted to do. She had too much work to be able to hover over her daughter all summer, and doing so would make Dallas nuts and drive a bigger wedge between them.

Tea. Tea was what she needed now.

Though it was nearly eighty degrees outside, the house was cool and yes, drafty. Vandermere had been right about that. On the hottest of days, a cold breeze could be felt, consistently winding its way through the estate. While it was welcome now, Terri worried about how uncomfortable the place would be in the winter, as they would be there past the end of the year; there was no doubt about it. As with all old homes, she'd no sooner fix one problem before she'd discover another, lurking behind the one she'd just repaired. She was relieved she hadn't found black mold under the water-damaged wall covering yet, but Terri was willing to bet it was there. Sometimes it was difficult to catch her breath in the house, as if her lungs were being squeezed.

Maybe this is a sign. She pushed the thought aside as she walked to the kitchen. Ever since her father had died of a heart attack at a tragically young age, leaving her alone with her kindly but ill-equipped-to-be-a-single-parent mother, dying the same way had been Terri's greatest fear. She'd driven herself to the hospital too many times to count, convinced that each minute was destined to be her last.

The diagnosis was the same every time: panic attack.

"There's nothing wrong with your heart, Terri," the last nurse had told her. He'd had kind eyes and a gentle voice, and had taken the time to sit with her for a moment, perching on the edge of the bed. She'd been hooked up to a frightening array of machines. "But if you don't learn how to deal with stress, there will be."

Dallas would be fine. She was strong and street smart, as much as any child with a comfortable life could be, and she had her phone. There was no reason to worry about her.

Except there was.

"The boy who stayed in my room before me. His name is Niles."

Screw it. What had she been thinking, leaving this until tomorrow? This kid could have a knife, or worse. How could she have thought they'd be able to sleep in this house tonight, with him wandering around?

She took her phone from her pocket and called Dallas.

"I haven't even been gone *five* minutes."

"I know. Sorry, but I can't help it. This Niles, or whoever he is, scares me. Everything all right?"

"Yes, Mom." Heavy sigh, mostly for effect. "No one's here but me and a bunch of spiderwebs."

Though her daughter wasn't the cuddly type, at least she wasn't scared of spiders. That would be impossible to deal with while doing restorations. "Find anything yet?"

"It's been five minutes, Mom. I just got here."

"Okay. Call me if you see anything."

Her daughter ended the call without a goodbye, and Terri tried not to be hurt, reminding herself that Dallas didn't mean to be abrupt or rude. She'd been telling herself that since the girl had learned to speak. Hopefully Vandermere would be less impatient.

If there was anything she hated, it was complaining. She prided herself on being a positive person, a *can-do* person. In the best-case scenario, her clients heard from her twice: when she applied for a job, and when she finished the job. However, this was far from the best-case scenario, and the sooner she let her employer know, the sooner it would be fixed.

"Ms. Foxworth. This is a surprise. I didn't expect to hear from you so soon. Are you and your daughter settling in?"

Startled, but not annoyed. That was a good start. "Everything's fine, Miss Vandermere. The house is beautiful, and I don't anticipate any problems with the restoration."

"But...." The older woman sounded bemused.

"Sorry?"

"I sense a 'but' coming. I somehow doubt you've phoned me to chat."

Terri mentally crossed her fingers. What if the boy were a relative? She hadn't considered that before. Even so, the woman needed to know the child had scared her daughter.

You mean he's scaring you. Dallas is fine, said the annoying voice in her head, but she pushed it aside. "There's a situation I need to talk to you about."

"Yes? I'm not much for beating around the bush. Tell me what's on your mind."

"I'm afraid one of your actors must have gotten confused. He's been in the house since we moved in, and he's frightening my daughter." She silently apologized to Dallas for throwing her under the bus.

"One of my *actors*? Whatever do you mean?" Vandermere still sounded amused, but now Terri could detect an undercurrent of irritation.

"You know, from the tours. The historical recreations," she said, feeling frustrated. Perhaps *actor* wasn't the best word, but surely the woman understood what she'd meant.

"My dear, I didn't mean to give you that impression. Some of our staff would dress up from time to time, just a simple show-and-tell. No actors or historical recreations. It's too fragile for that sort of nonsense."

"But…didn't I see a brochure with some actors in period dress showing people around?" Her heart was sprinting again, and she found it difficult to breathe. It was as if iron bands were wrapped around her chest, forcing the air from her lungs.

"Oh, we hosted a little event for the one-hundredth anniversary, but nothing since. Too much work, and too much hassle. Not to mention the cost to the house would be too great if we'd kept doing it. As I'm sure you're aware, the general public cannot be trusted with such a priceless artifact."

"Did a boy take part in that event?"

"No, no children." Terri could imagine Vandermere pursing her lips at the thought. Unlike a lot of women her age, she was not charmed by children, which had been quite apparent when she'd met Dallas. "Children are even worse than the general public. So destructive."

Deep breath. "Miss Vandermere, my daughter has seen someone in the house. A young man, wearing period clothing. He told her his name was Niles."

The woman sighed. "Do you know why I hired you?"

A million potential responses leapt to Terri's lips, each one more defensive or egotistical than the last. She settled for, "Aside from my recommendations and expertise, no. Not really." Remembering the other restorers, she prayed Vandermere wouldn't tell her she'd been the last choice.

"Oh, please. There are plenty of good people who have been in the restoration business longer than you've been alive. Recommendations and expertise come cheap. No, I hired you because you were brave."

Terri's mind reeled from the woman's not-so-veiled insult. *Brave?* But before she could ask what Vandermere meant, the woman continued. "When I heard you were the one who'd restored the Davis house, I thought, 'This is the right person for the job.' To be gauche for a moment, the fact that you needed the work didn't hurt either."

She'd missed the last barb, as the mention of the name *Davis* made her knees buckle. The Davis house had been the site of a multiple murder: a churchgoing couple gunned down by their eldest son, who had then turned the weapon on his three siblings. It hadn't been so much a restoration as a clean-up job. She had spent weeks separated from her daughter, scrubbing dried blood and brain matter off the walls, and had tried to erase it from her mind ever since.

"Are you saying something horrible happened in this house?" she asked once she'd regained her composure.

"Of course not, nothing like that. As you know, my brother passed away in that house, in the north bedroom, when he was sixteen. He had been ill for some time. There was certainly nothing nefarious about it. As for anything else you might hear, it's nothing more than idle gossip from those who forget sensibilities were quite different back then."

Terri was beginning to feel sorry she'd called. Rather than reassuring her, Vandermere's words were having the opposite effect. "What do you mean 'sensibilities were different'?"

"How people raised their children, for instance. What would be considered 'abusive' today was simply good discipline back then. Children weren't indulged, coddled, and handed everything on a silver platter. They had to earn their privileges, and were expected to behave."

The smugness in her voice, especially since the woman had never raised a child in her life, made Terri's blood boil. "And be seen and not heard, I suppose."

Her employer missed her sarcasm, or perhaps decided to ignore it. "Exactly. Children understood how to respect their elders back then. A little healthy fear never hurt anyone."

Healthy fear? She'd never heard a bigger oxymoron in her life. Best to bring this conversation to an end before she lost it completely. "I'm not sure what this has to do with the boy my daughter saw in the house."

"Do you remember what we discussed on the day I showed you the house?"

Damn. She'd been hoping Vandermere wouldn't go there. This had nothing to do with her imagination, or her daughter's imagination. Dallas hadn't had a clue who Niles Vandermere was. She couldn't have conjured that name up. "Yes, but—"

"It's an old house. Old houses have history. They make strange noises, and occasionally, one might see funny things. Do you remember me telling you this?"

"Yes, but with all due respect, we were talking about moving curtains. Not young men wandering around the house, claiming to be your brother. If he isn't an actor, I'd like to know who he is."

"Have you seen this young man for yourself?" The woman's voice was heavy with skepticism.

"No, but I believe my daughter."

"We talked about this, Ms. Foxworth. I told you that I prefer employees without overactive imaginations."

"This is hardly an overactive imagination. How would my daughter have known your brother's name? *I* certainly never told her."

"She has access to a computer, doesn't she? A cell phone? Information about our family is easy enough to find."

"That's what I thought too, but I asked her, and she swears she hasn't looked up a thing."

"And children never lie, do they?" Before Terri could explode, Vandermere continued, clearly not expecting an answer. "You remember what I told you about the other workers I hired. They had to be fired due to their flights of fancy and ridiculous notions. I'd hoped I wouldn't have to say the same about you."

"I thought it had been their choice to leave." Terri swallowed hard, digging her nails into her palms. "You told me they'd abandoned the project and left you in the lurch."

"I couldn't have you think I was difficult to work for, could I?" The amusement had returned to the woman's voice, like she was winking, and Terri felt ill.

"This isn't my daughter's imagination. There is a boy in this house, and he told her his name was Niles. She said he was wearing old-fashioned clothing." As she said the words, she realized how ludicrous it sounded. Still, she believed her daughter. Dallas wasn't the type to make things up, and definitely not something like that. How would she have known the name of Vandermere's brother? If she *had* researched the family, there would be no reason to lie.

"If you really believe a boy is in the house, the police would be the ones to contact. There isn't much I can do."

"Understood. Thank you, Miss Vandermere. I won't bother you again."

"I'll hold you to that," the woman said, and hung up.

Bitch. Terri had known Vandermere was set in her ways, but hadn't expected her to be so dismissive of Terri's concerns – or so rude. Not to mention her antiquated ideas about raising children. The idea of someone laying a hand on Dallas was enough to make her seethe. Not all of the old ways had been good ones, but try getting someone from that era to admit it.

Then there was the matter of the boy Dallas had seen. Maybe her daughter *had* imagined it, but that didn't seem likely, not if he had told her his name was Niles. If she saw him herself, she'd ask him to leave. No sense calling the police on a kid, especially a kid with a mental illness. Hopefully he'd get bored and leave on his own. Sooner rather than later.

Plugging in the electric kettle she'd brought with her, Terri wished she *did* have an overactive imagination. If she had, perhaps she could have convinced herself that it was going to be that simple.

CHAPTER THREE

"That is the box you want."

Dallas startled, but only a little. She'd known the boy was around; she could feel him watching her. Even her mom felt him — it was obvious from the way she kept looking around and rubbing the back of her neck. He made *her* neck prickle too, but Dallas found that interesting. She needed to ask him how he did that.

"You're not supposed to be here," she said in her best stern tone, the one she used with younger children, though Niles wasn't younger. Older or not, she wasn't going to let him boss her around.

He took a step backward, stumbling as if she'd hit him, and she instantly felt bad. "Whatever do you mean? I live here."

"My mom says that's not true. She said you're an actor, and that you're confused. She says you shouldn't be here."

"An actor?" He *did* look confused; her mother had been right about that.

"She says you're sick."

"It's true, I have been ill," he said, taking a seat on the floor. "It's called die-a-*beat*-tees."

"I know all about diabetes. My grandmother has it. It means you can't eat too much sugar. Right?" Seeing the deepening confusion on his face, she shrugged. "Never mind. That's not the kind of sickness my mom meant, anyway. She meant the kind that's in your head."

"I don't understand."

"You know, crazy-sick." Dallas spun her finger around her ear and made a face, even though she knew it was unkind. When people were sick in their heads, it wasn't their fault. But she wasn't trying to be polite. Niles scared her mother, and that meant he had to go.

"Thinking wrong thoughts, like believing you're Niles."

"But I *am* Niles."

Dallas exhaled, feeling very old and tired. How did this boy's parents put up with him? "Where's your mother?"

His brow creased. "I don't know. I haven't seen her for a long time. Have you seen her?"

"Of course not. How would I have seen her?"

"She lives here too."

"Look, my mom told me all about you, okay? She says you're an actor who *plays* Niles, but that you've gotten confused. She doesn't want you here."

His lip trembled. "But it's my home. She cannot make me leave my own home."

She returned to rummaging in the closet. "Whatever. But if she catches you, she's going to call the police."

"That is the box you want, the big one on the left. That one contains my belongings."

"You talk funny." Dallas wrinkled her nose.

"I am not the one talking 'funny'. *You* are the one who speaks strangely."

"Whatever." It was her best retort, and never failed to piss her mom off, but it wasn't having the usual effect on this kid. It didn't seem to bother him at all.

The box was heavy, and it was on the highest shelf. As he moved to help her, Dallas shrieked. "Don't touch me!" There was something about his closeness that made it feel like spiders were crawling on her skin. She had nothing against spiders, but she didn't want them *crawling* on her with their creepy little legs.

"I was only attempting to assist."

She could tell by his expression that she'd hurt his feelings. Despite what her mom had said about him not belonging here, she felt badly. She didn't like hurting people's feelings. And it wasn't his fault he was sick. Maybe that's why his face was so flushed all the time. Maybe it wasn't makeup.

"It's okay. I've got it."

The box was coated with dust. Before touching the flaps, Dallas carefully wiped them off with a rag she'd brought with her. Other kids would have used their sleeve, but she didn't like being dirty, and besides, sometimes the dirt stained if it was thick enough. She glanced at Niles, expecting him to make fun of her like other kids did, but he'd resettled himself on the floor, watching her with a blank expression.

She opened the box.

"Wow." Impressed in spite of herself, she examined the contents. It was like finding treasure. There were so many puzzles, and books, and games. She didn't know where to start. "This is all yours? This is really cool."

"Yes." He'd moved closer, but being distracted with the box's contents had kept her from noticing the spidery feeling. Maybe it was something she could get used to over time. She hoped so. It would be nice to have a friend here. "That one is my very favorite." He pointed to a board game, and she pulled it out.

"*The Checkered Game of Life*," she read aloud. "I've played this before, but this version looks different. The one I've played is called *The Game of Life*."

"It's the only one I've played. Perhaps there are others."

"It also looks really old. Mom won't want me playing with this." As much as she longed to open the box and see what the little cars and people were like in this version, she didn't dare. Her mom had told her over and over again how valuable old things could be. And besides, the contents of the house didn't belong to them. They were the property of the people who had hired them to fix this place.

"What do you mean? It's brand new. My papa gave it to me for my birthday. It's not 'old'. I've barely played with it." Niles's cheeks were redder than usual. "It is unkind of you to call it old."

"I'm sorry, but to me it looks like an antique. If we play with this, I could get in trouble."

He scowled. "Why? It's mine. It belongs to me. I can do whatever I like with it."

"Fine, here. Do what you want, but I'm not touching it anymore." She shoved the box at him harder than she'd meant, and he fumbled with it, nearly dropping it. Dallas cursed herself. She had to stop getting so angry all the time, or she'd never have any friends. But she *was* angry, a lot. She didn't understand why.

"I was angry much of the time as well," Niles said, startling her. The game remained on his lap, untouched. As excited as he'd been to find it, he didn't appear to be in a big hurry to open it. "I didn't like that I was ill so often, and that I had to stay in bed when other children were able to play. My sister used to tease me about it, and I hated her. Some days I would have liked to kill her."

Dallas was shocked. She'd never heard a kid speak like that. As furious as she felt sometimes, she'd never wanted to kill anyone. "You shouldn't talk that way."

"Why?" He looked at her in that intense way of his, and then lowered his eyes. "I have frightened you. I apologize."

"It's not me you should say sorry to, it's your sister. I can't imagine feeling that way about my family. It's not right." She tried not to think about all the times she'd told her mother she wished she were dead. She'd never meant it, not really. She'd just wanted her parents to stay together. When she'd heard her dad crying at night after Mom left, it hurt her heart. "I'd love to have a sister." *Or a brother.* Anyone to break up the boredom of being alone all the time.

"Not my sister, you would not. She is a monster." Niles made a face, clearly not paying any attention to her scolding. She'd noticed that about boys. They said and did whatever they wanted. They never listened to anyone, especially a girl.

"What does she do that's so bad?"

"I told you. She's forever mocking me, finding sport in having a laugh at my expense. It's not fair that she is healthy while I'm always ill."

"That doesn't sound very nice," Dallas conceded, "but maybe

she's teasing you." Angela, her one friend from her old school, had an older sister who'd teased them, but never in a mean way. Dallas missed Angela, and Angela's mother, who'd made the most amazing food, like tortillas and *real* Mexican tacos. At first she'd been disappointed that they were nothing like the kind from Taco Bell, but she'd decided that the real thing was much better, to the delight of Angela's parents. She'd loved how happy the family was, and how they talked about actual *stuff* at the dinner table, not just how school was going and other boring crap. She loved how Angela's mother rested a hand on her head when she walked past, and called her *mi reinita*.

"I cannot tolerate her. My other sister can ride a horse better than any man, and she's a wonderful shot and a good fencer too."

"Fencer? Like, with swords and stuff?" She'd seen fencing on the Olympics. It looked pretty boring to her, but she wasn't going to tell him that. He wasn't talking about wanting to kill his sister anymore, and that was a good thing.

"Yes. She's very impressive."

"That's cool."

"I have an idea of a thing we could do to pass the time."

"I told you I can't play that game with you. I wish I could, but my mom would get angry with me."

"It's not the game I'm thinking of. Why don't we put everything in the box back in my room, the way it was before?"

Dallas stared at the contents of the enormous box. "Everything?"

"Yes, everything. It will be a laugh – come on."

It didn't sound like a laugh to her. It sounded like unpacking, and unpacking was anything but fun. Packing wasn't fun either, but at least packing promised the excitement of a new adventure. Unpacking was boring. "But there's so much here. Where will I put my stuff?"

She wondered if she should have chosen another room. Niles was getting a bit controlling. She wasn't 'his bitch', as Angela would say.

"Please. I would love to see it all returned to the way it was. I promise there will be room for your things."

"Okay, I guess."

"Good. Then we're agreed."

She was a little annoyed when he let her struggle with the huge box all by herself, but if she dragged it along the floor, it wasn't so bad. Niles didn't look very strong. Maybe it was because of his illness.

Dallas had partly agreed to his idea because she couldn't wait to see her mom's reaction. Her mom loved old things, and she'd find some of this stuff super interesting. It would be a big surprise when she came upstairs and saw what they had done.

"This was a good idea," she said as they placed the old books on his desk. The desk was where it had always been, he'd said. They'd just had to remove the cloth that covered it.

"I'm blessed with many good ideas."

"Don't take this the wrong way, but you're kind of conceited."

"How shall I take it?" he asked, not appearing offended in the slightest.

"How – oh, never mind." Figures. She'd finally made a new friend, and he had to be a conceited dweeb who talked and dressed funny. It was just her luck.

Seeing the white knob on the door, she had an idea of her own. This couldn't be the *real* Niles – she knew that – but if he'd been part of the tours, maybe he had an answer. She could tell the strangeness of the mismatched knob had bothered her mom, and if she could figure out the mystery on her own, Terri would be so proud. "Hey, why is this like this?" Twisting the knob, she let it snap back, liking the sound it made.

"Why is what like what?" He ran his fingers over the board games again, appearing to be mesmerized by them. What was with him? She'd told him over and over again; she couldn't play with them. Maybe her mom was right, and he *was* funny in the head. But he didn't seem to be dangerous.

"Your doorknob. Why is it metal on one side and white on the other?" By now, she was careful to always refer to the room as his. It wasn't worth arguing about.

He barely spared it a glance. "I don't know. It just is."

"But white knobs are for servants' rooms. You know, so the people who owned the house could make sure their servants' hands were clean."

The atmosphere in the room shifted. It was as if clouds had obscured the sun. He scowled at her, his face flushing to a deep brick red, his eyes narrowing into slits. "What are you accusing me of?" He spit the words, speaking so loudly her mother might hear, even from downstairs.

For the first time, she felt afraid of him. She backed away, bumping into the wall, wishing her mother *would* come. She didn't care about getting into trouble, not now. "N-nothing. I'm not accusing you of anything."

He took a threatening step towards her. "Are you saying my parents thought I was a *servant*?" He said 'servant' as if it was the vilest word on the planet. If he was acting, he was really good – *too* good.

"Of course not. I-I was just asking—"

"Be careful, Dallas. You do not want to make an enemy out of me." Pushing past her, he stalked to the door, but paused when he reached the threshold. He smiled at her. It wasn't a nice smile, though. It gave her the creeps. How had she never noticed how pointed his teeth were before? "You would not like how nasty I can get."

CHAPTER FOUR

"Dallas Maria Foxworth, what have you done?"

Terri couldn't believe her eyes. Her daughter had never done anything like this before. She'd always shown so much respect for the properties they'd worked on and other people's things, and now here she was, sprawled on an antique bed, reading a book that was probably a first edition. It was all she could do to keep from snatching it out of Dallas's hands, but that would only damage it more.

To add insult to injury, instead of looking the slightest bit chastened, her daughter grinned at her. *Grinned.* What on earth was she thinking? Had she gone mad? Terri never should have left her unsupervised for so long.

"What do you think?" Clearly oblivious to her anger, Dallas stretched her arms wide, indicating her handiwork. Her horrible, horrible handiwork. "Isn't it great? It's like traveling back in time." She finally picked up on Terri's mood. "What's wrong? Why do you look upset?"

"Why do I look upset? You told me you were looking for a game."

"It's right there." She pointed to the stack of board games on a bureau. "It's the *Game of Life*," she said, sliding off the bed and hurrying to show her, "but it looks totally different from the one we have and the name is different too. Isn't it cool?"

It was cool, all right. Terri covered her eyes for a moment, praying for strength. "Do you have any idea what that game is probably worth?"

"That's what *I* said. But don't worry, Mom. I didn't play it. I just took it out of the box and put it where it used to be."

Terri felt her eyes narrowing. "That's what you *said*? To whom?"

It could have been a trick of the light, but she swore her daughter blushed. "I meant, that's what I *thought*."

"You haven't seen that boy again, have you? You promised you would call me."

Dallas shook her head. "No."

It wasn't like her daughter to lie, but Terri could tell she was hiding something. "I'm not going to get him in trouble, but if he's still here, he needs help. He's very sick, Dallas. He could hurt you – or me."

A shadow crossed her daughter's face, but she said, "I promise I'll tell you if I see him. I didn't do anything wrong, did I?"

Her anxious expression defused Terri's anger. Dallas hadn't meant to misbehave; she obviously thought she'd done the right thing, or maybe even had been helpful.

"You know you're not supposed to touch other people's things. We've been over this. Even though we're living here while I work on the house, it's not our home. Anything that was left behind isn't ours. How would you like it if Miss Vandermere messed with *your* things?"

"What if the person who owns them told me I could touch them? Doesn't that make a difference?"

Terri pressed a hand against her forehead. "Dallas...."

"He did! He asked me to do this."

"And what did I tell you? If you've seen a young man in this house who tells you he's Niles, he's mentally ill. The boy who owned these things is dead. He died a long time ago."

"Then maybe his ghost wants to see his things again. What's wrong with that?"

Ugh, there it was. What Vandermere was so afraid of. "You know I don't believe in ghosts, and that isn't funny."

"I don't think he is a ghost. He's too real. I couldn't see through him or anything, but I swear this was his idea. He insisted I do it. So it's not my fault. Really, Mom."

Terri considered the year that stretched before them. Where once it had been ripe with possibilities, now she foresaw Dallas doing terrible things with the ready excuse 'Niles made me do it'. The situation would quickly become intolerable. "Then he's mentally ill, just like I told you. He isn't truly Niles, Dallas. The real Niles, the boy who owned these things, is dead."

"Do I have to put everything back?" Her lip trembled, and Terri's heart ached for her. She'd done a lot of work, and had been so proud, so excited to show her. Terri went to put an arm around her daughter, but Dallas pulled away. Dallas *always* pulled away. You'd think that in time, that would start to hurt less. But it never did.

"I think that would be for the best. I'm sure you were careful, but these things are valuable antiques. We have to protect them." Seeing Dallas was about to protest, she hurried on. "Even the sunlight that's going to come through your window in the morning will damage them. That's not what you want, is it?"

Gesturing at the window, she noticed the white lace curtain, which reminded her of the first day she'd seen the house, and how a similar curtain had moved in an attic room. Terri no longer thought it had been Gertie, and suppressed a shudder. She didn't believe in ghosts, but the entire situation was beginning to freak her out. It wasn't like Dallas to do something like this, and it certainly wasn't like her to lie. *Damn this kid.* Why did he have to come along and complicate things for them? The situation was already complicated enough.

"No," her daughter said softly. "Can I at least finish the book I'm reading?"

It was unnerving – the whole thing was unnerving. Her child had recreated a dead boy's bedroom. Terri had to stifle her impulse to throw all of Niles's belongings back in the box herself.

"I guess so. If you're careful," she said against her misgivings. "But you have to put all this other stuff away and promise me you won't touch any of it again."

"I promise."

"*Now*, Dallas."

"*Okay*. You don't have to get *mad* at me."

"I'm not mad, but I am disappointed. It's not like you to do something like this. If you didn't see that boy again tonight, I don't understand why you did this."

"He asked me to do it this afternoon. I would have told you, but I wanted it to be a surprise." Dallas looked away, and this time Terri *knew* she was lying. She was sure of it. The back of her neck prickled.

"I think you should sleep in my room tonight."

Her daughter's head shot up as if she'd been slapped. "Why?"

"Because this doesn't feel safe. Dallas, Niles – the *real* Niles – died in this room. If this boy you've seen is pretending to be him, and told you to do this, he's sicker than I thought. I don't want you staying in this room. Not until we figure out who he is and get him out of this house." *Shit.* She was going to have to call the police after all, or Vandermere again. She wasn't sure which was worse.

"But you told me I could have this room. You *promised*."

She'd hardly promised; there hadn't been a need to. But she had told Dallas the room was hers if she wanted it. Her daughter would use this as ammunition against her for years to come, but that didn't matter. Dallas's safety came first.

"That was before I knew about this boy. You have to trust me. It's not safe."

"I don't want to sleep with you. I'm not a baby."

The venom in Dallas's voice was enough to make her recoil, and her response was harsher than she would have liked. "I really don't care what you want at this point. You lied to me, and could have damaged the owner's things. You have been speaking to this boy, and you told me you'd call if you saw him again. You *will* be staying in my room tonight. It's for your own good." She walked to the doorway, determined to leave before her daughter could throw the fit she knew was coming. "One hour. I mean it. I want all this stuff put back where it was within the hour."

Terri left the room, hearing a dull *thunk* a second later. Dallas had thrown something at her, probably the antique book. What was wrong with her? Her daughter had never done anything like this before – if she had, Terri wouldn't have trusted her in these homes. She'd always been respectful of the houses and everything in them. These stories of Niles were both troubling and scary.

With that in mind, she slowed her steps, and looked back at the room. The hallway was empty. Following her instincts, she crept back to where she'd left her daughter, careful to stay out of sight. If Dallas found her here, eavesdropping, she'd be horribly embarrassed. But something stronger than potential embarrassment was telling her to wait – to wait and to listen.

★   ★   ★

"I don't like her."

Dallas jumped, pressing a hand to her racing heart. "Would you stop doing that? It's not nice to sneak up on people."

The boy had an ugly look on his face. "Your mother is mean. Why does she keep saying I'm dead? Clearly that is not the case." He held out his arm to her, and though she didn't want to, she touched it. It felt solid enough under the stiff fabric of his jacket, and ghosts weren't solid. Everyone knew that.

"Maybe you are dead, though. I once saw this movie where the guy was dead through the whole thing, and had no idea." Was she like the other character, the kid who saw dead people? That would be too scary. But no, Niles – or whatever his name was – was real. She'd just touched him.

"That is preposterous."

"Well, my mom doesn't lie. And she says the boy who owned these things died a long time ago." She tried to look into his eyes, but he wouldn't let her. He paced around the room, making so much noise she was afraid her mom would hear. "Do you want her to come back in here? Settle down."

"Let her come in. This is my house and these are *my* things."

Dallas dragged the dusty box out from under the bed with a

heavy heart. Though she wouldn't have admitted it to her mother, she was tired of living here *and* of this angry boy. She wasn't sure she wanted to be friends with him after all. He'd gotten her in trouble, and that's not what friends did. And besides, he scared her. "I need to put them back."

"No!" He grabbed her by the wrist, and she pulled away in shock, almost expecting to see marks where he'd touched her. His fingers had been painfully hot but cold at the same time.

"Don't touch me," she snapped. "Don't you ever touch me. I did what you wanted, and it got me in trouble. I'm not allowed to stay in this room now, thanks to you."

"That is not my fault. It's your mother's. I have every right to say what I want done with my things."

"Didn't you hear what she said? These aren't your things. You're not Niles. Niles is *dead*. You're sick."

"No, I am not." The boy seized the first thing he could lay his hands on, which was *The Checkered Game of Life*. To her horror, he threw it against the wall, hard. The box opened and pieces flew everywhere.

Dallas cried out, but it was too late. Her mother stood in the doorway, staring at her with the most terrible expression she had ever seen.

"What have you done?"

"Mom, it wasn't—" The look on her mother's face stopped her cold. She was turning purple.

"Dallas Maria Foxworth, you pick up all these pieces right now. Then pack up everything in this room, and meet me in the parlor in one hour. Do you understand me?"

"But—"

"Do you *understand* me?"

Feeling frantic, Dallas looked everywhere for the boy, but couldn't find him. He'd been there a second ago – how did he manage to hide before her mom came in? He'd been so darn eager to give her mother a piece of his mind, so where was he? "Niles, tell her what you told me."

"Dallas, stop it."

"What? You tell me to put them away, and he tells me to leave them where they are. *He* was the one who threw the game, not me. He's furious with you. He wants everything to stay like this. I told you. I—" She felt the tears coming and stopped talking. She refused to cry in front of her mother, and in front of Niles, who had to be lurking around somewhere. Whatever. He was a wimp, bragging that he'd stand up to her mom and then vanishing whenever she was around. Sinking to her knees, she started picking up the pieces and putting them back in the game box. At least it hadn't been damaged when Niles threw it. He was too old to act like such a baby.

Her mother knelt on the floor beside her. "Dallas, wait. Stop for a moment."

Rubbing her eyes, she did as she was told, but refused to look at her mom. At that moment, she hated Terri with a fierceness that frightened her. Living with her grandmother had been so much better than this. Why had she come here? They didn't get along, and that was never going to change.

"There is no Niles."

"Of *course* there's a Niles," she said, tossing more pieces into the box. "He threw this game across the room. I would never do that."

Her mother touched her shoulder, but she flinched out of reach. Why did her mom always have to be so touchy? It was one of the things Dallas liked the least about her.

"I was here," Terri said. "I stood right outside your door. I could hear your voice, but you were talking to yourself, Dallas. There was no one else here."

"I *wasn't* talking to myself. That's crazy. I was talking to him. He's really angry with you."

"I'm telling you the truth. There was no one here but you. I checked, Dallas. You were the only one in the room."

The concerned look on her mother's face made her more upset. How could she not have heard Niles? He hadn't exactly been quiet.

Part of her had hoped her mother would catch him, and then the stubborn boy wouldn't have been her problem anymore.

"You're lying. He was here."

"Has this happened before?"

"What do you mean?" Dallas didn't like where this was going. Why would her mom say these things? If she'd been standing by the door, she would have heard Niles for sure. Why was she pretending she hadn't? But deep down, she knew her mom wouldn't do that. Her mom hadn't been the best parent, but she'd never been cruel.

"Have you ever seen Niles or talked to him before?"

"Before I came here? Of course not. He lives here. I never met him before we moved into this stupid house."

"Have you talked to other children before? Children your dad or your grandma couldn't see?"

Enraged, Dallas leapt to her feet. "I am *not* crazy."

"I'm not saying you're crazy. But sometimes children have imaginary friends. It's completely normal, especially if you've been lonely."

"He is not imaginary. Niles, where are you? Stop hiding, and talk to my mother. Tell her what you told me. Come on."

She looked around the room, but it remained empty, aside from her and her mom. The coward. The boy in the funny clothes was a big coward, a coward who had gotten her in trouble twice. That was it. She would not be friends with him, and she wasn't going to do anything else for him, either. He could pout all he liked; she didn't care.

"Do you see him?" The gentleness of her mother's voice made her angrier. Dallas wished she'd stop treating her like someone who'd fallen and hit her head.

"Of course I don't see him. I'm not crazy!" She was so frustrated she was dangerously close to tears again.

Her mother began to put the game pieces back in the box, which angered her even more. "Leave it. You told me to do it."

"Dallas, I know you're upset, but you need to calm down. I can't have you yelling and screaming at me like this."

"What do you expect me to do? You're telling me I'm crazy." And now the tears did come, spilling over her cheeks too fast for her to stop them.

"I never said that. And I don't think that, either." Terri got up from the floor and held out her arms, looking hopeful. "Are you sure I can't give you a hug?"

Dallas shook her head, taking some small satisfaction from the pain on her mother's face. "I don't like to be touched."

"Okay. I'll leave you alone, then. I'll see you in the parlor in an hour."

She left the room, and Dallas lowered herself to the floor again. In a few minutes, she heard Niles come in, and her face and chest burned with fury. His long, thin fingers dropped a game piece into the box.

"Leave it," she snapped. "I'll do it myself."

"I apologize. I should not have thrown it. I didn't intend to get you into trouble."

Dallas longed to rip his perfectly waved hair from his head, to smack his red cheeks. "Then why didn't you say something? You talked so tough when she wasn't here, but then she showed up and you disappeared. Where'd you go, anyway? How come she didn't see you?"

"I was in the closet." He pointed to the door, which had a white knob. "I was afraid that if I revealed myself to her, she would make me leave."

"Well, now she thinks I'm crazy. Thanks a lot."

"I apologize, Dallas. Please forgive me."

"Okay, I forgive you, but I don't think I want to be your friend." Niles drew back. "Please don't say that."

"I mean it. You've done nothing but get me in trouble. If my mom thinks something's wrong with me, she won't let me live with my grandma again. She'll make me live with her, and I can't stand the thought of that, I really can't."

"I told you I didn't mean to cause problems for you."

"Yeah, well, you did. You could have helped me talk to her, and you didn't. You hid in the closet like a coward. So I'm done with you."

The boy's face darkened, and for a moment, she was scared again. He might have been a coward, but Niles was bigger than her, and he had a bad temper. If she went too far, he might hit her, and that would hurt. "Again, I'm sorry for what happened with your mother. I thought it was for the best that she not see me."

"The best for you, maybe, but not for me. Please leave me alone."

He stood there, watching her as she closed the lid on the game and put it back in the box. She stacked the other games on top of it and then started on the books, hoping he would go away. When he didn't, she turned on him in frustration. "Are you going to stand around and stare at me all night? I asked you to leave. Please go, or I'll call my mother in here, and you'll have to deal with her then."

Niles glowered at her. "You will regret this. I told you before, I do not make a good enemy."

"Oh, I'm sooooo scared."

"Perhaps not now, but you will be."

CHAPTER FIVE

Unable to focus on her work any longer, Terri sank into a slip-covered armchair. Her mind raced. *On the spectrum.*

She remembered the school psychologist who'd suggested it as the solution to all of Dallas's problems. Her sullenness. Her moods. Her inability to connect with her peers. Her aversion to being touched.

Terri had refused to believe it. Not her perfect baby girl, not Dallas. She'd tried to explain that her daughter hadn't always been this way, that something irreparable had broken in the girl when her parents divorced. But she couldn't bear to see the look of pity and judgment on the other woman's face, that look that said her daughter's problems were all her fault.

Maybe she should have stayed with Derek. Maybe leaving him had been her biggest mistake, the most selfish thing she'd done. God knows this wasn't the first time she had considered this. Things between them hadn't been fantastic, but they hadn't been unbearable, either, except in her own head. What if he'd been right about her?

"Nothing is ever good enough for you. You're never happy. You're never satisfied."

Except that wasn't true. After the pain of breaking up the family and dealing with her increasingly angry, resentful child had eased, she *had* been happy. She loved getting up in the morning and finding her apartment was exactly the way she'd left it, not filled with dirty dishes and other messes he'd left for her. Even when he ate a banana, he'd leave the peel on the counter rather than putting it in the compost bin, and this never changed, no matter how nicely she asked him.

"What's the big deal?" he'd say. "I clean up after you."

Except he didn't. It had always been her doing the cleaning, always. And nothing she did was good enough. She'd rush home from working on a house and spend two hours making lasagna from scratch, only for him to complain there was no garlic bread.

"I guess I'll go get some," he'd say with a sigh, leaving their meal to get cold while he went to get the store-bought loaf that was always coated with so much butter it made her feel slightly sick.

They never had fun anymore. Even on the weekends, Derek had been too tired to go anywhere or do anything, other than laze around in front of the television or read a newspaper (which he then left on the floor for her to recycle). She'd gone out anyway, taking their daughter to the planetarium and garden centers and the zoo. She would have taken Dallas to the mall too, but her daughter had never had an interest in shopping and she hated crowds. Fair enough. Terri didn't mind the zoo, though she preferred to see animals in the wild. The cages had begun to remind her uncomfortably of her own.

There had never been arguments, or harsh words between them. Dallas had never woken up to hear them screaming at each other. Derek had been too mild-mannered for that. But when he reached for her in the night, which happened with less and less frequency, her skin crawled. That was when she realized she wasn't in love with him anymore. She wasn't sure she had loved him at all.

Terri could have kept up the charade of her marriage for years, as her own mother had. It wasn't pleasant, but it was tolerable. In some respects, it was comfortable. The idea of dating again, of having to go to nightclubs and singles' events like her divorced friends, also made her skin crawl. But she wanted more for her daughter. She didn't want Dallas to grow up thinking this was what marriage was supposed to be like, believing that women should be responsible for everything, while men watched television and read newspapers that they left on the floor. She wanted her daughter to see that her mother could be happy *and* satisfied.

So Terri had left.

And Dallas had been furious with her ever since.

But what if it was more than that? What if her daughter's mood swings and prickliness had nothing to do with the divorce, but with her own brain? It was a horrible thought.

Still, she'd seen her daughter arguing with someone who wasn't there. She hadn't seen her throw the game – she'd been too slow for that – but there was no way anyone could have gotten past her. If this 'Niles' existed, he would have been in the room when she'd burst in. But he wasn't; he didn't. Dallas had been alone.

The fact that her daughter's imaginary friend had the same name as the boy who'd once lived in this house and died in that room was troubling, but like Vandermere had suspected, Dallas must have read about Niles online. It was the only explanation. Her daughter had sworn she hadn't, but if she was having auditory and visual hallucinations, she easily could have forgotten reading about the Vandermere family. Terri could no longer trust her daughter's word, and the thought filled her with dread.

She considered calling her mother to ask if she'd noticed anything unusual about Dallas's behavior, but discarded the idea as quickly as she'd come up with it. Helen Foxworth hadn't thought taking this job was a good idea. She didn't think it was safe for her granddaughter to live in an old house, where there could be asbestos, rotten floorboards, or any number of hazards lying in wait. She'd use Terri's worry and concern against her as leverage to push for her granddaughter to be returned. Getting Dallas for the summer, and maybe the year, had been a big enough fight as it was.

No, she had to figure this out on her own. She had to be brave. If her daughter *was* on the spectrum, she'd get her the help she needed, no matter how much it cost. The important thing was that they spend the summer together in this house, restoring their relationship.

"Mom?"

Terri jumped. She'd been so deep in thought that she hadn't heard her daughter come into the room. Dallas's face was blotchy, her eyes red. It was obvious she'd been crying, and Terri felt terrible. Nothing that had happened upstairs was Dallas's fault. She couldn't control hallucinations, and she certainly couldn't control her brain.

"All done?" she asked, trying to sound cheerful. She had to show Dallas she wasn't angry. Now she regretted yelling at her, and snapping at her earlier in the evening. She was going to have to be more patient. A lot more patient.

"I'm scared."

Those two words were the last thing she'd expected, and they broke her heart. "I'm sorry I scared you. I shouldn't have gotten so upset. I apologize. I know it wasn't your fault."

Dallas looked taken aback. "You do?" When Terri nodded, she said, "So you believe me about Niles?"

Terri hesitated. "I believe he's real to you."

"Mom, he *is* real. He told me he went into the closet when you got to the room, so you wouldn't see him." Dallas wrinkled her nose. "He's a jerk. All he does is get me in trouble, and I'm sick of it."

Terri's mind raced. What was the right thing to do? Should she be honest, or play along? What was best for Dallas? She had no idea. "That's impossible," she said as gently as she could. "There was no time for him to get into the closet – I was right outside your room. It took me a second or two to get there, at most. And I didn't see anyone but you."

"You're saying I'm crazy again."

"No, not crazy. Of course you're not crazy. But what would you think about taking a day off tomorrow? We could drive back to the city, go for lunch, and you could talk to Miss Akinlade for a bit. What do you think?"

"I think it's stupid. I don't like Miss Akinlade. I don't want to talk to her."

Terri knew Dallas wasn't being honest. She'd liked Miss Akinlade a lot, and had been upset when the visits with the psychologist had stopped. "Why don't you like her? I thought she was really nice."

"It's a dumb idea, okay? I want to stay here tomorrow. I have to unpack, and you have a lot of work to do." Her daughter's tone was so accusatory, Terri felt like *she* was the child.

"That can wait. If Miss Akinlade has an opening tomorrow, we're going."

Dallas rolled her eyes. "Then why even ask me?"

Because I thought you'd agree with me. Because I thought you'd say what I wanted you to. Because I thought you'd be happy.

But that was ridiculous, wasn't it? Dallas was never happy when they were together, though her mother claimed that the child was always euphoric when she was out of Terri's sight. Perhaps *she* should be the one who spoke to Miss Akinlade.

Before she could respond, a loud crash sounded from above. It shook the house, startling them.

"What on earth was that?"

"That's what I was trying to tell you, Mom. That's why I'm scared. Niles is really angry. At both of us."

★   ★   ★

Niles's room was a disaster.

The wallpaper was in shreds. The curtain rod had been torn from the window. The box of belongings that her daughter had repacked had been turned on its side and crushed flat. Games, books, and model planes were everywhere. Torn pages littered the floor, and Terri's stomach churned. Miss Vandermere was going to be furious, might even fire her over this, and who could blame her? These items were priceless.

Her daughter hadn't done this. No matter how upset or frustrated Dallas had been, she wasn't destructive. She loved books and respected them. She would never have destroyed them like this.

"Mom!" Dallas had tears in her eyes again.

"It's okay. I know you didn't do this. Let's go." Taking her daughter by the arm, she hustled her out the door and away from the room. The girl was in such shock she didn't attempt to pull away.

"Where are we going to go?"

"We'll stay in a hotel, just for the night. I'll figure this out in the morning." She paused, trying her best not to worry about how much it would cost. "Do you need anything from the room?"

"No, I brought all my stuff to yours."

"Good, let's grab what we need for the night and get out of here."

For once, there were no complaints. No whining, sighing, or rolling of the eyes. Dallas hurried to the room Terri had chosen to temporarily call her own, and they worked in companionable silence, stuffing things into their carry-on suitcases.

Before they left, she took the time to make a phone call.

"Hello, police? I'd like to report an intruder."

CHAPTER SIX

It was hard to tell who was more reluctant to return to the house the next day.

"Do you want me to quit?" The very thought made her want to go back to bed and stay there, but her daughter's comfort and safety were way more important than any job. Leaving Vandermere in the lurch would do untold damage to her professional reputation, not to mention her bank account, but she'd figure out how to deal with that. There would be other jobs, even if they had to move again. When she saw the destruction of Niles's room, Vandermere would probably fire her anyway.

Dallas considered it for a moment before shaking her head. "No. Niles is a brat. He's used to getting his own way. He wants us to leave, so I think we should stay."

Other than the destroyed room, the police hadn't been able to find signs of anyone else in the house. They couldn't find a point of entry, either. Sounding irritatingly weary, the officer she'd spoken to on the phone had told her it was safe for them to return.

But what did he know? Not so long ago, she hadn't believed in Niles either.

Once back at the house, Terri's heart leapt into her throat when she saw a woman waiting for them on the veranda. This was no police officer, and thankfully, it wasn't Miss Vandermere, either. She didn't think she would have been able to bear that, definitely not before coffee.

The woman's age was impossible to determine. Though her face was smooth and unlined, it had the tight, pinched look of someone much older, someone who didn't suffer fools. Whoever she was, Terri had a feeling she wasn't going to like her, and probably vice versa.

"Who is *that*?" Dallas asked as they got out of the car.

"I'm not sure." She reached for her daughter's hand out of nerves, and to her amazement, Dallas gave it to her.

The woman stood as they approached. She was wearing a wool coat, even though it was summer and the temperature was already climbing. "Ms. Foxworth?"

"Yes?"

"Please forgive me for dropping in on you like this, but I work here. Or, I should say, I *worked* here. Before you were hired. My name is Gertrude Phillips."

"Gertie?" The nickname slipped out before she could think better of it.

The woman smiled, which improved her features considerably. The pinched look disappeared. "I see Miss Vandermere has mentioned me. She's the only one who calls me that. I hate to think what she must have told you about me."

"That you were a dedicated and loyal employee who was extremely committed to the house."

Gertrude's eyes flashed, taking on a mischievous look. "Well, that's a nice change. I'm glad to hear it."

"She also said you might drop by. She actually thought you were here while she was giving me the initial tour of the house." Terri wasn't sure why she'd added that, except for the fact that she was praying Gertrude would tell them it was she who had moved the curtains in the attic.

"Really? I certainly wasn't, but I'm glad to meet you now." Gertrude extended her hand, and Terri reluctantly let go of Dallas's to take it. The woman's handshake was strong and confident, belying her meek appearance. "Do you mind if we chat for a bit? There are a few things I think you should know if you're going to be working at Glenvale."

"Sure." The woman seemed a bit strange, but it sounded like she had information, and information was something Terri was in desperate need of.

"Mom, can I weed the garden? It looks like it needs it."

She wasn't fooled. As much as Dallas liked gardening, this was a stalling tactic. She didn't want to go back in the house yet, and Terri couldn't blame her. How were they going to last the summer, let alone the year? "That sounds like a good idea." Before she could remind Dallas of her manners, her daughter was gone, running around the side of the house to the shed. She smiled at Gertrude, shrugging. "Sorry about that. Kids."

"Not a problem. There's certainly enough to keep her busy out here while we talk." When they got to the door, she turned. "Would you mind opening up? I'm afraid Miss Vandermere took my key when she fired me."

Terri gasped. She couldn't help it. Though she'd never laid eyes on Gertrude before today, not even in a photograph, she'd come to think of her as the ideal employee, the house manager, Miss Vandermere's right-hand woman. A woman who had been laid off because of the economy, not fired. "She *fired* you?"

"Yes, I'm afraid she did. Right before she hired you."

"But she spoke so highly of you."

Gertrude smiled. "Yes, she did, didn't she? Like I said, it was a nice change. However, she apparently forgot to take my name off the contact list, so the police called me early this morning. That's why I'm here. There are some things about this house that you need to know."

As Terri led the way inside, she couldn't help feeling nervous. Miss Vandermere had made Gertrude sound as if she was obsessed with Glenvale, unable to resist checking on the house, even during the off season. Why would she have fired her? Was there a chance Gertrude was unhinged, maybe dangerous? Miss Vandermere had told her that she'd never gotten Gertrude's key, while Gertrude claimed Vandermere had taken it. Who wasn't telling the truth? She wasn't comfortable having the other woman behind her, and waited until they were walking beside each other. "Should we talk in the kitchen? I could make us some tea."

Though the temperature outdoors was approaching seventy-eight degrees, inside the house it was cool and drafty. She felt a chill.

"Tea would be nice. Thank you."

She didn't seem deranged, but then again, Ted Bundy hadn't, either.

"I don't mean to pry, but I don't understand why Miss Vandermere would fire you. Like I said, she spoke so highly of you. She led me to believe you'd been laid off."

"She didn't say anything about my overactive imagination?" Gertrude sounded amused.

"No, not about yours. She did complain about some other restorers, who she'd said abandoned the project."

Gertrude snorted. "Abandoned? Try fired. She let them go too, for the same reason she fired me."

Terri joined her at the table, feeling weak behind the knees. All thoughts of tea were forgotten. "What reason is that?" It couldn't be Vandermere's hate-on for anyone with an imagination. That would be insane.

"We got too close to the truth. She's willing to do anything to prevent that, whether it's firing loyal employees, threatening to sue us, or God knows what else."

"She threatened to *sue* you?" Terri struggled to picture the elderly lady being that vindictive.

"Oh, I received a lovely little cease-and-desist letter from her attorney, but I didn't let it bother me too much. She did it out of fear, and the need to protect the family name. Besides, she knows I have nothing worth taking. Especially since I don't have a job anymore."

"I'm sorry." She didn't know what to say. Whether Gertrude had deserved to be fired or not, her predicament was unfortunate. Terri had experienced lean times herself, but she'd always been able to find more work. There probably weren't a lot of museums in town in need of house managers.

"It's all right. It honestly was for the best. You wouldn't know it to look at me, because my sister is a miracle worker, but my hair has gone almost totally gray from stress. Working for Miss Vandermere – working *here* – was taking years from my life."

Looking at Gertrude's smooth brown bob, Terri had to concede that at least the part about the woman's sister was true. She wouldn't have known it wasn't Gertrude's natural color. Before she could think of what to say, the other woman leaned forward, pinning her to her chair with a look so intense it was unnerving. "Ms. Foxworth, do you believe in ghosts?"

Ghosts. There it was again. "A week ago, I would have said no, but now, I'm not so sure."

"You must believe in them if you're going to work here. You *must.* Otherwise, you'll drive yourself and your daughter crazy. Your daughter will certainly see them, even if you don't. Going by the phone call I received from the police, I'm guessing one or both of you has met him already. And someone upset him greatly."

Terri couldn't have been more shocked if Gertrude had started speaking in tongues. "You know about Niles?"

"Of *course* I know about Niles. As you've noticed, he's not exactly shy. And I'm convinced Miss Vandermere knows about him too, though she'd die before admitting it."

"Then he's not a mentally ill child? He's not...real?"

Gertrude laughed. "Oh, he's perfectly real, but he's not alive, if that's what you're asking. Poor thing died almost a hundred years ago."

Remembering the seemingly one-sided conversation she'd overheard Dallas having the night before, Terri shivered. "I thought my daughter was having hallucinations."

"You're not the first. Niles isn't a fan of adults, for obvious reasons, but he can't resist children. It takes a lot of time and trust before he'll appear in front of an adult."

"Why isn't he a fan of adults?" Terri asked, though she could scarcely accept that she was having this conversation. "Because they don't believe?"

"Oh, he couldn't care less whether you believe in him or not. *He*

knows he's real. No, it's because he was treated poorly by adults."
Gertrude glanced around the kitchen. "Any chance of that tea? My
mouth is feeling dry."

"I'm sorry." Terri jumped up from the table, feeling embarrassed.
"I got distracted by all this." She went to the box of items she'd
brought to the house, which thankfully was still on the counter. At
least Niles's rage appeared to be confined to his own things. "Earl
Grey okay?"

"That'll be fine, thank you. I get it, trust me. It's not every day
someone shows up and tells you the house you're working on is
haunted. But you specialize in restorations. You must have had
some experience with this kind of thing before, working on all those
old houses."

"Honestly, no. Or if I did, I never noticed." She thought
uncomfortably of the Davis house again, but that had been disturbing
for other reasons. Tangible reasons.

"You've experienced something. I can see it on your face."

"Oh, I was hired for a clean-up job once. A family had been
murdered in the house." She filled the kettle with water, hoping
Gertrude wouldn't notice her hands were trembling. "It was – well,
it was an upsetting experience, to say the least. Their blood…and
other things…were all over the house."

"I'm so sorry." Gertrude looked sympathetic, but not appalled,
the way others had when she mentioned it. "That must have been
extremely difficult."

"Thank you. It was. But this work is always difficult, for different
reasons every time. Each house poses its own challenge."

"And in this one, you have Niles." She was quiet a moment
before asking, "Forgive me, but wasn't that a strange thing to hire a
restorer for? What you do takes real skill. It's an art, bringing these
houses back to life. Seems to me they could have hired a cleaning
company for that job."

"I guess no one else was willing to do it, and I needed the
money, so…."

Gertrude raised her hands. "Say no more. I understand all about needing work."

"How do you know Niles was badly treated?" Terri asked, bringing a small carton of milk and a sack of sugar to the table with two spoons. She didn't want to interrupt Gertrude's train of thought by asking how she took her tea. "I thought his father doted on him. I've heard Howard Vandermere was never the same after Niles died."

Gertrude shook her head. "That's what the family wanted people to think, and as far as I can tell, they managed to fool everyone. Forensics weren't what they are today, and no one would have suspected a father of killing their own child in those days."

Terri realized her mouth was hanging open and closed it with a snap. "*Howard* murdered him? Did Niles tell you that?" Wait, had she just asked that question, as if Niles were able to communicate? Did she believe this wild story? But if she didn't, who else had destroyed his room? Dallas had been with her when they'd heard the commotion. Her daughter hadn't made that mess. Unless there had been a highly contained earthquake, or an intruder who'd left before the police arrived, there was no other explanation.

"Not exactly. I don't think Niles knows *who* killed him, though he might have an idea. There were some signs at first, clues I picked up on from working here. Once Niles began to communicate with me, my suspicions were confirmed." Gertrude's hazel eyes bore into hers without blinking, and Terri looked away, shifting on her seat. Something about the other woman was unnerving, and she was beginning to regret inviting her in. What if Gertrude wasn't just obsessed with the house, but psychotic?

She laid her hand over Terri's, startling her so much that Terri had to bite her lip to keep from crying out. "I know what you're thinking. I can see it on your face. Others have thought the same, but I am *not* crazy."

"I-I wasn't thinking that." Was there anything in this room she could use as a weapon? The kettle wasn't heavy enough, but hadn't she seen a poker for the kitchen stove? That could work.

"You were. I've seen it before. I didn't believe any of this at first, either. Vandermere kept insisting everything I saw and heard was the product of my 'overactive imagination', until I thought I would go mad," she said. "I wasn't someone who went around wearing crystals to open my chakras or giving tarot card readings, Ms. Foxworth. Niles was my first encounter with something of this nature, but he *does* exist. Surely you can't have any doubts about that?"

But in the harsh light of day, she *did* have doubts. At night, with the police telling her there was no one in the house, and that there were no signs of a break-in, other than the destroyed room, it had been easier to believe. "I was so sure he was an actor. I guess I did a good job of convincing myself."

"An actor?" Gertrude raised an eyebrow, a bemused expression on her face.

"From the historical recreations. I thought the boy who played Niles had gotten confused and stayed behind. It sounds a bit ridiculous now."

"But there never were—"

"There weren't historical recreations. I know that now. But that's what I thought initially. I didn't have any other explanation."

"You have one now. I'm telling you the truth."

"I'm sorry, I don't mean to give the impression that I'm doubting your word. It's just difficult for me to wrap my head around all this. Why would his father have killed him? To end his suffering?"

That was the most benign reason she could give, and it was almost understandable. Diabetes was a cruel disease now, but back then, when so little had been known about it, it would have seemed like a monster. It must have been unbearable to watch your own child struggle and not have any clue how to help him.

"This wasn't a mercy killing. Do you think Niles would be hanging around if it was? He wants justice. If his father had killed him out of kindness, however misguided, there would be no need."

"What, then?" Terri wasn't sure she wanted to know, but something made her ask in spite of herself. Would she be able to work there after Gertrude was finished? Or would her fear of the house – and yes, Niles – have become too great?

"The Vandermeres had three children. Emma, Niles, and Henrietta. Niles wasn't the eldest, but as the male, he was the intended heir, and the fortune he was expected to inherit was unprecedented. The family was worth millions over a hundred years ago, which is probably like billions today." She paused to sip her tea. "If my accounting is a bit off, forgive me. Math was never my best subject."

"But Niles was sickly," Terri added, the uncomfortable truth becoming clear. "I'd read that his father was beginning to show him the ropes of the family business, even so."

"He was. While Niles was alive, Howard loved his son, and never stopped hoping a true cure would be found for his disease, something that would free him of it completely. The boy's death shattered him. I'm sure the guilt he felt was a large part of that."

Gertrude pushed back her chair and rose, stretching. "Do you mind if I move around? It helps me think. After Niles grew ill, Emma – the eldest child – was the most likely heir. Some would argue that she'd always been. She was smart, with a good head for business, unlike poor Niles, who leaned toward more creative pursuits." She paused long enough to make a face. "You can imagine how well *that* went over in those days. Niles was bullied and called a pansy, in addition to other lovely names. Meanwhile, Emma was the better 'son' for the Vandermere family. She excelled in typically masculine pursuits, including horseback riding, skeet shooting, and fencing. Rumor has it that she was an accomplished huntress as well."

Rumor has it? Who would be spreading rumors about a family that had last been high profile decades before? She could see why Vandermere might be concerned with Gertrude's 'dedication' to Glenvale, and by extension, her family.

"It was the very fact that she was so accomplished that makes her death so strange. A riding accident…most unusual for a woman who had won countless ribbons for her expertise with horses, don't you think?"

Terri could scarcely believe what she was hearing, and the

woman's pacing in the cramped room was making her nervous. With the baking table, original wood-burning stove, china cabinet, and sinks, there was barely any room to move around as it was. "You're not saying Emma was murdered too?"

"I haven't encountered Emma's ghost, so I can't be sure, but it's suspicious, no? Someone wanted to make sure Henrietta was the one to inherit the family fortune."

"But why? That doesn't make any sense."

"It doesn't seem to make much, no. One could argue that Henrietta's stewardship didn't hurt anything. The Vandermeres remain one of the wealthiest families in the state. But she didn't improve matters much, either. Emma would have grown the family empire considerably if she'd had the chance. The best Henrietta could do was keep it in a kind of holding pattern."

"I don't believe Howard murdered two of his children, just to make sure Henrietta inherited. Especially when, as you say, it didn't end up doing the family much good. I can't see any parent being that cruel."

Rather than appear offended, Gertrude shrugged. "It's a theory. I was never able to prove anything. As soon as I got close, I was fired."

"You said you found clues that led you to this theory. What clues? What did you find?"

Gertrude gripped the back of a chair, studying Terri's face. "Not yet. I don't know you well enough to be sure I can trust you."

It was understandable, but frustrating. Why had Gertrude come here, if it wasn't to reveal what she'd learned? How did she expect Terri to earn her trust, when they'd most likely never see each other again?

She didn't have to wonder long. With Gertrude's next words, all became clear.

"I have a proposition for you. Let me continue my investigation." She held up her hand before Terri could respond. "Please, hear me out. I'll stay out of your way entirely. You'll find having me here will be quite helpful. No one living, aside from Miss Vandermere, knows this house better than I do. I can make the meals and entertain Dallas while you're working."

She looked so hopeful that it was difficult to say no, but the thought of this strange woman spending time with her daughter was more frightening than the prospect of living with a ghost. "I'm sorry, but I can't jeopardize this job. If Miss Vandermere fired you, she doesn't want you on her property any longer. I can't risk her finding you here. I'm a single mother – this income is crucial for us."

Gertrude nodded, her lips tightening. "I understand. I'll be going then." She reached for her purse, and Terri felt an unexpected sense of loss. She *did* want to learn more about the house, and Vandermere had praised this woman's loyalty and work ethic. *Then why had she fired her? Was it really that she'd gotten too close to the truth, or was it something else?*

"Wait. I can't have you living here, but maybe there's something else we can do."

"What do you have in mind, Ms. Foxworth?"

"Please, call me Terri," she said, playing for time. What *did* she have in mind, that was the question. "How about regular visits? If you were to come by, say, once a week, we should be able to hide that from Miss Vandermere, right? I'm guessing you can predict her schedule better than anyone, but she hasn't been by to check on things since she hired me." It was still a risk. She couldn't imagine what would happen to her and Dallas if they lost this job, and she didn't want to.

"Honestly, it's less likely to be noticed if I'm living in the house. Otherwise, people will see me coming and going." Noticing the expression on Terri's face, she quickly added, "But I completely understand why you're not comfortable with that yet. Perhaps you'll change your mind once you know me better."

The *yet* was troubling. Terri couldn't imagine ever being that comfortable with Gertrude, and hoped the woman wasn't deluding herself. Say what she wanted about Miss Vandermere, her employer had told her the truth – Gertrude *was* obsessed with the house.

"And don't fool yourself, Ms. – Terri. Vandermere has ways of keeping an eye on things, even if she's not physically on the property. She knows exactly how things are going here, and she knows all about your visit with law enforcement yesterday. She'll also know you stayed in a hotel last night, rather than in the house. So be careful. As you're aware, she doesn't have a lot of patience for those who flout the rules."

That didn't make sense. If Vandermere was aware the police had been there, why hadn't she called or come by? If she cared so much about the house, wouldn't she have checked to make sure everything was okay? "But if that's true, how did you expect to live here without her finding out?"

Gertrude smirked. "Years of experience."

A long, low moan echoed through the room. Terri froze. It was an unearthly sound, but she instantly knew it was *not* air in the pipes. Rather than seem spooked, Gertrude brightened.

"I'd almost forgotten. He can eavesdrop on anything we say when we're in this room. He's probably listened to our entire conversation."

Before Terri could ask who she was talking about, the woman had moved to the speaking tube and was cooing into it. "Hullo, Niles. I'm back for a visit. See, I told you I would never abandon you."

Another moan. This time, the pitch rose at the end, turning it into more of a wail. She might be going insane, but Terri could have sworn she heard someone crying.

"Don't cry, Niles. Of course I still love you. Your mean old sister sent me away. I had no choice." She looked over at Terri and winked. "But I have a feeling I'll be back."

CHAPTER SEVEN

"Is Niles a ghost, Mom?"

"Huh?" Terri had been so lost in thought that she'd forgotten her daughter was there. The Hamburger Helper she'd made for dinner sat mostly untouched on her plate. It was awkward to eat without a table, in any case. Following Gertrude's visit, Terri had made the executive decision to move their meals into the parlor. To protect the fine furniture, they sat on the slip covers and balanced their plates on their laps. She was thankful it was early enough that light still streamed through the window. After dusk, the sheet-covered furniture looming over them would feel ominous.

There was no way she'd feel comfortable in the kitchen again. Even making a meal in there had been nerve-racking, but fortunately, the speaking tube had remained silent.

"I said, is Niles a ghost? Like, for real?"

"I think so." As bizarre as the situation was, she had to accept it. While there was a possibility that a living boy had found the world's best hiding place in this house, she'd heard Dallas's conversation and seen the aftermath of Niles's rampage. Either she believed in ghosts, or believed her own daughter was insane. "Does that bother you?"

Part of her wanted Dallas to say it did, to beg her to quit. It would have been a welcome excuse, although it wouldn't have done their finances any favors. She was willing to move in with her mother again, if that's what it took to get back on her feet. Anything was better than her daughter feeling unsafe.

"Not really, I guess. It's kind of cool. I never talked to a ghost before."

Damn. "You don't find it scary?"

Dallas thought for a moment, and then shook her head. "No, only when he gets upset. But that happened because I was telling him to go away. I won't say that anymore. Now that you know he isn't dangerous, I can go back to being his friend."

But I don't know that. If Niles could destroy his room, what could he do to her daughter? "I think you should keep your distance as much as possible. I want you to choose another room to sleep in."

She'd expected a pout, but perhaps last night's episode had bothered Dallas more than the girl had let on. "Okay."

"When Niles talks to you, what does he say?"

"Not much of anything, really. He's bossy. He kept pressuring me to find his things and put them back where they belonged. Can't we leave them there, Mom, just while we're living here? Otherwise, he'll never shut up about it."

Terri had been eager to pack everything associated with Niles away in a box and hide it in the far reaches of a closet, but if leaving it out meant less harassment for her daughter, what was the harm? "As long as you promise not to touch anything."

"I think it's too late for that, Mom. Don't you remember what he did last night? He trashed everything."

With a sinking heart, Terri remembered what she'd been trying to forget. Someone had to clean up the mess in Niles's room, and that someone was going to be her. No way she'd let Dallas near it.

"Who was that woman today?"

"Oh, that was Gertrude Phillips. She used to work here."

"Is she going to come live with us?"

"No, why? Did she tell you she was?" If she had, Vandermere's ex-employee was even more unstable than Terri had thought. So much for the weekly visits.

"No, not exactly. When she left the house, she stopped to compliment me on how I was fixing up the garden. Niles had told me she wanted to stay with us, so I asked her."

"What did she say?"

"She winked at me and said, 'Ask your mother.' She's not, is she?"

Terri's fear turned to anger. "No, she's not." Whatever Gertrude's obsession was with the house, she wanted no part of it. For all Terri knew, everything she'd said was a product of her own delusions. There was absolutely no proof that Niles and Emma had been murdered. If there were, surely Gertrude would have gone to the police as soon as she was fired.

The house phone rang, making them both jump. It sounded unusually loud in the quiet heaviness of Glenvale. Terri hurried to answer, as it was an old rotary-dial model that didn't have voice mail.

"Hello?"

"I heard you had a visitor today." The voice was cold, female, and more than a little accusatory.

Ugh. The last person in the world she wanted to talk to, aside from Gertrude. "Yes, I was going to call you about that. We had an incident here last night, and I wanted to make sure everything—"

Vandermere cut her off. "I'm not talking about the *police*, Ms. Foxworth. As you may recall, I'm the one who told you to contact them in the first place. I'm glad to see you're taking my advice in some regard."

"I'm sorry, if you don't mean the police, I'm not sure I understand—"

"Oh, we're going to play games, are we?" The fury in her employer's voice was unexpected. "I didn't realize you were a game player."

"I'm not. But I—"

"Please drop this silly charade, Ms. Foxworth. We both know I'm referring to my lovely former employee, Gertie Phillips."

Terri's cheeks grew hot. *Damn that woman.* Gertrude had known Vandermere had eyes on the back of her head, and she'd taken it upon herself to come here and jeopardize Terri's job anyway. "But isn't she still welcome here?" she asked, her instinct for self-preservation kicking in. "Didn't you tell me she was laid off because of the economy?"

"You may be a wonderful restorer, but you're no actress. I'm sure she told you about my little white lie during her visit."

"She did, but what I don't understand is the reason for it. If you don't want her on the property, why didn't you tell me?"

Vandermere sighed. "I have no time or inclination for petty gossip. I thought I was being kind. I also thought she'd have the decency to stay away from the house while you were working there. I am one hundred years old, Ms. Foxworth – did you know that? And yet, people never fail to surprise – or disappoint – me."

A hundred years old. She had assumed her employer was at least twenty years younger. It didn't seem possible for Vandermere to be that age and in such good shape. Against her misgivings, she decided to trust her. "She had a rather disturbing story. I have to admit it unnerved me."

"Was it that outrageous theory she came up with about my father killing my brother?"

Another shock. Terri had never imagined Vandermere would know. Perhaps Gertrude was right, and the older woman didn't miss anything that went on in this house. But how was that possible? Bugs? Any listening device would be disturbed, and most likely destroyed, during the extensive restoration. She would most definitely find it. "Yes, and your sister."

"Oh, she's made it even more ludicrous now. Lovely. As if murdering one child wasn't enough." Vandermere didn't sound angry, or even mildly concerned, which filled Terri with relief. Surely if there was any truth to Gertrude's theory, she'd have been desperate to keep it a secret.

"So it's not true."

"Of course it's not true. I'm going to be frank. Miss Phillips has mental issues. She appeared to be fine when I hired her. In fact, I'd wager she was more than fine. She was a model employee. But she became obsessed with the house. I'd find her talking to the walls, and listening as if someone was speaking back."

Terri thought of the eerie episode with the speaking tube. Someone *had* been speaking back – or had they? Come to think of it, she'd never actually heard anything more than moans coming back through the tube, but Gertrude had responded to them as if she were having a conversation. At the time, she'd thought the woman had the ability to understand Niles, but now there was another explanation. One that was much more probable.

"She did that today, only she used the speaking tube."

"That dreadful speaking tube will be the death of me. Whenever the wind blows, it makes this ghastly moaning sound. Gertie was convinced someone was sending her messages from beyond the grave. If it wasn't considered such a quaint feature now, I'd ask you to get rid of it."

"I might be able to stop it from moaning." Terri wasn't sure how wind was reaching an internal structure, but whatever was causing the noise could most likely be fixed.

"Would you? That would be delightful. Perhaps it will help preserve the sanity of my future employees."

"I'll do my best."

"Then you wish to continue working at Glenvale?"

The question took Terri aback. "I do, but it sounded like you wanted to fire me."

Vandermere chuckled. "Not at all. You have a good head on your shoulders. You had no reason to think Miss Phillips wasn't welcome on the property. You did nothing wrong. I should have been more honest about my dealings with her."

Whew. "There is something else." Might as well get everything over with at once.

"Yes?"

"Well, as I'd mentioned, I called the police last night. Someone trashed your brother's room, and I was afraid there might still be an intruder in the house."

"What do you mean by 'trashed', exactly? What was the extent of the damage?"

"I was about to go set things to rights when you called, but it looks like Niles's model planes had been thrown around and some pages torn out of his books. Some of the planes and games may have been damaged."

"I must admit I'm confused. That room was left empty, except for a few pieces of old furniture. His models and books were in storage."

Damn. "I'm sorry, Miss Vandermere, but my daughter found them. She was taken with the idea of putting the room back the way it had been when Niles was using it, but she didn't touch anything other than that. I made sure of it. I know how valuable those items are."

"I wouldn't worry about that. I hardly think the loss of a few old models and books is going to destroy the family fortune."

Of course. How could she have been so silly? If Niles's belongings meant anything to his sister, it was sentimental value, not monetary. For Terri and her daughter, the money that could have been earned by selling them would have made a substantial difference, but for Miss Vandermere, not so much.

"Anyway, I'm very sorry about what happened. I should have made my daughter put them back. But it is upsetting that someone broke in here and destroyed them."

"I believe you met your intruder today, Ms. Foxworth. You'll be fine."

"You mean...you think Gertrude?"

"Yes, I think Gertrude. Who else would trouble themselves with a young man's playthings? For all her obsession with Glenvale, it paled in comparison to her obsession with my brother."

"But why would she destroy his belongings if she cared for him?" As strange as the woman had been, it had been obvious that she *did* care for Niles Vandermere. Terri tried to imagine Gertrude going on a rampage and tearing up the boy's books, but she couldn't. Vandermere may claim that she was forever surprised by people, but Terri believed *she* was a good judge of character. Gertrude might have some outlandish theories, but she wasn't capable of the destruction in Niles's room.

"Do you know what it's like to be mad and suffer from delusions?" Clearly not expecting an answer, Vandermere continued. "Nor do I. Who knows what was going on in that mind of hers when she did it?

Perhaps she was furious that someone else had handled Niles's things. She was quite protective of them."

That made sense, she supposed, as much as any of this did. What a strange thing to be obsessed about, but perhaps Gertrude desperately wanted children, and didn't – or couldn't – have any. She'd witnessed the desire for a child turn other women a bit squirrelly.

Terri wanted to ask about the possibility of a ghost. Even if Gertrude were responsible for the disaster in Niles's room, it didn't explain her daughter's experience of seeing and talking to a young man in old-fashioned clothes. But she didn't dare. If she mentioned it, it would lead to another lecture about overactive imaginations, and Vandermere might suggest Dallas was 'mad' too. That conversion wouldn't end well.

"I'll do my best to salvage what I can. Hopefully there's not too much damage."

"Thank you. I appreciate that, but please don't spend too much time on it. The restoration is more important. For my part, I'll send the police around to pay Miss Phillips a visit, and make sure she hasn't acquired another key."

"When she came here this afternoon, I had to let her in. She said you'd taken her key – that's why she let me know she'd been fired."

Vandermere was silent for a moment. "That's good to know. Thank you. Still, it's an old house and she knew it well. She may have found another way in."

★　　★　　★

It felt like the door stared back at her, regarding her as warily as she regarded it. She never left any of the doors shut on this floor. The rooms needed all the 'airing out' they could get. Before her imagination ran away with her again, Terri told herself that the police had probably closed the door behind them. There was always a rational explanation. She'd forgotten that last night.

Gertrude's story of a double murder and a brutal quest to ensure

Henrietta had been the heir at all costs had been disturbing, to say the least. Vandermere's calm rejection of it had made her feel better, but now that she was up here alone, that sense of peace had vanished. Was Gertrude capable of doing all the things Miss Vandermere believed, or was she merely a convenient scapegoat?

Terri grasped the filigree knob, wondering again why it didn't match the other half. Standing out here ruminating wasn't going to get the job done, but the truth was, she dreaded what awaited her.

Taking a deep breath, she opened the door.

What awaited her was the last thing she could have expected.

The room was perfect.

The bed was neatly made, and all of the games and books had been returned to where Dallas had put them the day before. No torn pages or game pieces littered the floor, and none of the planes appeared the worse for wear. Somehow, Dallas must have found time to do this, but she had no idea when, or whether to be pleased or upset. She didn't like the idea of her daughter being in the room alone, not after everything that had happened. Cleaning up in here must have taken hours. When had she found the time?

After setting the cleaning equipment on the floor next to Niles's closet, Terri ventured further into the room. It was perfectly silent and still – no wind blowing, no draft, and no young man in old-fashioned clothes loitering about. The room *was* several degrees colder than the rest of the house, but that was hardly supernatural. If she had to guess, she'd choose poorly insulated windows as the culprit.

As if reading her mind, one of the lace curtains fluttered, and Terri headed in that direction. What had Niles looked at during all those lonely hours when he'd been stuck in bed? How had the view changed over time?

Looking out, she couldn't see much, other than the silhouettes of shrubs and trees, standing in stark relief against a periwinkle sky. It remained light out later and later now. Soon it would be the longest day of the year. Terri wondered how much Dallas had managed to do with the garden, and felt guilty that she hadn't taken the time to check out her daughter's handiwork. Tomorrow; she'd do it tomorrow.

Bang.

Terri whirled around. Niles's closet door had flown open, sending her cleaning supplies sprawling. "Shit!" She ran for them, envisioning the bleach leaking onto the hardwood floor, destroying it. But all the bottles were still closed.

Terri approached the closet as carefully as one would approach a snarling dog, and looked inside. It was empty, but large enough to conceal several people. Gertrude, maybe? Or whoever was pretending to be Niles, assuming she was abandoning the ghost theory. The closet door was a single piece of solid wood with the ubiquitous white doorknob – white on both sides this time. It was extremely heavy, nothing like the hollow-core doors used in modern homes.

She closed it and tested the latch to see if the door would let go and swing open again, but it was a tight fit. She knew it had been closed when she'd entered the room.

"Niles?" she whispered, feeling foolish but also scared. She turned her back to the closet once more to see if the same thing would happen. Nothing. Perhaps there was a loose joint in the floorboards that had triggered the closet door? She retraced her path to the window, over and over again, at one point even hopping across, putting as much weight on the floor as she could. Still nothing.

There was no rational explanation for the closet door flying open the way it had, and no Gertrude lurked within. But there was also no reason for her to stay – no cleaning nor salvaging needed to be done. The room was in better shape than most of the others.

Unnerved, Terri left, closing the door behind her.

CHAPTER EIGHT

Dallas clicked the light off and turned on her side, closing her eyes. She found it hard to sleep in this house, and no wonder. Why couldn't her mother have a normal job, like other moms? Or better yet, it would be great if she could afford to stay home all day like Angela's mom. Her mom didn't have enough money to do that, though, and her dad wasn't helping. She didn't like to think that way, because she loved her dad, but he would have made it a lot easier on them if he'd given her mom a little money now and then.

The light snapped back on. Heart pounding, Dallas flipped over, expecting to see her mother. But it was Niles standing by her bed, his rosy face looking even pinker in the lamp light. "Oh, it's you."

"Why aren't you in my room anymore?" His lower lip protruded in a pout.

"If you keep making that face, it'll freeze that way," Dallas said, parroting one of her grandmother's all-time favorite sayings. Then again, maybe the saying wasn't much of a threat if you were dead. She supposed not.

"I like you being there. Please come back."

"I can't, thanks to you. You had to throw that big tantrum and scare my mom. Now I'm not allowed anywhere near your room."

"I apologize for my behavior. I was upset."

"Being upset is no reason to throw your stuff everywhere. If you were alive, you'd be grounded." Dallas bit her lip. *Oops.*

"What do you mean?" Niles's protruding lip trembled. "I *am* alive, same as you."

She tried to remember that movie. It shouldn't be that hard; she'd watched it a thousand times. What did one do with a ghost who didn't realize it was dead? Was it kinder to tell them, or to let them figure it out on their own?

Before she could say anything, she felt a vicious pinch on her upper arm. "Hey!" The attack sent hot waves of pain running down her skin, and tears sprang to her eyes.

"I'm speaking to you," Niles said, and though his smile wasn't obvious, she could see one in his eyes. He *enjoyed* hurting her.

"Well, I'm no longer speaking to you." She rubbed her arm, glaring at him. "You're a brat. Go away."

She turned off the light, though the idea of trying to sleep with him standing there watching her was unbearably creepy. Squeezing her eyes shut, with her hand covering the place he'd pinched her, she prayed that he would get bored and go away.

"You are being extremely rude."

"I said, I'm not talking to you, Niles. You hurt me, and you're not very nice. Go find someone else to pick on."

"Pick on?"

"Go away!" she roared, sitting up enough to throw a pillow at him. It soared harmlessly through him and landed on the floor.

"I thought we were friends." The accusation is his voice was clear, and it made her angrier. It wasn't *her* fault they weren't getting along, now was it?

"People don't pinch their friends."

"I apologized."

"No, you didn't! You didn't say sorry once. You were *happy* about it."

"It appears we're at an impasse. Perhaps I'll allow you some time to calm down."

Dallas didn't know the word to describe his attitude, but if she had, it would have been patronizing. He acted like he was so much more mature, but he was the one who'd had a fit and trashed his room like a little baby. Furious, she used the worst insult she could think of.

"You are dead, Niles. *D-E-A-D*, dead. You're a ghost. So why don't you find some chains to rattle somewhere else?" She turned her back on him and shut her eyes again.

The cover was yanked off her body, exposing her to the cold air. As usual, it was freezing in the house. It didn't seem to matter how hot it was outside. "Hey! Stop doing that. I need to get some sleep."

"I cannot believe you would say such an appalling thing. I am as alive as you are."

She clicked on the lamp again. He obviously would never believe her without a demonstration. And, although she was frustrated, she also didn't blame him. She probably wouldn't have believed it either, especially if she was still in the same house she'd lived in during her life. *God, please don't let me end up in* this *house after I die. That would be the worst.* Dallas could hardly stand being there now. "Okay, then, hold out your arm."

"Why?" He scowled at her. His features were so gentle that the expression resembled a parody.

"I'm going to pinch you back. If you're alive, it will hurt like hell, but if you're dead, you won't feel a thing."

"Fine." He thrust his arm out, the stiff fabric of his suit protecting his skin like armor.

"Can you take your jacket off? It would be easier."

"I'm not sure that is appropriate," he said in that haughty tone of his, and she wanted to slap him. If the place had to be haunted, why did it have to be by the world's most annoying ghost?

"Um, you're in my bedroom and I'm in my nightgown. How is that appropriate?"

"You have a point." Niles removed his jacket and carefully folded it, laying it on a chair in the corner of the room. Dallas watched in fascination. She hadn't been sure he could do it. For a ghost, he was incredibly real. What if her mother's first theory was correct, and he was a confused kid? What would she do when he cried out? He rolled up the sleeve of his thin white shirt and thrust his arm straight out in front of her face. "Very well. Do your worst."

In that moment, she hoped she *could* hurt him. Her own arm

throbbed, and she wanted very much to get revenge. Gritting her teeth, she reached for his arm, but her fingers couldn't get a grip. They didn't go *through* him like one saw in the movies; he wasn't transparent. It was as if his skin had a life of its own, moving underneath her fingers whenever she tried to pinch him. It was like trying to pinch water. "See?"

"You are not putting in an honest effort. Repeat, please."

Exhaling, Dallas took another deep breath and tried again. She showed him how her fingers couldn't close on his arm.

"This is a waste of time." Glowering, he rolled down his sleeve and put his jacket back on. "You did not make a strong attempt."

She brought her arm straight back, and — using all of her strength (which she'd been told was considerable; people were always telling her how strong she was) — she aimed a slap at Niles's cheek. Dallas had never hit anyone before, and she hoped she wasn't making a big mistake. This time, her hand *did* go through him, and she felt a twinge of pain as her shoulder joint overextended.

Niles had been fussing with his cuffs, but at the slap, his head shot up. "What did you do?"

"I slapped you, but I knew it wouldn't work. I wanted to prove it to you."

"It proved nothing. I *felt* that, so I suppose that means I'm not a spirit."

"If I'd really hit you, it would have made a loud noise." She clapped her hands to demonstrate. "Haven't you been in a fight before?" Boys always seemed to be fighting back home.

"No, I was too ill. I never had the opportunity to make male friends. I was always shut up in my room."

"I'm sorry, that sucks." In spite of his bratty behavior, she sympathized with him. Aside from a cold or the occasional flu, she'd never been sick. She hadn't even broken a bone.

"In any case, you said you would pinch me. That was what we agreed to. You never said a word about slapping."

"I was trying to prove it to you. I've been doing my best to pinch you, but it isn't working."

"Perhaps you're a bad pincher."

"Oh yeah? Maybe you're dead."

Niles looked more offended than when she'd hit him. "Friends do not strike each other, and they do not say unkind things."

"How do you know what friends do if you've never had one?" It was cruel, and she felt badly about it, but right now all she wanted to do was sleep. If she insulted him enough, maybe he'd leave her alone.

"I have had friends. Before I fell ill. I had *lots* of friends."

"Great. I'm happy for you. Can you leave my room now, please?"

"This is not *your* room. This is my sister Emma's room."

Dallas seized another opportunity to enlighten him. "And where is Emma? How come I'm here, and she's not?"

He shrugged. "Emma is always traveling. She could be in Paris, or Milan. She likes to compete in equestrian events. I'm certain she will not mind you making use of her room while she's gone, but once she returns, you are welcome to stay in mine."

"Emma isn't traveling, Niles. She's dead."

"Why do you persist in saying such awful things?"

"Because they're true. I'm sorry, but the only one of your sisters that's still alive is Henrietta, and she's *old*. Can't you see how old she is? Even if you hadn't been sick, you probably would have died by now anyway. People don't live forever."

Missing the point of what she was saying entirely, Niles made a terrible face. "I cannot stand Henrietta. I wish she were not my sister. She is horrid and cruel."

Dallas was startled by the venom in his voice. The elderly lady hadn't been overly friendly, but she had seemed nice enough. "Yeah, well, you're lucky. I don't have sisters *or* brothers, and since my mom travels for work all the time, I'm alone a lot."

"That's why I anticipated that you would welcome my friendship. And yet, you have not welcomed it. You have treated me with derision."

She didn't know what that word meant, but she guessed it wasn't anything good. "Can you let me sleep now, please? We can talk about this in the morning." *Or never.*

"You are not my friend."

"Fine, I'm not your friend. Whatever. Can you go away now, please?"

"You will rue this day."

She rolled her eyes. He always had to be so *dramatic.* Turning off the light, she sighed. "Okay, Niles. Whatever you say."

Crash.

She flinched at the sound of breaking glass. "What did you do?"

"You should have been my friend," he said. "I keep telling you, you will not like me as an enemy."

★   ★   ★

Terri's eyes flew open. She'd fallen asleep in the parlor with a pile of water-damaged wallpaper around her. She startled to see a young man standing over her, watching her sleep.

She recognized his image from photographs. Even his suit was the same. "Niles."

His angelic features contorted until they looked demonic. He sneered at her. "I despise you."

"What? Why? We've just met." The boy's aggression unnerved her. Why was he so furious? What had she done to upset him?

"I despise you and your daughter. You are terrible, wicked people. I do not want you in my house."

"I thought you liked Dallas. I thought you were friends." It was strange, referring to this boy as her daughter's friend. He was so enraged he appeared deranged, and she was afraid of what he would do.

"She is no friend. She is evil."

"Hey, that's not—"

"Leave Glenvale, and leave it now. This is your first and last warning."

She opened her eyes, her heart tripping in her chest. *Where am I?* This wasn't the parlor. Pushing herself into a sitting position, she heard a bed creak, and felt a mattress sag underneath her. So she'd made it to bed, even though she didn't remember it. Still, it didn't feel like the master suite where she'd set up camp. Something troubled her, something that nagged at her and wouldn't let her relax. It was more than the nightmare.

A small window let in light, but the moon was almost new. She could make out white curtains fluttering in the draft. Squinting, she strained to see any other details. Furniture hovered in the corners, the darkness and the uncertainty of her situation turning them sinister. She looked to where a nightstand would typically be, and relief washed over her when she detected a familiar shape. Her fingers slid over the ceramic surface until she found what she'd been looking for: a switch.

Please let it be plugged in.

Click. The light temporarily blinded her, and as her eyes adjusted, more objects wavered into focus. Books. Peeling wallpaper. Model planes.

Planes?

When she spotted *The Checkered Game of Life* on top of a stack of games, her suspicion was confirmed. She was in Niles's room, but why? How? She never would have come in here deliberately, and certainly never at night. Even in daylight she avoided it like the plague.

Terri pressed her back to the headboard, struggling to get her breathing under control. This wasn't the place to have a panic attack.

There's nothing to be afraid of. If Niles is here, he's a ghost. And ghosts can't hurt you.

Once she felt calmer, stronger, she pushed aside the velvet coverlet. The room was freezing, and she shivered in her thin T-shirt and shorts. All of the house was cold, but Niles's room was like an icebox. She didn't understand how Dallas had managed to sleep here, even for a single night.

Wishing for slippers, Terri touched her feet to the hardwood, which felt like ice under her toes. The powerful sensation that someone was watching her made the skin on the back of her neck prickle, and without thinking, she turned.

The young man from her nightmare was there, his face mere inches from her own. Terri screamed.

His lips curled back in a snarl, and before she could run, his hand lashed out at her cheek, his fingers hooked into claws.

The searing pain of his nails digging furrows in her skin snapped her out of her daze. She ran for the door, but the closet flew open in front of her. She extended her arms to absorb the impact. The heavy wooden door slammed into her palms, sending sickening pain through her bones.

"Mom? Mom, where are you?"

An equal mix of relief and terror flooded through her. She had to protect Dallas, had to warn her daughter. But the only sound that escaped her lips was a gasp. She couldn't speak.

"Mom!"

The fear in her daughter's voice freed her own. "I'm in here. In Niles's room." She prayed that thing, whatever it had been – surely it wasn't human – was gone.

Terri flinched when the doorknob rattled.

"It's locked," Dallas cried. She pounded on the door. "Mom, it's locked. Let me in."

"I don't understand, Niles," Terri said under her breath. "What did we ever do to you?"

She closed the closet, making sure it was shut tight before she leapt for the door. The porcelain knob was slick under her hands, but she forced it to turn. There was a popping noise, and the door opened.

Dallas stood shivering in the hallway, her feet bare and her hair disheveled. Her eyes were wide and panicked, and her chest hitched with every breath. "What were you doing in there?" she asked, her eyes widening. "And what happened to your face?"

CHAPTER NINE

The warmth of the sun on their backs belied the gravity of their conversation. The bench was solid and comforting, the worn wood like an old friend.

Dallas tilted her chin upwards and closed her eyes. "This is nice. So much better than that stinky old house."

Their love affair with Glenvale was over.

Her first instinct was to be defensive, to claim the house wasn't *that* bad. That she was doing this for them, for their future.

But then her cheek burned, and she remembered.

It *was* that bad.

"It's always so cold in there, no matter how hot it is outside. What's with that?"

"Old houses are drafty," Terri replied absently, her mind a million miles away. When she gave her notice, how hard would Henrietta Vandermere work to destroy her? Would she write it off as another employee with too much imagination, or would it become an all-out vendetta? Would Terri be able to find another job before their savings ran out?

The feeling of being trapped was never a pleasant one, and in this case, the cage was an iron maiden with spikes instead of bars. Her failed marriage had been easier to escape.

"Mom, I'm really sorry about your face."

"It's okay. It doesn't hurt," Terri lied, though it stung something awful. She'd applied aloe vera to the deep scratches, and the resulting pain had nearly made her scream. She raised her hand to touch the wounds, but thought better of it.

"It looks sore. Is it my fault?" Dallas's voice cracked, and Terri put an arm around her daughter, gratified when she didn't pull away.

"Of course not."

"But I'm the one who made him angry." She'd reiterated her conversation the night before, but Terri found it difficult to accept that they were talking about a *ghost*. A ghost with the capability of gouging her face and trashing the house. Before attacking her, he'd shattered the Tiffany lamp in Emma's room. "I just don't understand why you were in his room."

"I don't either. I must have sleepwalked." The notion was unsettling. The last thing she remembered was working in the parlor. The final remnants of the wallpaper had detached from the walls under her steamer, and though she'd been exhausted, she was determined to clean up the room before going to bed. She couldn't recall even thinking of Niles's room, let alone going there.

Dallas's brow creased, making her look much older than her ten years, and Terri longed to smooth the lines from her forehead. She hated that she'd been the one to put them there. "You don't sleepwalk, Mom."

"Maybe I do now. Maybe it's the stress." Lord knows there had been plenty of that.

"I don't think so." Dallas leaned against her, settling her body against Terri's as if it were no big deal. The events of the night before had changed her daughter, at least temporarily. She'd gone from standoffish to craving affection. "I think he *did* something to you, something that made you go in there so he could hurt you. I called him a brat last night, but he's more than a brat. I think he's evil, Mom."

Her words were an eerie echo of last night's dream.

She is no friend. She is evil.

But had it been a dream? The wounds on her cheek were all too real.

"Maybe. The question is, what do we do about it?"

It was nicer out here, in the garden. In a few short days, Dallas's hard work had made a noticeable difference, and some perennials that had been strangled by weeds were beginning to thrive again. It was wonderful to let the sun chase the chill out of their bones, and feel actual warmth upon their skin again, but that wasn't why they were outside.

Neither of them was comfortable discussing anything of importance in the house, even when far from the speaking tube. The atmosphere of Glenvale had always had weight to it, but it had grown heavier since last night. It felt like someone was forever watching and listening.

"In the movies, the family always gets a priest."

"I think you have to be religious for that, hun." Terri had been raised by agnostic parents, and had raised Dallas the same. Derek was a lapsed Catholic, so he couldn't have cared less about religion. It wasn't like he would muster up the energy to take their daughter to church.

But Dallas was right; in the movies, the family *did* always get a priest, and they made it look so easy. One phone call, and a man in black robes appeared, Bible and holy water in hand. She wouldn't know where to start. Could you drop by any church and tell them your house was haunted? Did every priest know what to do, or was it only special ones? "Besides, I'm not sure Miss Vandermere would approve."

"You can't quit. You're thinking of quitting, aren't you?"

"It's not safe here. You've seen what happened to me." Terri gestured to her face. "I couldn't stand it if something like this happened to you."

"You always told me not to be a quitter." The stubborn edge had returned to Dallas's voice, and the girl shifted to face her. "You told me not to run away from my problems."

"That's true, but I have to protect you. When you're a mother, you'll understand."

"I'll never be a mother. Kids suck," she said, making Terri laugh. "They *do*. Always needing stuff and asking for things. It would drive me crazy. Anyway, I'm not scared of Niles. He's an asshole."

"Dallas, your language." But she had to bite her lip to keep from smiling.

"Well, he is. Look what he did to your face. I'm not afraid anymore. I want to go into that room and tell him exactly what I think of him."

"Please don't," she said, picturing the snarling creature from the night before. The thought was enough to drive her mad. It hadn't resembled anything human. Whatever Niles had been during his life, he wasn't a young man anymore – more like a monster. "It might make things worse."

"We need the money, don't we?" her daughter asked in a sad, scared voice that broke her heart. Terri decided to be honest.

"We do, but there will be other jobs."

"Right away, though? Sometimes it takes you months to find another one."

Jesus, this kid got straight to the heart of the problem, didn't she? She had the makings of a fine financial advisor, or maybe an accountant. "I have some savings. It'll be okay. If things get really desperate, maybe your dad will help us out."

Dallas snorted. "Yeah, like that's going to happen."

She had a point, so Terri didn't bother arguing. She didn't have the energy to defend Derek today. It was a strain, always defending the indefensible. "Do you really want to stay? Honestly."

As she asked the question, Terri stared up at the house, which towered over them. Overactive imagination or not, Glenvale was forbidding. It wasn't the type of place that inspired happy thoughts. She wondered if Niles's death on the premises had forever changed the feel of it.

A curtain twitched in the attic room, and this time there was a silhouette behind it. Someone *was* watching them, and it wasn't a ghost.

"Dallas, stay here for a sec. I have to go back to the house."

"Now? But I didn't answer your question yet."

"Stay here. If you don't get a signal from me in ten minutes, call 911."

"Wait! What kind of signal?"

"I'll wave at you if everything's okay. From that window." She pointed to the attic room, but the silhouette was gone. Magically, so was the 'draft'.

"Are you sure, Mom? You could get hurt."

Touched by her daughter's concern, she spared a second to run her hand over Dallas's hair. "I'm sure. I'll be right back."

Running for the house, her exhaustion and fear replaced with rage, Terri thought about all the things she planned to do to her unwelcome visitor. The idea of working off some of her stress was so appealing that she managed to pick up speed. She hadn't run this fast since she was in high school.

What if it's locked? she wondered, but apparently Niles wasn't up to his old tricks today. The front door opened without protest. After thundering up the two flights of stairs, she tried the door to the attic, half expecting it to be locked as well, but no.

She flung the door open and burst into the room, scanning the surroundings for her target.

The room had been used for storage, just as Vandermere had told her. It was crammed with drop cloth-covered shapes. Any one of them could have concealed a person. As she seized the cloth closest to her, about to rip it off – rip all of them off – a woman stepped out of the shadows.

"What's wrong, Terri? You look upset," the woman said in an exaggerated singsong. "What happened to your face?"

"What are you doing here? I said you weren't welcome." It was all she could do to keep from striking Gertrude, though she'd never hit another woman in her life. Logically, she knew Gertrude had nothing to do with the events of the night before, but emotionally was another matter. "You know Vandermere doesn't want you here."

"Tough titty said the kitty." Gertrude laughed.

"What the hell is that supposed to mean? You need help, Gertrude. You're not making sense."

"It means I'm staying. You're just the contractor," the woman said, her tone heavy with disdain. "You can't make me leave."

What was she, twelve? 'You can't make me'? Next she'd be double daring her. "Maybe I can't, but I'm sure the police can."

"You're cute, but I'm not doing anything illegal."

"How do you figure? Trespassing on private property is illegal, last time I checked."

"They know me here. All the police, everyone knows me." Her voice changed, rising into a falsetto. "'Poor Gertrude gave her life to this place, and mean old Henrietta shunted her out. It's natural she'd get a little confused, poor thing. It was an honest mistake.'"

While Terri was tempted to write the woman's words off as delusional, Gertrude was probably right. No one would arrest a white woman for being so confused she'd still reported for work, even though she had been fired. Gertrude was fully aware of her privilege, and she wasn't afraid to use it. She tried another approach. "You need to move on. This isn't healthy. You can find another job."

"Not until I avenge Niles's and Emma's deaths and see Henrietta Vandermere pay for what she's done." Gertrude sounded as if she were talking about ice cream and puppies instead of murder.

"Christ, the woman is a hundred years old! What kind of paying do you expect her to do? Besides, if your theory is right – and that's a big *if* – she was a little girl when her siblings died. She shouldn't be held responsible for what her father did."

Gertrude clicked her tongue. "Oh, Terri. You're so naïve."

"*I'm* naïve? I'm not the one who's obsessed with an employer who doesn't want me. Why don't you spend your time and energy looking for a new job, instead of making it impossible for me to do mine?"

"I shouldn't have expected you to understand, but I care about Niles. I couldn't leave his spirit here forever, wandering these halls and wondering what happened to him. I promised to set him free." She indicated Terri's face. "It's obvious you've managed to upset him."

"I didn't do a damn thing to him, but *he* trashed his room, shattered a priceless lamp, and attacked me. I don't understand your devotion to him. Dead or not, that kid is a creep."

Gertrude put a finger to her lips, her eyes darting this way and that, as if she expected Niles to appear from out of the shadows. Maybe she did. Who the hell knew? Terri only knew she didn't care. Let him hear. The monster deserved to hear everything she'd said, and so much worse.

"You need to be careful. Niles can be dangerous if he's angered."

Her warning reminded Terri of the one she'd given her daughter, back when she'd believed Niles was some confused kid in a costume. "I don't give a fuck about Niles, *Gertie.*"

"You should," the woman said, ignoring Vandermere's nickname for her. "If this is his first attack, can you imagine what he'll do next? And what if he goes after your daughter?"

"You know what? I don't need this. I don't need *any* of this. I restore houses, not sanity. You win — you and Niles can have Glenvale. I'm going to tell Vandermere I quit, which I'm sure will not surprise her, and then you can have the place to yourself."

"You don't understand. I don't want you to leave. I want to help you."

"I don't give a fuck about you or what you want, either. You're the one who needs help. You should be finding yourself a good doctor instead of obsessing over this stuff."

"Please, Terri — be reasonable. I could tell when we spoke yesterday that you care about this place, and that you love children. I get that Niles attacked you, and I'm not saying that was right, or that you should forgive him. But please try to understand where he's coming from. That poor fellow was murdered. Don't you want to help me find justice for him?"

"That's not my job. I'm here to restore the house, not help you with your obsession. Whether Niles died from natural causes or was murdered is not my problem. I can't see how you would prove it, anyway."

"There has to be evidence in the house. Don't you see? If there weren't, Vandermere wouldn't have fired me. She could see I was close to finding something, so she took my key and sent me away. She wouldn't have done that if there was nothing to find."

Wow, talk about delusional. "Maybe she sent you away because you were so obsessed over this so-called mystery that you weren't doing your actual job. Did you consider that?"

"That isn't true. I was an excellent employee. You said it yourself – when Miss Vandermere spoke of me, it was of how dedicated I was. Any investigating I did, I did when I was off the clock. And I was open about it at first, until she started getting defensive."

"And what, you think that indicates guilt?" Terri asked, incredulous. "I think most people would be defensive if someone started accusing their dead father of doing horrible things – the *most* horrible thing. Howard isn't around to defend himself any longer, so that responsibility falls to his daughter."

"You don't understand," Gertrude said again, looking weary. "She wasn't just defensive, she was threatening."

"That's to be expected too. The Vandermeres are an important family. She can't have you nosing about, trying to ruin their reputation with your half-baked theories."

"They aren't half baked, Terri. I promise you they aren't."

Terri shrugged. She didn't care anymore, and she no longer had the inclination or energy to punch Gertrude in the nose. The poor woman was mentally ill, obsessed like Vandermere had told her. She needed help, not recriminations, but Terri wasn't the one who could give it to her. "Well, good luck with that. But if you manage to move past this, think about what you're doing to an old woman who's at the end of her life. Niles is dead, but Henrietta is alive...for now. Why torture her this way?"

Pushing past Gertrude, she pulled aside the lace curtain. Dallas still waited on the bench far below, her pale face turned upward. Terri waved, and her daughter waved back. *Good. No sense getting the police involved.* Terri went to leave.

"Where are you going?"

"I told you – I'm going to give Vandermere my resignation, and then I'm going to pack up our stuff and leave. You'll have the place to yourself again in an hour or less, depending on how my call with her goes. But I'm going to have to tell her you're here. She deserves to know why I'm leaving."

"What if there was a way for you to successfully restore this house, and get the money you were promised? Without having to worry about Niles or any of this other stuff?"

It was a nice thought, but Terri didn't think she had it in her anymore. The money would have been nice, but Dallas was smart enough to succeed without it. She would earn scholarships to help pay for college. Nothing was worth this much aggravation, especially money.

"It's too late for that. We're leaving."

"How can you say it's too late? You've only been here a few weeks."

"You have no idea how long those few weeks have been."

"Give me a chance, Terri. If it doesn't work out, you won't have lost anything, except maybe some time. But imagine if it does work out."

"Time, and the other half of my face."

"Oh no, nothing like that will happen again. I give you my word."

"How much is your word possibly worth, Gertrude?"

"It's the only thing I've got left, so I'd say it's worth a lot. But you have to trust me."

It was a tall order, but deep inside Terri, a tiny spark of hope had flared. She *did* love this house; the deranged occupants were not its fault. She *did* want to restore it. And she wasn't a quitter. She wanted to make her daughter proud. If Gertrude could somehow keep Niles from tormenting them while she finished the work, the aggravation she'd suffered would all be worth it.

"If that were possible – and I'm not saying it is – what about Vandermere? You're not supposed to be anywhere near Glenvale. If she finds out you're staying here, she'll fire me anyway."

"You were going to quit, right? Sounds to me like you've got nothing to lose."

"I don't feel good about this." It was true; she didn't. She'd never deceived a client before. "What exactly is your plan? What are you going to do?"

"You'll see," Gertrude said, and grinned. "Trust me."

CHAPTER TEN

"Can you keep a secret?" Terri asked.

Dallas's expression was comically serious as she nodded. She made a zipping motion across her mouth.

"I'm not sure this is the right thing to do, so feel free to tell me if you think it's crazy. Do you remember that woman who spoke to you in the garden yesterday?"

"Gertrude? She's going to be staying with us, right?"

Terri was well aware of how smart her daughter was, but sometimes it unnerved her how quickly Dallas figured things out. She was always two steps ahead – at least two steps. "How did you know?"

"Niles told me. He's really excited and happy about it. And he says he's sorry about what happened last night." Seeing the fear that must have crossed Terri's face, she added, "But don't worry. I told him there was no excuse for his behavior and that we would *not* be forgiving him."

"He's still talking to you? When?"

"When I was unpacking the rest of my things in his sister's room. He's lonely, Mom. He can get as mad as he wants, but he never stays away for long."

The idea of her daughter conversing with that…that *thing* from the night before was enough to give her hives. "Are you sure Emma's room is the best one? That could be what's attracting him. If you stayed in Henrietta's old room, I bet he wouldn't bother you."

"That's okay. I don't mind. I think Emma was cool, and I like the stories he tells about her."

When her daughter was an infant, Terri had braced herself for the difficult years ahead. The rebellious years, the pulling away Dallas would inevitably do before they could come back together again. She'd expected her daughter would have friends she didn't agree with, people she couldn't stand. But never in a million years had she imagined that friend would be a ghost.

"I don't think you should talk to him, Dallas. He's not safe." She pointed at her wounded cheek. "I don't want this to happen to you."

"It won't. He wants to be my friend, and he understands that if he did anything like that to me, I'd never speak to him ever again."

"Still, I want you to avoid him as much as possible, okay?"

"Okay. He doesn't bother me when I'm in the garden, only when I'm in the house."

Terri took a deep breath, trying to collect her thoughts. All she wanted to do was focus on her work without worrying about the dead. Was that so much to ask? "Are you all right with Gertrude staying with us?"

"Sure. Niles — sorry — well, he says she knows more about the house and his family than anyone else. He says she even knows more than Henrietta because of the things he's shown her. I think she'll be able to help you with the restoration. And if she keeps Niles happy, that's good too."

"You're absolutely positive?" Part of her had hoped Dallas would give her a reason to tell Gertrude she couldn't stay. There was something off about the woman, and Terri didn't think she'd ever feel truly comfortable around her. How could you feel comfortable around a woman who enjoyed talking to ghosts? "This was supposed to be our summer together, and I don't want you to feel that's changed. Gertrude is going to be doing her own work in the house. We'll probably hardly see her."

Dallas patted her arm. "It'll still be our summer, Mom. Don't worry."

How she wished it were that easy. "If Miss Vandermere or anyone who works for her comes to the house, they can't know about Gertrude. Okay? The fact that she's staying here has to be our secret."

"Niles told me. He said that Henrietta hates her and has done everything she could to keep Gertrude away from Glenvale."

Now *that* was interesting. "Did he say why?"

Her daughter nodded. "He says that Gertrude never worked for his sister. That, from the first day she arrived, she's been working for him."

★   ★   ★

Any hope that Terri had of Gertrude keeping to herself and doing her own thing was quickly dashed. When dinnertime rolled around, and Terri took a break from removing the peeling paint from the upstairs doorframes (she had to admit, it had been a lot more peaceful working up there than she'd expected), Gertrude was in the kitchen. She looked up and smiled when Terri entered. One would have never believed they'd come close to blows that morning.

"Hungry?" She stirred something on the stove, and as much as Terri resented her presence, it smelled delicious. Her stomach growled, and she realized she'd missed lunch with all the drama taking place in the house. She was starving.

"You didn't have to make dinner for us."

"Oh, don't be silly." Gertrude waved the comment away. "I love to cook, and this is a nice change from making food for myself. I'm happy to do all the cooking while I'm here. That way, you can focus on your work and you won't have to worry about the meals."

"But you have your own work to do. I don't want to keep you from that."

"Honestly, it's no bother. I enjoy doing it, and if it makes things easier on you, that's great." She gave whatever was in the pot another stir, and then held a spoonful out to Terri. "Want to taste?"

Her curiosity and hunger getting the better of her, Terri accepted the wooden spoon. On it was broth and a bit of shrimp. The flavors exploded in her mouth, and she was surprised by the complexity. It was rich and buttery, with a sharp tang of tomato, accented by a taste of the sea. She'd never tasted anything quite like it. This was a far cry from boxed mac n' cheese. "That's incredible. What is it?"

"Cioppino. It's an Italian-American seafood stew. My mother used to make it all the time, and I thought it would be just the thing to warm us up a bit. Do you think Dallas will like it?"

"I can't see how she wouldn't. It's fantastic. Is your family Italian, then?"

Gertrude laughed. "No, English. We just like the food."

Terri's stomach rumbled louder, and though she felt as if she was giving up something too easily, her misgivings about Gertrude taking over the meals faded. "I can see why. But that tastes like such a complicated dish. You didn't find the ingredients for this in the fridge." Terri was embarrassed to think of what the woman *had* found in the fridge: some cheese slices, a loaf of Wonder Bread, a jar of peanut butter, and few sad-looking apples. "Where did they come from?"

Gertrude's face flushed. "I brought them with me."

"You brought all that…with you?"

"I had a feeling we'd come to an understanding, and that you'd let me stay."

Terri sank into a chair. "That was a huge assumption."

"I was right, wasn't I? I don't want to get in your way. I'd like to be your friend, and Dallas's too, if she'll let me. When it's time to work, you'll do your thing, and I'll do mine. Maybe if I get bored or need to think, I can help you out a little. Remember, we're on the same team. We want the same thing."

"Do we?" Terri was shaken by the thought of Gertrude lugging shrimp, tomatoes, and who knows what else to the house in her purse, confident everything would turn out exactly the way she wanted. It gave her the creeps. The woman was too overconfident for her liking.

"Of course we do. We both want Niles to leave you alone, for starters."

A long, low moan came from the speaking tube on the wall, and

Terri flinched, her hand flying up to touch her cheek. The scratches were healing, but they were still tender to the touch.

"You behave, Niles," Gertrude said, not bothering to use the tube. "No one is talking to you right now."

Located near the tube, an ornate wooden box was installed above the pantry door. Each of the home's most important rooms had its own carefully labeled circular cutout with a small, red flag contained within. Terri's eyes were drawn to one of the bedrooms, where the flag waved furiously. Gertrude followed her gaze.

"Emma's room. Either your daughter has figured out how to use the call box, or Niles wants our attention."

As she said the words, all of the flags began to wave, faster and faster. Gertrude returned to the stove, but Terri couldn't stop staring at the call box. The movement of the flags was hypnotic. "What does he want?"

"Justice, I think. The poor thing was so young when he died. Or maybe attention. Niles has always been lonely. Dallas is the first child who's stayed here in decades. Remember, he was ill for most of his youth, so he was practically a shut-in. He missed a lot of his childhood."

Terri felt a twinge of sympathy until she remembered they were talking about the creature that had clawed her the night before. "That's sad," she managed, because Gertrude appeared to expect her to say something.

"I get that you haven't had the best experience with Niles, but a lot of that stems from his frustration. He has a sweet side too. I thought I'd help you get to know him better after dinner, if you like."

The intense prickling sensation returned to the back of her neck, and Terri shook it off. "I'm not sure that's a good idea. Aren't we encouraging him if we keep talking to him? If we ignore him, he might go away."

"Niles's spirit has been here since before we were born. He's not going anywhere," Gertrude said, taking a small foil-wrapped loaf of bread from her purse and sliding it into the oven. "Do you and Dallas like garlic?"

"Yes." She *thought* Dallas liked garlic. There was so much about her daughter's tastes she didn't know, and the processed foods she relied upon when feeding her child hadn't helped with that particular fact-finding mission.

"I make my own garlic bread. It's so much better than the store-bought stuff. Not so salty." Gertrude made a face. "Anyway, I get that it's difficult, but when it comes to Niles, try to think of him as a kid." She lowered her voice, glancing at the speaking tube. "That's what he is, a teenage boy who was murdered by his own father."

"He didn't seem like much of a kid when he attacked me last night. I hadn't done a thing to him, and he scarred my face."

"What happened to you was very unfortunate. I've spoken to him, and it won't happen again."

"Well, that's a relief." Terri recognized her sarcasm sounded harsh, but she didn't care. After what had happened to her, she was in no mood for this Niles-was-such-a-good-boy talk.

"I apologize for his behavior. I get that it will be difficult for you to forgive him, but I hope you can. It may sound strange, but over time, I developed a relationship with Niles – a friendship, I'd like to think. He got used to me being here most days, and when Henrietta fired me, it made him frustrated and furious. Probably lonely too. Now he had no one to talk to again. And then your daughter came. When she rejected him yesterday, it sent him over the edge. I've never seen him do anything like that before."

"Don't you dare blame Dallas for this," Terri snapped. "She has every right not to talk to him, and she was trying to get some sleep. She doesn't owe him anything."

Gertrude raised a hand in surrender. "Sorry, I didn't mean that the way it sounded. What happened wasn't Dallas's fault at all. The blame lies with Niles. I was just trying to explain why he acted so out of character.

"He got to like me, I think, and maybe look forward to me

showing up every day. At first, there were subtle things. I'd see movement out of the corner of my eye, or things on my desk would be moved overnight." Gertrude sampled the stew and added a bit of freshly ground pepper from a pepper mill she pulled from her purse. Terri was beginning to think the woman's purse was an enchanted bag with no bottom. How on earth had she fit everything in there? "I thought the volunteers were playing a prank on me, but they all swore they had nothing to do with it. One of them finally said, 'Maybe it's Niles.' Everyone laughed, like it was some terrific joke, but it got me thinking – maybe it *was* Niles.

"When he showed himself to me the first time, we were alone. It was near Christmas, and I was working late at my desk, finding things to keep me busy." She looked over her shoulder at Terri. "Since my father died and my mom got sick, the holidays aren't so fun anymore. So I'd rather stay here. But finally I'd done every bit of work that needed doing, and some that didn't. I was doing my rounds, turning out the lights, and there he was, this young man standing in the doorway of his father's study.

"It scared the bejesus out of me, let me tell you. But then I saw how sad he looked, and the strangest feeling came over me, as if I was going to cry. Which isn't something I do often. I asked him if he was lost, and he told me he lived here. That's how I figured out he was Niles.

"I wasn't the only person on staff to see him, you see. Other employees and some of the volunteers talked about him too. But with them, it was all ghost stories and trying to scare each other. I wasn't interested in that. If Niles was here, it meant there was something in his short life that had gone unresolved, but how could that be, if he'd died from natural causes? An illness is one of the most natural ways to die, an open-and-shut case. So I started asking questions."

"And he told you his father killed him?" Terri asked, fascinated in spite of herself.

"Oh no, I started piecing that together on my own. I don't think he knows how he died, to be honest. Sometimes he refuses to believe he's dead at all."

"It doesn't make any sense to me." She wished she could take the words back after she'd said them, or tactfully rephrase them. What right did she have to criticize Gertrude's theory when she didn't have one of her own? "Why would Howard murder his son? Niles was the male heir, and from everything I've heard, the man was devastated after he died. It ruined him for anything else. If it weren't for the acumen of his wife and daughters, he could have lost everything."

Gertrude opened the oven and checked the bread. "You can tell Dallas dinner is ready, if she'd like to set the table. I don't think Howard was responsible. Not directly, anyway. His failure was not opening his eyes to what was happening around him."

Wait a minute. Was she going crazy, or hadn't Gertrude repeatedly blamed Howard for his son's death? She decided to play along, but she could see how Henrietta had lost her patience. "Then you think his wife killed her son?" That made even less sense to Terri. Matricide happened back then, just as it did now, but it was hardly common. And what reason would Elizabeth have had? She'd been a wealthy woman with a gorgeous house, three children, and by all accounts, a happy marriage.

"I'm not sure yet. That's why I'm here. I'm determined to find out the truth."

CHAPTER ELEVEN

To Terri's relief, Dallas loved the meal and cleaned her plate, asking for a second helping of the stew. She felt only the slightest twinge when her daughter proclaimed it the best meal she'd ever tasted.

Gertrude shifted in her chair, looking uncomfortable. "Now, I'm sure that's not true. Don't forget all the wonderful meals your mother has made you."

Before Dallas could completely embarrass her, Terri jumped in. "To be honest, I'm not much of a cook. Since I started restoration work, the best meals have been the ones that are quick, easy, and don't use too many dishes. Often the water has been shut off, and I have to haul it in with me. So keeping things simple is key. Macaroni 'n' cheese is as wonderful a meal as Dallas has gotten from me – mac 'n' cheese from a *box*."

"And it was delicious, Mom." Dallas patted her hand, looking guilty.

"Thanks, but it was nothing like this, let's be honest. This was a gourmet feast. Thank you, Gertrude."

"You're so welcome. And now that dinner's over, I can help you get to know my friend Niles, as promised." Gertrude walked over to her purse, that bag of wonders, and withdrew a small, square board and something that looked like a wooden triangle. She carried them to the table and unfolded the board to reveal an alphabet painted in ornate scrollwork.

"A Ouija board!" Dallas said, bouncing on her seat. Terri couldn't help staring. Was this the same girl who was never interested in anything, who responded to everyone with a roll of the eyes and a sigh? "How cool."

Though she was thrilled to see her daughter showing some genuine enthusiasm for a change, she had misgivings. "Are you sure this is a good idea?"

"Sure, this is the best way to talk to spirits." Gertrude put the wooden triangle on the center of the board, and gestured for them to move their chairs closer. "It's perfectly safe."

"I've always wanted to use one of these things." Dallas paused, frowning. "But why do we need it to talk to Niles? I can't get Niles to shut up."

The woman laughed. "Maybe this will help with that. You never know. But there are other spirits in this house too, spirits who aren't as chatty as Niles. This board brings them out of their shells, so to speak. Just wait, and you'll see."

Gertrude reached for the triangle, but Terri took hold of her arm. "I'm not sure encouraging more spirits to come forward is the best idea. We've already had plenty of problems with the one we've met."

"This will help, Terri. Please trust me." Before she could argue further, Gertrude closed her eyes and pressed her fingers to the triangle, moving it in a slow figure eight. "Is there anyone there who would like to talk to us? Don't be shy, we're here to listen."

The triangle slid to the word 'Hello' so suddenly that it made Terri flinch. Dallas smiled at her, her eyes sparkling with excitement.

"That didn't take long. Hello to you. What is your name?"

Gertrude's hands moved in a predictable pattern. N-I-L-E-S.

"Hello, Niles. I'm glad you're here. As you can see, Terri is with me. Is there anything you'd like to communicate to her?"

Terri was tempted to say that whatever Niles might like to express, she wasn't interested in hearing it. Teenager or not, murdered or not, the kid's ghost was an asshole. A *violent* asshole. She wanted nothing more to do with him. But she held her tongue for Dallas's sake.

I AM SORRY, the board spelled.

"See, Mom? He wants you to forgive him."

"That's nice," Terri said, unable to keep the sarcasm from her voice.

Gertrude opened her eyes long enough to give her a look. "You're not going to do anything like that again, are you?" she asked. The triangle under her hands shot to NO.

"He better not do anything like that again," Terri muttered. Could one fight back against a ghost? Probably not, but she would sure like to try.

"Terri is a good person, and she and Dallas want to help you, like I do. Do you understand?"

YES.

"Good," Gertrude said. "Now, what can you tell us about—"

"Wait a second. How do we know you're not moving that thing on your own?" Terri asked.

"This *thing* is called a planchette, and you can see for yourself." Gertrude moved her fingers over to one side of the triangle, making room for Terri's. "Once you've placed your hands on it, don't take them off until I tell you. Okay?"

Terri nodded, squeezing her fingers next to Gertrude's on the planchette. The wood was warm from the other woman's touch.

"Go ahead," Gertrude urged. "Ask him anything you like."

"Why won't you leave my daughter alone?" Terri asked.

"Mom!"

"No, it's okay. She has the right to ask whatever she wants," Gertrude said.

For a moment, the planchette didn't move, and Terri thought Niles – if it actually was Niles and not some trick Gertrude was playing on them – wasn't going to answer. But then it *did* move, slowly at first, but gradually gaining speed.

FRIENDS.

Her jaw tightened. The little bastard. The last thing Dallas needed was a friend like him. This was supposed to have been a good summer – *their* summer – and now this brat had threatened to ruin it. "She doesn't need friends like you. She wants you to leave her alone."

"*Mom!*"

"That's not a question, Terri." Gertrude raised an eyebrow. The planchette was still.

"Okay, then. Will you leave us alone?"

The planchette moved so quickly under their hands that Terri's nearly slipped off. She leaned forward, struggling to keep her fingers pressed to the wood.

NO.

"Great." She sighed. "This has been very helpful."

"You're not doing it right. You shouldn't be saying mean things to him and telling him to go away," Dallas said. "He came here to talk to us."

Terri tilted her face so that her wounded cheek pointed up. "Have you forgotten?"

"I know, Mom, but if you're not going to take this seriously, what's the point in doing it?"

What's the point, indeed?

"Niles, I understand this is difficult for you, but can you tell us what it was like when you were sick?" Gertrude asked.

The planchette made a sharp motion to the left. YES.

"Did anyone come to visit you while you were ill?"

YES.

"Who came to visit you?"

MOTHER.

FATHER.

EMMA.

"Not Henrietta?"

Terri could feel the planchette trembling under her fingers, as if the object couldn't make up its mind.

Finally, it moved to YES.

"Henrietta did come to visit you?" Gertrude asked.

YES.

"Why didn't you mention her before, with the rest of your family?"

This time, there was no hesitation.

HATE.

Gertrude clicked her tongue. "Hate is a strong word, Niles. Henrietta is your sister. Why would you hate your own sister?"

Look at how he treats his 'friends', Terri thought but did not say. The other two were getting something out of this, so let them. It was one night. She'd never get suckered into it again.

MEAN.

"What did Henrietta do that was mean to you?"

NAMES.

It didn't mean anything to Terri, but Gertrude clearly had a lot more experience with this kind of communication. "She called you names?"

YES.

"Mean names?"

That one was obvious, Terri thought.

YES.

Gertrude sagged, as though she'd been expecting something more dramatic. Like what? This was ridiculous. She couldn't honestly expect to find out anything this way.

"My brothers do that too. It's called teasing. It isn't meant to be mean, though it can feel that way sometimes. It hurts, doesn't it?"

YES. And then, slower, SHE MEANS IT.

"Did Henrietta do anything else mean to you?"

PUSH.

HIT.

IGNORE.

PULL.

HAIR.

Gertrude's eyes met Terri's. She looked startled, but to Terri, the only thing it proved was Henrietta had been a bratty kid. Nothing unusual about that. And why was she focusing on Henrietta anyway, if she believed Howard or Elizabeth had killed him?

"I see," she said. "That is pretty mean. I wouldn't like her either."

NO.

HATE.

"Mom, that's the woman who hired you, right?"

Terri nodded. "Remember, though, this might not be true. We can't prove it, and we're not hearing her side of the story."

"Why would Niles lie?" her daughter asked, and she shrugged, not wanting to say in front of Gertrude that she wasn't sure the whole thing wasn't faked. It didn't feel like Gertrude was the one moving the planchette, but there was no way to be certain.

Gertrude cleared her throat. "Did Henrietta do anything nice for you?"

YES.

"What did she do?"

CANDY.

"She brought you candy?" Gertrude appeared to perk up at this, applying enough pressure to the planchette that her fingernails turned bright pink, but Terri wasn't sure why. So far, talking to a ghost had been more boring than talking to a human being.

YES.

LOTS.

"Where would she get lots of candy?"

Terri groaned inwardly, and sure enough—

STORE.

"Did your parents know she was giving you candy, Niles?"

The triangle quivered under their fingers. Then it shot from YES to NO and back again. "What does that mean?" Terri asked.

"I think he doesn't know, or remember. How often did she give you candy?"

Why all these questions about candy? Next she'd be asking him for the servants' grocery shopping list. Who cared? But the question triggered a flurry of activity on the board. Terri could hardly keep up with the letters until she figured out the pattern, and then it was easy.

MONDAY.

TUESDAY.

WEDNESDAY.

THURSDAY.

FRIDAY.

SAT—

"Did she give you candy every day, Niles?"

Terri imagined both she and the ghost were relieved when Gertrude cut to the chase. YES.

"How did you hide this from your parents?"

NO TELL.

SECRET.

NOT ALLOWED.

LOVE.

CANDY.

During the strange conversation – strange mostly for how banal it was – Gertrude had grown pale. She turned to Terri, her eyes glistening. "Is there anything else you'd like to ask him? Not tell him, *ask*."

Here was her chance. Maybe Gertrude had nothing better to do than ask this board tedious questions all day, but she had work to do. If she got to the point quickly, she could show the woman her theories were wrong, and then Gertrude wouldn't have to stay with them after all. Perhaps Niles would leave them alone too. It was worth a shot.

"Did your mother kill you, Niles?"

Gertrude's eyes widened. *No*, she mouthed, but Terri pretended she hadn't seen.

NO.

"How about your father?"

NO.

"Henrietta? Did Henrietta kill you?"

NO.

The table shuddered under their hands. At first, Terri thought Gertrude was doing it to get her attention, but a glimpse of the woman's face put that to rest. Her eyes bulged, and her skin was the color of curdled milk.

NO NO NO NO NO NO NO NO NO NO NO NO NO

NO NO NO NO NO NO NO NO NO NO NO NO NO NO NO
NO NO NO NO NO NO NO NO NO NO NO NO NO NO NO
NO NO NO NO NO NO NO NO NO NO NO NO NO NO

"Who killed you, Niles?" Terri raised her voice to be heard over the roaring in her ears. "Tell us."

The light fixture above them swayed back and forth, faster and faster.

NOT DEAD. NOT DEAD. NOT DEAD. NOT DEAD. NOT DEAD. NOT DEAD. NOT DEAD.

"Of course you're dead. You died decades ago."

"Terri, stop!" Gertrude yelled.

The light bulb above them popped, plunging them into near darkness, and Dallas screamed. Terri gritted her teeth, keeping her fingers pressed to the planchette. She was going to end this, once and for all. "Haven't you seen Henrietta when she comes to the house, Niles? Haven't you noticed how old she is? Even if you'd survived your childhood, you'd be dead by now."

The table tilted abruptly to one side, almost sliding the board to the floor. It rocked back and forth, like a teeter-totter.

NO NO NO NO NO NO NO NO NO NO NO NO NO
NO NO NO NO NO NO NO NO NO NO NO NO NO NO NO
NO NO NO NO NO NO NO NO NO NO NO NO NO NO NO
NO NO NO NO NO NO NO NO NO NO NO NO NO NO

"Were you murdered, Niles?"

NO.

I AM ALIVE.

Another bulb exploded in the kitchen, and from elsewhere in the house, Terri could hear glass shattering. "You're not alive. *We're* alive. You're dead."

Now her daughter was shrieking for her to stop as well, but Terri tuned her out and kept going. If this brat insisted upon hanging around, she wasn't going to make it easy for him.

"If you're alive, where is your mother? Your father? Where is Emma? Why don't they live here anymore, Niles? Why did they leave you?"

The moaning came from the speaking tube again, but it was louder than ever before. Between that, Gertrude and Dallas yelling at her, and the sounds of breaking glass, Terri was afraid the spirit wouldn't hear her. She raised her voice as loud as she could.

"The only one of your family that's alive is Henrietta, and she's an *old* woman! Everyone else is dead. *You* are dead!"

Papers fluttered on the counter and went flying. A cold wind swept through the room, moving Dallas's ponytail so it smacked Terri's uninjured cheek.

The Ouija board continued to spell out NO NO NO NO NO NO NO NO NO NO NO NO NO NO NO NO NO NO NO NO NO NO NO NO NO NO NO NO NO NO NO NO NO NO NO NO NO NO NO NO NO NO NO NO NO NO NO NO NO NO NO NO until it flew out from under their fingers and hit the opposite wall, splintering.

"Let go, Niles," Terri hollered. "You're dead. Go to the light. Go to the light!"

She wasn't sure why she'd said that last bit, but she'd seen it in a horror movie once, and it sounded good.

The heavy stockpot containing what was left of the cioppino hovered above the stove before soaring toward them. It slammed into the wall inches from their faces, splattering all of them with red stew. Then it dropped to the table with a thud.

The chaos ended as abruptly as it had begun. Torn papers drifted to the floor. One light bulb sputtered and flared, illuminating a godawful mess. Dallas and Gertrude stared at her, their expressions alternating between terror and fury, stew dripping from their noses and eyelashes. Terri had to fight the urge to laugh.

"I think that went well," she said.

CHAPTER TWELVE

Over the next few days, Terri experienced what *persona non grata* really meant. It was almost enough to make her regret she'd tormented Niles – almost, but not quite. She was tired of having their lives revolve around a sixteen-year-old brat. A *dead* sixeen-year-old brat, but still.

Her daughter and Gertrude had started an exclusive club where they'd talk to each other but not to her. Long after the last of the cioppino had been scrubbed from the kitchen walls, they continued their silent treatment, as if Glenvale now served as a bizarre version of high school. Well, fine. Let Gertrude deal with Dallas's moods and sullenness, the pervasive whines of "I'm bored" that were bound to begin any day now.

The thing was, aside from giving her the cold shoulder, they both appeared to be happy. Terri had stumbled upon them in the garden several times, chatting and laughing, but they became silent as a mortuary when they saw her.

She didn't care about what Gertrude thought of her, but she did care about Dallas. While she refinished the estate's hardwood floors, her eyes burned as she thought about the lost potential of 'their summer' and what a joke that had turned out to be. Several times she'd considered sending Gertrude home, or somehow tipping Henrietta Vandermere off and having *her* do the dirty work, but it was Dallas who kept her from doing so. Her daughter would see right through any excuse she provided to the jealousy and inadequacy that festered in Terri's heart. She'd never forgive her.

Thus, the ostracism dragged on. She'd haul herself to the kitchen for a glass of cold water and some supper, only to find Gertrude there, fussing over something that smelled amazing. Sometimes Dallas would be keeping her company, and Terri would linger as she made yet another peanut butter-and-honey sandwich, thinking that this would surely be the day when her daughter would break down and talk to her again. But so far, that hadn't happened. They continued to talk through her and over her, as if she weren't there at all. Was this what it was like to be a ghost?

Cruel remarks sprang to her lips, about how she wouldn't eat any of the crap Gertrude made if you paid her (what was wrong with processed food, anyway?), and how both of them were choosing their undead little friend over her, but she left the room before she could make the mistake of voicing them. Glenvale *was* high school, and she'd survived high school the first time with her sanity mostly intact. She'd had no inkling she'd have to repeat the fun and excitement in her mid-thirties, but she remembered well how to beat the silent-treatment game. *She who is the most silent wins.*

Not everyone left her alone. Terri often felt someone watching her as she did her work, and glimpsed the dreaded Niles out of the corner of her eye. A smell accompanied him sometimes, the nondescript medicinal smell of sickness that hadn't changed much over the ages. It reminded her of hospitals and palliative care, not of someone dying in their bed at home. She continued to steer clear of his room, intending to leave it until the end, along with the attic.

Then there was the woman. The woman had begun to show up a day ago, startling Terri into thinking Vandermere or one of her assistants had arrived, until she'd noticed the clothes. Corsets and wasp-waisted day dresses; jodhpurs, jackets, and hats that looked like they'd sauntered off the pages of *Horse and Hound* magazine. When she wasn't dressed for riding, the woman's hair was styled in a waved bob, making her look like a 1930s valentine come to life.

Elizabeth? Terri thought, unsure who the woman was. Her presence was more disconcerting than Niles's, even though Niles had been the one who'd mauled her cheek (which was healing nicely, finally). The woman held her head tilted at an unnatural angle, with her ear nearly touching her shoulder, and an expression of equal parts disgust and loathing upon her face. Terri couldn't figure out what she had done to provoke this reaction, unless it was yet more fallout from the doomed séance. Which hadn't been her fault in the first place. Gertrude never should have brought a Ouija board to Glenvale – that was like turning up at a knife fight with a flamethrower. What had she expected to happen?

Terri ignored it all. The persistent snubs from her own child, the unwelcome spirits, the irritation that was Gertie. She shut it out, and as she engrossed herself in her work, at times she felt a bit of relief. *This* was her destiny, bringing beautiful homes back from the dead. This was what she should have focused on all along: her work, not what the Vandermere family may or may not have done in the past, or what secrets the house may or may not conceal.

Thy Work Be Done, indeed.

She never imagined it would be Glenvale's ghosts who broke the silence, but break it they did.

The fourth day of Operation Cold Shoulder dawned as drearily as the others. Cloud-covered skies and oppressive humidity. Terri worked in Emma's room. It was a natural progression, but she'd also moved the bedroom up on her list in the hopes it would encourage Dallas to talk to her. However, her daughter had just moved her things to a different room.

She set to work dismantling a lovely wooden window seat in desperate need of repair. When she removed the rotten boards, she discovered there was a hidden nook where Emma had stored a number of treasures: an antique sparrow brooch wrapped in an embroidered handkerchief so delicate that it felt like it would crumble under her fingertips; a mother-of-pearl tussy mussy for carrying a small bouquet of flowers to ward off unpleasant smells; and a small, leather-bound book. The book tumbled onto the floor at her feet when she revealed its hiding place, and as Terri stooped to pick it up, a feeling of foreboding caressed her. Which didn't make any sense, as the book was likely just a Bible.

But it wasn't.

She opened the creaky book and found line after line of elegant script. It seemed like she'd found Emma Vandermere's journal. A lock of dark hair, glossy and wavy, fell into her hand as she turned the pages. It could have been anyone's, but she instinctively knew it was Niles's. Without thinking, she lifted it to her nose, but whatever smell he'd had, it was long gone.

Aware that she had no right reading the diary, and that she had no claim to anything she found during the restoration, Terri still couldn't help herself. Though she scoffed at Gertrude's theories and never-ending obsession, she *was* intrigued by the mystery of these unquiet spirits.

Had Niles been murdered? Had Emma known her own days were numbered? Terri sank down on the bed and began to read. It wasn't long before she found something troubling about the deathly ill male heir.

My little pussycat has gone missing, and its absence breaks my heart. It is the fourth creature who has suffered such a fate in as many months, and I am certain I know the identity of the culprit. For years, I have warned Mother about Niles's curious behavior, even telling her about the abomination I discovered in the cellar, but she refuses to listen. He is ill again, and she coddles him so, never accepting how dangerous he is. She believes he is as meek as a little lamb, but any animals we have adopted into this house would beg to differ. They know the truth, as do I.

Freezing fingers traced a path up her spine again, and Terri felt a cold draft that appeared to come from everywhere and nowhere all at once. They'd believed Niles was a victim – either a young man murdered while too ill to defend himself, or one cut down in the prime of his life by a treatable condition. But Emma's words told a different story. There were few things that bothered Terri more than the abuse of animals, but those who hurt animals were capable of hurting people too. Animal cruelty was often a training ground for serial killers.

She recalled how Niles had looked the night he'd attacked her, his angelic features twisted and contorted into something demonic, his teeth sharp and pointed when he'd hissed at her. Could she believe someone like that was capable of making kittens disappear? Without a doubt.

Who would believe her, though? Dallas and Gertrude had fallen so hard for the victim story, she wasn't sure they'd believe his own sister.

I had suspected Niles knew I was aware of his behavior and his foul collection of oddities in the cellar, and now I have proof. He has taken to following me, ensuring I do not have a moment alone with our parents or even Henrietta. He appears to be fearful of Henrietta, but what hold she has over him, I do not quite understand. The last few nights I awoke to feel that he had cloistered himself in here and was watching me slumber. I hate to think for what purpose! I have come to sleep with my epee alongside me, and though it is an impractical weapon, in my capable hands it should suffice.

Terri shut the volume for a moment, marking the place with her finger, fighting to collect her thoughts and catch her breath. She kept picturing Emma awakening to find someone was in her room, watching her. Though he had been her little brother, how terrifying that must have been. Had she heard his breathing? How had she known it was Niles? Scootching back on the bed so her back was pressed against the headboard, Terri surveyed the room. Though Emma had been the eldest daughter, her bedroom was one of the smallest, and from the photographs she'd seen, it had been packed with stuff. The woman's sporting equipment, musical instruments, including a Stradivarius violin whose price would have been astronomical today, dressmaker's dummy, and armoire full of fine clothing wouldn't have left much room for Niles to maneuver, but would have provided him with several objects to hide behind. Emma also had a walk-in closet that was its own separate room, a rarity in those days. Her brother could have concealed himself in there while he waited for her to fall asleep.

I hate to think for what purpose!

The same question troubled Terri. Had Niles hoped to catch his older sister off guard so he could hurt her? Was he wanting to intimidate or scare her? Or was it some sort of perversion that urged him to her room at night?

I could no longer bear it in silence. Though mortified, I told Mother about Niles's nocturnal visits. And once again, she refused to believe the truth! She refused to believe me, though I am honest as the day is long. She instead accused me of hysterics.

My brother has kept to himself more than usual lately, and I know he is plotting some nefarious deed. Most perturbing of all is that one of my beloved shotguns has gone missing. There is no point in telling Mother; I shall be wasting my breath. Once Father returns from his business trip, I shall request a private audience with him and reveal everything. I pray he will take my warning seriously, or it could very well be the death of us all!

The door flew open and, startled, she cried out, expecting to see Niles leering at her. Dallas burst into the room, her cheeks flushed and her eyes glowing. Terri's chest ached at the sight of her, and at how her smile disappeared when she spotted her mother on the bed.

"Oh. You're in here. I didn't know." She began to back out of the room.

"Wait! Hasn't this gone on long enough?"

Dallas's eyes narrowed. "Hasn't what gone on long enough?"

"Oh, Dallas, let's not pretend either of us is stupid. This silent treatment. It's getting to be ridiculous."

"I guess it'll last until we're not mad at you any longer." Dallas's hand clutched the doorknob, and she glanced behind her. "I should go. I'm playing Hide and Seek with Gertrude."

"Hide and Seek? Since when do you like to play Hide and Seek?" Or any games, for that matter. Since she was a toddler, Dallas had refused to participate in any organized games, never failing to let Terri know how dumb they were.

"Since I have someone fun to play it with, I guess."

Ouch. "She's not here to play games. She's supposed to be investigating."

"Everyone needs a break, Mom."

"It doesn't matter to me. She's the one who's going to regret it if she wastes her time here."

"Yeah, well, nice talking to you. I'll be going now."

"Can you just tell me what I did that was so terrible?"

"You know what you did," Dallas said, scowling. "Don't pretend you don't."

"But I don't. I mean, I don't understand why it's enough to make you stop speaking to me for days. Did Gertrude tell you not to talk to me?"

"God, Mom. She's not like that. She would never do something like that. I haven't been talking to you because *I'm* mad at you."

"Thanks for your honesty. I appreciate it. But why are you so angry with me?" As long as she kept her daughter talking, they could resolve this. Dallas would be reminded that she wasn't an ogre, and this silliness would end.

"You drove Niles away," her daughter yelled, voice breaking. "He won't talk to me anymore."

Ugh, Niles again. She was tired of hearing his name. He had been dead for so many years, and he was still causing problems. "Maybe that's not such a bad thing. You wanted him to leave you alone."

"That was before I knew his sister killed him. It's not his fault he's weird. Anyone would be if their sister *murdered* them."

"Hey, where are you getting this from? I don't think Emma had anything to do with Niles's death." She considered the book in her hands. Had Emma's meeting with Howard gone as badly as the ones with her mother? Did she finally feel she had no other choice than to kill Niles before he killed her? What a strange and troubled family. She wondered, not for the first time, what she'd gotten into by taking this job.

"Not Emma, Henrietta. The one *you're* working for."

"Dallas, she hired me to restore Glenvale. I'm hardly in cahoots with her. Gertrude worked for her too, a lot more closely than I have. The only difference is that Henrietta fired Gertrude."

Her daughter rolled her eyes. "Whatever. She's still a murderer."

"And where is the proof? Has Gertrude discovered anything concrete? Or is this just more accusations with no evidence? It's illegal to accuse people of things they haven't done without proof, you know. She could be sued for saying stuff like that."

Dallas stared at her as if she'd grown another head. "What are you talking about? Gertrude hasn't said anything. Niles told us! He told us with the Ouija board. You were there, and you made fun of him."

"I did not make fun of him. I told him he was dead, which is the truth. I don't remember him saying Henrietta killed him. How could I have missed that?"

"Mom, come *on*." She crossed her arms. "He told us about Henrietta giving him candy. Lots of candy. *Secret* candy. He was a diabetic. He shouldn't have been eating any candy. She obviously meant to kill him, and she did."

Terri hadn't considered the ominous implications of the candy, and now Gertrude's barrage of questions about how much candy he'd eaten made sense. "We don't know that," she said gently. "Henrietta was a child, and her brother was sick. She could have been giving him candy to cheer him up. There's no proof she meant to kill him."

She wasn't a doctor, but she wasn't certain the candy would have killed him, in any case. "Unlike her brother, Henrietta is alive. We have to be careful what we say about her, especially when there's no proof."

"But there *is*. Niles told us." Dallas continued to look and sound furious, but Terri knew her daughter well enough to see her conviction was wavering.

"*Did* he tell us? Gertrude could have been moving the planchette on her own, and might not have known she was doing it. I had my hands on it too, and I couldn't tell either way. In any case, the evidence you might think we have wouldn't stand up in court. We could hardly use the testimony of a ghost."

"Did I hear my name?" Gertrude popped her head into the room, smiling that fake smile of hers. Terri had never loathed anyone more than she loathed Gertrude at that moment. "Oh, you two are talking again. Glad to see it. It was feeling a bit tense around here."

Unbelievable. "You weren't talking to me either, Gertrude. If the tension bothered you so much, why didn't *you* say something?"

The woman's smug smile vanished. "You seemed very upset with me, Terri. I thought it best to give you a respectful distance for a while. The last thing I wanted to do was make things worse for you."

"Are you sure? Because for someone who doesn't want to make things worse, you're doing a great job of it."

"Mom! Why do you have to be so rude? Gertrude is trying to be nice."

"No, Gertrude is pretending that she wasn't an equal partner in the silent treatment I've been getting. Do you want to take the blame for it?"

Dallas bit her lip but didn't say anything. Her eyes went from Terri to Gertrude and back again. Terri hated every second of this, hated that the perfect summer she'd envisioned for them had gone up in smoke. Her daughter should have been having fun, enjoying the nice weather and the gardens, and instead she was entangled in adult drama. *Immature* adult drama. Two women bickering like a pair of teenagers.

"I agreed to give this a try, Gertrude, against my considerable misgivings. But clearly it's not working out. I think you should leave."

Gertrude's mouth gaped open like a fish's. "But…it's too soon. I haven't found what I need yet."

"And you're never going to, if what you're looking for is evidence that Henrietta murdered Niles with candy. What are you expecting to find, an old bag of M&Ms? A scrawled note that says, 'I did it'? Henrietta was a child. Even if she had more malicious motives than trying to cheer up a sick brother, there's no proof. None of us can say what was going through her head, and if she told anyone, they'd be long gone by now."

"There's something in this house. Niles told me. He was working with me until you scared him off. Now we might never find it. The truth might never come out."

"Henrietta Vandermere is one hundred years old. What exactly were you intending to accomplish? Do you want her thrown in jail for her remaining weeks or months of life, so she can die of old age in prison?"

Gertrude straightened. "I want everyone to know what she did. I want to find justice for Niles."

"Well, I'm afraid you're going to have to do it somewhere else. Like I said, this hasn't been working out."

Dallas's face fell. "Mom, don't send her away. She hasn't done anything wrong."

"I'm sorry, sweetheart, but this summer was supposed to be for us. You and me. I'm not going to let her come between us and cause more damage." *Even though she already has.* She returned her attention to Gertrude. "I can't believe I trusted you and let you stay here, and you repaid me by convincing my daughter not to talk to me."

"That was my idea, Mom. She had nothing to do with it," Dallas protested.

"She didn't help, though, did she? If you and I had been here alone, it never would have lasted four days. But you had an adult encouraging you, acting like you were a team of two against me. You're both so upset about Niles being gone, but if I 'drove him away', why is he always around me when I'm working? He hasn't gone anywhere."

Gertrude glared at her. "You're lying."

"Why would I lie about something so ridiculous? We're talking about a *ghost*. You're both furious with me because I told a ghost he was dead. Christ, you should hang me for my crimes. If you hadn't brought that damn board into this house, none of this would have happened."

A small voice piped up. "My mom doesn't lie, Gertrude," Dallas said, and Terri knew her daughter had found her way back at last.

She could have wept with relief. "You shouldn't say stuff like that."

"You're a sweet girl, Dallas, but I don't think you have any idea what your mother is capable of."

"Next you'll be saying *I* killed Niles. Is that your latest theory? I want you gone within an hour. And if I ever see so much as a hint that you're back in this house, my first call will be to the police. My second, to Henrietta. I'd love to see you explain how she killed her brother with candy."

The woman looked so furious Terri thought she might snap. Her lips were pressed together so tightly they'd gone white, and her throat and cheeks were flushed with anger. "Fine. You got what you wanted. Admit it, you never wanted me here in the first place."

"No, I didn't. You're right about that."

"I hope you're happy. Because of you, no one will ever find out what happened to Niles."

"That's where you're wrong." Feeling spiteful, but also pretty damn good, Terri held up Emma's journal. "I have the truth right here. You're the one who's never going to find it."

CHAPTER THIRTEEN

"I'm sorry, Mom."

Terri put a hand on her daughter's head. Gertrude had left them hours ago, and already the house felt lighter. Perhaps *she'd* been the one truly haunting the house. She'd definitely been poisoning the atmosphere. "It's okay."

"No, it isn't. I feel really bad. I should never have sided with her over you."

"*I'm* the one who's sorry — sorry you're back to eating like this again." She looked ruefully at the grilled cheese sandwiches and oven fries she'd prepared for dinner. Gertrude would have undoubtedly made chicken fricassee or some other fancy shit. Terri couldn't compete in that department. But her daughter was still here, and Gertrude was not.

"I'm not. It's great. Gertrude's cooking was nice and all, but it was a bit too weird for me."

Terri laughed, even though she knew she shouldn't. "Me too. It was a lovely cioppino, though."

"Until it ended up all over the walls."

"Yeah. It took forever to get that stuff off. Mac 'n' cheese would have come off in a snap."

"I really do feel bad, Mom." Dallas lowered her gaze to her plate, but not before Terri saw a glimmer of tears.

"Hey, forget about it. We're together now, we're talking now, and that's what's important. You know I don't hold grudges. I'm glad you came into Emma's room."

A smile tugged at the corners of her daughter's mouth. "Me too. To be honest, I kind of hoped you'd be in there."

"Really?" That had been the last thing Terri expected to hear. Dallas had looked so angry when she'd first seen her sitting there.

"Yeah. I wanted to talk to you, but I didn't know how. After so many days, it felt weird."

"If that ever happens again, and I hope it doesn't, now you know. Just talk. You're my daughter. I'm never going to shut you out."

"I got so caught up in wanting to find out what happened to Niles. I wanted to prove his sister killed him." Dallas sighed, the weary sigh of a much older person. "But you were right. We shouldn't have been going around saying Henrietta did it without any proof. I'd hate if someone did that to me."

Thrilled that her daughter was displaying empathy after three days of showing none, Terri was also furious with Gertrude for involving her child in her sick obsession. "I'm glad you see that now. Honey, Henrietta fired Gertrude, and Gertrude is angry about that. It doesn't have anything to do with Niles at all."

Niles was a convenient excuse, had always been an excuse.

"I apologize for letting her stay here," she continued. "It wasn't a healthy environment for you, but I'm going to do my best to make up for it with what's left of the summer."

"Can I stay with you for the school year too?"

Terri could scarcely believe what she was hearing. While it was her greatest wish that Dallas would choose to live with her full-time again, she'd assumed that ship had sailed. "Are you sure you want to do that? I'm probably going to be stuck here for the year, so that means leaving your old school and all your friends."

Her daughter shrugged. "That's okay. I didn't have many friends there, anyway. The only one I really liked was Angela. Maybe she could come and stay with us sometime. She's nothing like Gertrude."

"I would love that." When was the last time she'd met one of her daughter's friends? It had been ages.

"Did you get a lot done in the house while I was with Gertrude?" Dallas asked, sounding shy. Terri's chest ached again. So much damage had been done in the past few days, so much progress erased. At least now they had a chance to get back on track again.

"I did. If you like, I can show you after dinner."

"Okay. What was the book you showed Gertrude?"

The book that Terri was determined to carry everywhere until she had an opportunity to read it from cover to cover and have a copy made. It was too valuable to let out of her sight. "It's Emma's journal."

Dallas instantly brightened, looking happier than she had since Gertrude had darkened their lives. "Cool! Can I see it?"

Terri hesitated, wondering how Emma's story would affect her daughter. She'd loved scary books and movies when she'd been Dallas's age, but that had been fiction. This was real life, which made it so much more frightening. "We'll see. I'm going to need to finish reading it first. It might be better if you waited until we aren't living in this house anymore. It's...well, it's quite disturbing."

Rather than appearing the slightest bit put off, Dallas sounded more eager. Of course she did. Terri would have been the same way when she was ten. "What does she say?"

"I'll tell you when we go for our walk tonight. I don't want to talk about it in the house." Terri glanced at the speaking tube. Though she wasn't obsessed with Niles like Gertrude was, she had a healthy respect for the ghost – respect that had come courtesy of the scratches on her face, which had yet to fully heal. Had Niles used the speaking tube to eavesdrop when he was alive too? The thought was enough to make her shudder. There was that goose, walking over her grave again.

"Okay."

She'd expected her daughter to protest, and was relieved when she didn't. Terri wondered how long this new, tentative respect was going to last. Probably not nearly long enough.

"Were you telling the truth about Niles? Have you really seen him?"

"Of course I have. Like you said, I don't lie."

Dallas beamed. "I know you don't. Has he said or... done anything?"

"No, he's been pretty quiet. He's watched me, mostly. Maybe he's curious about what I'm doing to the house." It had felt a lot more menacing than that, but there was no reason to scare her daughter more. Terri was beset with guilt whenever she thought of the doomed séance and how Dallas had screamed. She should have dropped it before it had ever gotten to that point. "He hasn't been to see you at all?"

"I don't think so. I don't feel him around anymore, and he doesn't talk to me. I haven't had any nightmares, either."

"You've had nightmares? Why didn't you tell me?"

Her daughter shrugged. "It didn't seem like a big deal. Anyway, they're gone now."

More relief. Terri felt the weight of her worries leave her, and sent a silent thanks to the ghost. All she'd wanted was for him to leave her daughter alone, and it sounded like that had been accomplished. "The fact he's leaving you alone – that's not such a bad thing, is it?"

Dallas sighed again. "I guess not. I feel bad saying this, because he wasn't nice to you and scratched your face, but I kind of miss him. He could be a brat sometimes, but he was someone to talk to."

Terri put her arm around her daughter and gave her a hug. "I'm sorry, honey. I understand that it's lonely for you here, but once school starts, you'll meet other children in the area. You'll make *real* friends."

"I hope so."

"I know so."

"You're not going to tell Henrietta, are you? About Gertrude staying here?"

The question was so out of the blue she was at a loss for words. "I've thought about it, but haven't decided yet. Why do you ask?"

"Gertrude was really scared about that when we weren't talking to you. She thought you'd call Henrietta, and Henrietta would make her go to jail."

Terri felt another wave of anger that Gertrude had said those things to Dallas in an attempt to drive a wedge between them. "That's not the way it works, honey. But yes, she would have gotten in trouble for trespassing." *And I would have lost my job when Gertrude immediately threw me under the bus.* The woman probably had proof that Terri had allowed her to stay in the house, however briefly.

"Please don't tell Henrietta. I get that you don't like Gertrude, but she can't afford to go to jail. Her mother is sick, and she's the only one who can take care of her."

"It's not that I don't like Gertrude," Terri said. *'Despised' would be a better word.* "She's ill, and she needs help. Now that she's not living here, able to proceed with her 'investigation', she might go after Henrietta and seriously hurt her. Henrietta is well aware Gertrude has issues – that's why she fired her – but I don't think she realizes how disturbed Gertrude is, or that Gertrude is convinced she murdered her brother."

Dallas's eyes widened. "You really think she'd hurt Henrietta?"

"Yes, I do. And I wouldn't put it past her to do something to us, either, so if you see her in the house or around the yard, you have to promise to tell me, okay? Don't let her approach you."

"Okay." Her daughter thought for a minute. "That's scary. She seemed so nice."

"Remember when you were little, and we taught you about stranger danger? Just because people *seem* nice doesn't mean that they are. Look at Niles." Terri hesitated for a moment. Dallas had to understand the gravity of their situation, but she didn't want to make her paranoid. "I'm not saying you shouldn't trust anyone. It's important to trust other people, but they should *earn* that trust. Don't give it to them before they deserve it."

"Do you think Gertrude will come back here, Mom?"

Terri recalled the fury on the woman's face when she'd told her to leave. "Yes. Yes, I do."

* * *

Father told me he would take care of things. He seemed to take me seriously, much more so than Mother did. I am not sure what he said to Niles, if anything, but my brother has stopped coming into my room while I sleep. However, I am positive he has done something to the horses.

He has been in the barn. I am at a loss to imagine what he has been up to, but Midnight is badly spooked, and she ordinarily has the calmest disposition. I cannot prove anything, of course – I can never prove anything with that Niles! But I would swear to it all the same. I am considering cloistering myself in there until I see what he is up to. If Father revealed that I was the one who aroused his suspicions, Niles could very well be plotting to destroy me...or the creatures I love most.

The lightness Terri had experienced when Gertrude left the house faded when she read Emma's words. Had Niles been capable of killing his sister? He'd been a kid, and a critically ill one at that. And yet, children *had* killed at that age and younger. Mary Bell. Robert Thompson. Jon Venables. Children had proven time and time again that they could be every bit as sadistic as adults.

Many times she'd thought she glimpsed the figure of a woman out of the corner of her eye while she worked. A woman in formal dress, with an anxious expression. Was it her imagination, or was Emma trying to influence her, urge her to discover the truth about Glenvale and the Vandermeres, as Gertrude had insisted Niles had done to her? The idea was disquieting, to say the least.

Once she'd finished with the journal and made a copy, she would ask for a meeting with Henrietta. If Niles *had* killed her sister, Henrietta deserved to know, and unlike Gertrude, Terri wouldn't keep this from her. She had no desire to go public and ruin the Vandermere name. As long as Henrietta understood the truth about her family, that was all that mattered.

She wished her daughter had agreed to share a room with her, but Dallas had insisted on retaining her independence. She'd moved out of Emma's quarters as Terri restored them, and into the smaller cook's room nearby. They would be able to hear each other if either of them cried out, but that wasn't much comfort.

Terri was tempted to leave the door open, but the darkness lurking outside the room was too unnerving. She imagined the Vandermere ghosts parading by as she slept, looking in on her, watching her, as Niles had once spied on Emma. She shivered, and decided to check on Dallas one more time.

She heard a rustling noise in the hallway as she stepped out, as if someone had hurried out of view as she approached. She was at the point where she wished for rats over ghosts. At least rats were predictable. Dallas's door was closed, the white doorknob gleaming in the dim light. It reminded Terri that she'd never asked Henrietta about the door to Niles's room. With all of the recent drama, she'd forgotten about the strangeness of it.

"Mom?" The voice, small and frightened, startled her. She opened the door and looked inside, relieved to see that Dallas appeared to be fine, snuggled in the small bed with Rufus, her old teddy bear.

"I heard someone in the hall. I'm so glad it was you."

"Yes, it was me," Terri said, forcing the thought of the rustling out of her mind. "But to be honest, I'm a bit spooked. Are you sure you won't share a room with me? We could move into the master suite." Hopefully there were no ghosts in there. Gertrude hadn't said a word about Howard or Elizabeth haunting the place, but then again, she hadn't mentioned Emma either.

"I'm too old to share a room with my mom. What would my friends think?"

"I won't tell your friends if you don't, but I think they'd say you were brave for staying in a haunted house. I bet none of them would stay here."

Why *were* they staying there? When she'd first made the decision to board at Glenvale, it had made sense. It was the most convenient – wake up, and you were already at work. But the more she learned about the tragedies that had shadowed the Vandermeres, along with the whispers of murder, the less convenient it felt. And then there was Gertrude, who'd managed to get inside the house. What if she came back? What if Terri awoke to find the deranged woman standing over her with a knife? Or worse, what if she went after Dallas? She'd never be able to live with herself if something happened to her daughter.

"We'll be fine, Mom. Ghosts can't hurt us."

It was an odd thing to say, given the scratches on her face, but Dallas was clearly adamant about them sleeping separately. There was no point pushing it. Terri wasn't going to make her daughter act as her security blanket.

Still, she thought longingly of the hotel that was a few short blocks up the road. They could hardly afford it, but her fee for the restoration would more than cover it. Terri was reluctant to spend money she hadn't earned, but in this case, it might be worth it to preserve her sanity.

"Okay…if you're sure."

"I'm sure." Dallas laughed. "Your room is right there. You'll hear me if I call out, right?"

Terri nodded, though her mind strayed to how heavy those wooden doors were. They were highly effective at muffling sound. "Where's your phone?"

Reaching under the covers, Dallas retrieved the cell and held it up, still smiling. As scared as she had sounded only a moment before, she appeared a lot more confident than Terri felt herself. "See? I promise I'll call you if anything happens, even if it's just a spooky dream."

"Looks like you're all set." Her lips curved in a smile that felt as natural as plastic. "Sweet dreams, honey."

"Sweet dreams, Mom. And don't worry. Nothing's going to happen."

Leaving her daughter's room, Terri could feel the weight of the darkness pressing against her back. Someone was standing in the shadows, watching her. She could see them waiting there, hear them breathing.

Hands trembling, she flicked on the hallway light. No one was there. The shadow had been just that – a shadow. She stood there for several seconds, her heart racing. When nothing appeared, she returned to her room, fighting the temptation to run. She left the light on.

But as soon as her door closed, someone else turned it off.

CHAPTER FOURTEEN

Gertrude added another blanket to the bed, even though it was warm in the room.

"Is it raining?"

Tilting her head, she listened. She couldn't hear anything, but that didn't mean much. Her mother had always been able to sense things, and that ability had only increased as Death drew near. "I don't know, Mom."

The older woman nodded, her eyes gleaming unnaturally in her gaunt face. Gertrude could barely stand to look at her, to witness how the cancer had ravaged her. Not so long ago, Esther Phillips had looked years younger than her age. She'd run the most popular bed and breakfast in town all by herself, and everyone had said how pretty she was.

No one would say that now. Cancer had stolen that from her, as it had so many things.

"I think it is. I always feel a chill when it rains."

"Is that better?" Gertrude tucked the afghan around what was left of her mother's body, an afghan that Esther herself had knit, never imagining that she'd be the one to need it.

"Yes, darling, thank you." Before Gertrude could leave the room, she added, "How is work?"

The question startled Gertrude so much, she nearly dropped the glass she was carrying. "Huh?"

"I asked about your job. It's hardly an unusual question." Her mother attempted a smile, but she'd lost so much weight it looked like a grimace. Gertrude averted her eyes.

"I know, Mom. It seemed to come out of the blue, that's all."

"When your days are numbered, you don't have time to beat around the bush. I want to make sure that old battle axe is treating you well."

"I haven't seen her much," Gertrude said, relieved to speak the truth. She hated lying to her mother, and there had been so many lies already, out of necessity. She was sure lying to a person on their deathbed was a sin. She only hoped it was a forgivable one.

She hadn't seen Henrietta since the day she was fired, and had taken great pains to avoid her. Thankfully, after working for the old woman for so many years, she knew her routines well. She knew when Henrietta did her shopping, and where. Which restaurants she frequented and when. The one place she risked a confrontation with her former employer was at Glenvale, and once Henrietta had left Terri in charge, that risk had been greatly minimized.

"Is she ill?" In spite of Esther's condition, she had great sympathy for anyone else's suffering, even an 'old battle axe' like Henrietta Vandermere. There had been a time when Henrietta had considered turning Glenvale into a bed and breakfast, and she'd asked Gertrude if it was possible to 'pick her mother's brain'. Esther was excited to meet her daughter's boss, and to see the infamous Glenvale from the inside at last, but the meeting hadn't gone well. Instead of wanting advice, Henrietta had used the opportunity to deliver vague and not-so-vague threats about how Esther should consider other lines of work, since Vandermere's new venture was sure to put its rivals out of business. Esther had been so mortified that she hadn't told her daughter the truth about the exchange until months later. By then, she'd been diagnosed, and any concerns about the bed and breakfast had been relegated to another time, another life.

"I don't think so. She's probably busy." Gertrude took a deep breath, deciding to tell her mother more of the truth. "Glenvale is being renovated."

"Now *that* is a surprise. I never thought she'd finally get around to it. When did that start?"

"A few weeks ago."

Esther frowned. "But…this won't affect your job, will it?"

"Don't worry, Mom. They still need me. No one knows that house better than I do, except maybe Henrietta herself." Gertrude knew full well that she'd discovered places in that house that the Vandermere heir would never dare go. The woman was extremely cowardly when it came to the family home. She wouldn't go near her brother's bedroom, and Gertrude was pretty sure she knew why.

Niles's blood was on Henrietta's hands. All she had to do was prove it.

But Terri Foxworth had asked some troubling questions today, and as infuriating as those questions had been, she couldn't stop going back to them, the way she'd continue to work a sore tooth with her tongue. What exactly *was* she hoping to accomplish? Even with proof, assuming she could find it, few prosecutors would be willing to throw such an elderly woman in jail for her actions over eighty years ago. Would anyone care about what had happened to Niles? Another rich, white dude, and the public had lost sympathy for rich, white dudes long ago. Did she *want* to see Henrietta thrown in prison, and if so, was it about justice for Niles at all? Or was it revenge she was after, revenge for the terrible way Henrietta had treated her and her mother? Such thoughts weren't worth considering, and yet, she *had* to consider them. Achieving justice for Niles was one thing, but petty vengeance was quite another.

Her mother settled back against the pillows, wincing as that most miniscule of movements pained her. Life wasn't fair. Esther Phillips had worked hard every day of her life. She'd deserved a good retirement, where she could put her feet up and have someone else cook her breakfast. Nothing like these days of pain clouded by the morphine she hated to rely on. It made her sleep too much, she said. As agonizing as life had become, she didn't want to miss a minute of it.

"I'm glad to hear it. For a moment, I was worried you'd lost your job."

This time it was Gertrude who winced, but on the inside. Her mother was too sharp, even now, and she couldn't risk Esther figuring out what was going on. The loss of her job at Glenvale had been devastating. Her mother's illness was costing them hundreds, if not thousands, of dollars a day. Gertrude's one hope was to find the proof Niles had promised her, and for Henrietta to care enough about the family name to pay well to protect it.

Her own days were numbered as much as her dying mother's. Henrietta might be fortunate enough to maintain her faculties to the end, but how much longer could she be expected to live? Forming that alliance with the Foxworths had been a godsend, and then Gertrude had gone and blown it with her temper. She'd thought her friendship with the daughter would be enough to keep her in the house, no matter how strong Terri's objections, but she should have foreseen what had happened that afternoon. Blood was thicker than water. She understood that better than anyone.

"You don't have to worry about that. Henrietta may be an old fool, but she's not foolish enough to lose me. She needs me to run the place, always has." That wasn't a lie, either. The house had suffered in her absence, and would suffer more with no one supervising Terri Foxworth. The woman was clearly out of her depth. She hadn't been able to see what was happening at Glenvale when it was right under her nose until Niles attacked her. And now that Gertrude had been banished from the house again, Niles was bound to get nasty.

The restoration appeared to be progressing painfully slow, if it was progressing at all. The one thing the woman had managed to accomplish during her month in the house was removing the wallpaper from the parlor, which looked terrible now, and tearing apart the window seat in Emma's quarters. As bad as the damage was, Gertrude wished she had done it herself. That had to have been where that hateful woman had found her so-called 'evidence'. Why hadn't she guessed that Emma would have concealed something personal in the window seat? It was the perfect hiding place, but almost too obvious. The truth was, she'd given Emma more credit. Out of the three Vandermere children, she'd been the standout – the most compassionate, the most intelligent, and the most skilled. In other words, Emma Vandermere had been doomed from the start.

"If it's not your job, what's troubling you? I know something is, so don't try to deny it."

Gertrude cursed her mother's ability to accurately assess a situation and read the minds of those around her, and then immediately felt guilty. The doctor had warned her that Esther's astuteness would not last forever. Eventually the cancer would find its way to her mother's brain too, and when that happened, Gertrude would be lucky if Esther recognized her, or remembered her name. As difficult as it was to face her questions, and as much as she hated lying to her, it was far, far preferable to what was to come. The future was the darkest of dark clouds.

"I don't have a clue how I'm going to make it without you. That's all," she said, and this was true as well, though her mother didn't like to talk about it. Hopefully this would bring the conversation to a merciful end so she could get back to Glenvale. The clock was ticking so loudly she could actually hear it.

Her mother's eyes glimmered with tears, and Gertrude instantly regretted her words. Though they talked plenty about Death, they neatly sidestepped his cousin Loss, understanding that this cousin would be the most difficult to deal with.

"Don't be silly," Esther finally managed. "You hardly need me hanging around, making all this extra work for you. You'll be fine. And someday, a wonderful man is going to sweep you off your feet and treat you the way you deserve."

"I don't need a man, Mom. You didn't need one, and I don't, either." Not only did Gertrude not need a man, she didn't want one. But as much as she wished her mother understood who she really was, that was not a conversation she was going to burden her with on her deathbed. As far as secrets went, this one only hurt her, not Esther. So it was well worth keeping.

"That's true. All I meant was you're going to be fine. And you are. You'll see."

"Thanks, Mom." She returned to her mother's side and kissed her forehead, which felt as thin and dry as tissue paper under her lips. "Why don't you rest now? Maria will be here in case you need anything, and as soon as she gets here, I'll need to go back to work for a bit."

Esther frowned. "So late? How can Henrietta expect you to keep these hours? It's not decent."

"It's only temporary, just while the restoration work is going on. It's better if I'm there at night so I'm out of their way." The lie slipped so smoothly off her tongue it frightened her. She was getting to be too good at lying, but it was most likely because she'd had so much practice while staying with the Foxworths. Practically everything she'd told poor Dallas had been a lie.

Her mother's face cleared. "I suppose that's all right, as long as it's temporary. You can leave now, dear. I'll be fine until Maria gets here. Can you turn off the light? I think I'd like to sleep for a bit."

It was tempting to leave, but Gertrude was determined to wait for her mother's nurse. She'd heard horror stories about what happened to the elderly and infirm when people thought no one was watching, that no one cared. She wanted to make sure Maria understood exactly how much she cared about her mother. Even when she'd been staying at Glenvale during those few short, blissful days, she'd kept a close eye on how things were at home. Besides, waiting for Maria gave her some time to plan her attack on Glenvale.

Not a *real* attack. In spite of what Terri Foxworth believed, she wasn't insane (but she was uncomfortably aware that crazy people didn't think they were crazy), and she had no desire to hurt the restorer or her daughter. Getting revenge on Terri for destroying her séance had been amusing for a time, but look how it had backfired. She'd been pushed out of the house again, and now her mother was worried she'd been fired. This time, she couldn't make any mistakes.

She'd shown Dallas a few of her secrets, enough to keep the girl interested, but she hadn't shown her the way in through the cellar. Niles had hinted that the proof she was searching for was in the basement, so all she needed to do was slip in without either of the Foxworths hearing her, and slip back out again. No one needed to be the wiser, especially if Henrietta paid for Gertrude's silence. If not, the Vandermere name would be splashed all over the evening news, their reputation would be permanently destroyed, and Niles would have finally found his justice.

All because of her. It was a heady thought.

By the time Maria showed up, Gertrude was in her raincoat. (Her mother had been right, as always.)

The nurse was visibly startled. "Going out, Ms. Phillips? But it's so late."

"I've been cooped up all day. I need some air. I also thought I might visit a friend."

Maria looked pointedly at her watch. She was one of the few people who still wore one, which might be the reason she was also one of the few people who were always on time. "A friend? At midnight?"

"A very good friend," Gertrude said with a wink, and the nurse smiled.

"Ah, I see. Well, have a good time, Ms. Phillips. You deserve it. I'll look after things here."

"Thank you. You'll call me if anything happens?"

"Of course." The nurse crossed herself, as she often did when making a promise. Maria was also a fan of pinky swears. "Please, try not to worry. Your mother is in good hands."

Was she? Gertrude considered this as she left the house. Maria Martìnez was a decent woman and a capable nurse who genuinely cared about her mother. Gertrude believed this, or she never would have left Esther alone with her. But how quickly would that change if Maria discovered Gertrude didn't have the money to pay her? That soon she wouldn't have the money to pay the electrical or water bill, let alone hundreds of dollars for a homecare nurse? Medicaid helped a bit, but didn't come close to covering all of her mother's expenses. Gertrude couldn't bear to find out what would happen when she ran out of money, but she couldn't tell Maria the same lie she'd told Esther. Unlike Esther, the nurse wasn't bedridden. She interacted with many people during the course of her day, and was bound to say something. If Maria believed Henrietta Vandermere required her employees to work through the night, that would be much too tempting to keep to herself. She'd tell people, and those people would tell other people, until it finally reached the source, who wouldn't hesitate to call the police once she discovered her ex-employee was still lurking around Glenvale.

Not that Gertrude liked to think of herself as lurking. *Lurking* had evil connotations, and she was hardly the villain of this piece. That would be Henrietta. *Gertrude* was the hero. Truth be told, she liked to think of herself as an avenging angel. Once she solved this mystery, everyone would be able to see her halo.

Assuming Henrietta wasn't willing to pay.

If the elderly woman did the right thing, no one would ever have to know. Gertrude was willing to give up any glory, as long as her mother was able to live out her remaining days in comfort.

Flipping the hood of her black raincoat over her head, Gertrude set off toward Glenvale at a brisk pace, blending into the night.

★　　★　　★

Her feet, smaller than she'd seen them since childhood, were encased in narrow boots with pointed toes. Though they looked painful, they felt as natural as if they'd been painted on, as did the stirrups beneath them.

Instinctively, she lifted her weight from the saddle and her horse began to move faster and faster, breaking into a canter and then into a run. Her hair flew out behind her, and she loved the freedom of it. These early mornings were for her and Midnight; there was no one around to judge her for not being feminine enough, or to tell her she needed to stop giving the mare her head. During these moments, these precious minutes together, she was tempted to let the horse keep going, to leave Glenvale far behind and never return.

She never got the chance.

As they neared the edge of the property, her brother stepped out from behind the trees, startling her. He held something in his hand, something she couldn't see. "Niles!" The horse stopped short, and she narrowly avoided being catapulted over Midnight's head.

"What are you doing out here?" she asked, but Niles said nothing. He slowly raised his arm, and she saw what his hand contained and understood his purpose. It was too late for her to avoid his trap, but she attempted to anyway, struggling to turn the horse around. Midnight fought her – the mare didn't want to present her back to Niles, and for good reason.

Her brother threw the snake at Midnight's hooves. The reptile hissed, and her horse reared. She did her best to stay on, but she hadn't had the chance to regain a stable position. She tumbled to the ground, falling in such a way that she wouldn't be badly hurt. Squealing, her mare galloped back to Glenvale.

With the wind knocked out of her, she was temporarily helpless. She hoped she'd have the chance to regain her footing and run back to the house before her brother did anything further. Though in her heart she knew that Niles had much bigger plans for her than simply knocking her off a horse.

The only thing to do was retain her composure. She'd learned long ago never to show fear around her brother. Fear just encouraged his cruelty.

"I suppose you think that was amusing," she said as he approached. "Very funny, but I have a feeling Mother and Father will not be nearly as amused."

"You are not going to tell our parents about this. Or anyone else, for that matter."

"Niles, please consider your actions," she said, as she realized what was about to happen. She fought to stand, but he kicked her legs out from underneath her. The pointed boots had no grip, and she went down hard. The resulting pain told her she'd been more injured from the initial fall than she had thought. She would never make it back to Glenvale on her own; she'd have to be carried.

"Oh, I *have* considered them, dear Emma. I have dreamed of this moment for longer than you could imagine."

The stone was large. Large enough to blot out the sun, and the features of her attacker.

When it hurtled toward her, crushing her neck and silencing her forever, there was a brief flash of pain before oblivion claimed her. In that fleeting second, the perspective shifted, and Terri woke up, gasping for breath.

She'd seen the killer's face.

CHAPTER FIFTEEN

For a second, Gertrude feared the cellar doors were locked, and relief flooded through her as she ran her hands over the slick wood and found no obstruction. The rain pounded against her head and back, giving her a headache. As damp and dark as the cellar was, the shelter would be a welcome respite.

The doors creaked as she opened them to reveal the stairs, and she paused, waiting for lights to flare below and for the voice of Terri Foxworth to demand an explanation. Or maybe to tell her she was crazy again – that was always nice. If Dallas had been the one who was dying, Gertrude wondered how crazy Terri would find this. But it didn't matter. She didn't care what Terri thought of her, and the cellar remained silent and pitch black.

She turned on her phone's flashlight and carefully made her way down the stairs, moving slowly so her sneakers didn't squeak. The one light was a bare bulb with a chain, and she took the risk of using it. She couldn't let her battery run out, lest something happen with her mother and Maria needed to reach her. The cell was her connection to the outside world.

She crept along the dirt floor, trying to be as quiet as possible. She had no idea where the Foxworths had chosen to sleep that night, but it had never been consistent. Dallas had told her she'd wanted Niles's room, but then Niles had lashed out at her mother, and that was the end of that.

Someone appeared in front of her and she almost screamed before she saw the face of her friend. He had never appeared ghostly to her, but as real as any flesh-and-blood person. At times, it was difficult to believe he was dead. Only his old-fashioned clothes served as a constant reminder of what he had lost. He beckoned at her, urging her forward.

Over here.

Gertrude hesitated when she saw the size of the crawl space under the stairs. It was the perfect spot for a child, but adults would find it a challenge to squeeze through. Niles went in first, ducking low to show her the way through, reaching for her hand. She imagined she felt the pressure of his fingers closing on hers, but couldn't tell if the sensation was real or in her mind. The scratches on Terri Foxworth's face had been real enough. Her friend was capable of incredible things, but she had never doubted that.

The ceiling was higher than she'd thought. She was able to stand, the top of her head brushing the planks of wood above. The space was claustrophobic, crammed with crudely made shelves, shelves that were full of all manner of jars and containers. This was what he had been leading her toward; this was where she'd finally find her evidence.

It was darker in here, and Niles's spirit felt oppressively close. Gertrude imagined she could feel his breath on the back of her neck, but that was ridiculous. Ghosts didn't breathe. Taking her phone from her raincoat pocket, she turned on the flashlight again. Light reflected back from dozens upon dozens of jars. She leaned closer, sweeping a thick layer of dust from one in order to see its contents. The liquid inside was murky, and she gasped in revulsion when she finally glimpsed the pink, hairless creature inside.

Smoky, read the label. Though the contents looked more like a rat, Smoky was a cat's name. Someone had skinned a small cat or kitten and put him in this jar – but why? And why had Niles led her here? Why had he wanted her to see this?

Each jar was worse than the last. They'd clearly been family pets at one time, but now they were preserved in this macabre laboratory. Poor Smoky had fared better than most, as she was able to see evidence of dissections or mutilation on the others. Aside from his skin, Smoky had been intact.

Gertrude's stomach churned, and she felt dizzy. After taking care of her mother for months, she'd witnessed all manner of gruesome things. She was not squeamish. This, however, was something else. She had a soft heart when it came to animals and couldn't understand why anyone would have done these things. Though she desperately wanted to believe the pets had died of natural causes, and that some curious child had taken the opportunity to experiment, this wasn't the case. It was obvious how some of the poor creatures had died, and there was nothing natural about it.

She choked back the bile that rose in her throat and kept looking. As horrific as this was, somewhere among this revolting display was the evidence she'd been searching for. The evidence that would prove Henrietta was a vicious murderer who'd taken the life of her own brother. She'd just have to push through.

A small jar at the very back had a reddish tinge to the liquid inside. With shaking hands, she lifted it from its shelf. *Emma* was written on the label in ornate script. Someone had taken more care with this one.

Emma? No, it couldn't be….

Praying to see nothing more than a lock of hair or some other ghoulish but standard memento, she peered into the jar. At first, the contents appeared to be a blob of grayish jelly, but as her focus sharpened, she saw the familiar segmentations. Her gorge rose when she realized she held part of a human brain.

Emma's brain.

She couldn't throw up, had to control herself. Gertrude managed to set the jar down, and clung to the shelf, closing her eyes and taking deep breaths until the dizziness and nausea subsided. Maybe it wasn't Emma's brain, but some kind of macabre joke, keeping a grisly tribute to her with the other dead.

But it wasn't a joke. Gertrude didn't know which was worse – one of Emma's siblings discovering her body after the accident, and having the composure to scoop up part of her brain and preserve it, or the possibility that Emma's death hadn't been an accident at all.

She swooned, and struggled to think of something else, something that would make her less likely to vomit. As she clung to the shelf, eyes still closed, rough hands seized her breasts and squeezed them. Gertrude gasped, whirling around, but saw only the ghost staring back at her.

"Niles!"

Had that really just happened? He wouldn't touch her that way, would he? She was his friend, the one who'd been trying so hard to find justice for him. Folding her arms protectively across her chest, she waited for him to speak, tears stinging her eyes.

"I see you have found it," he said, as casually as if they were sitting down for tea and he'd invited her to select one of his favorite books to read.

"F-found what?" she stammered, not quite trusting her voice.

He rolled his eyes, looking so alive and solid, nothing ghostly about him at all. She wished he *had* been transparent. Then maybe he wouldn't seem quite so dangerous. "Emma, of course. You've found what is left of my dear sister."

"Niles, did you...touch me?" If he admitted it, she would leave, never to return again. She would find another way to pay for her mother's medical bills and keep the power on. There were other jobs, and if worse came to worst, she could always fundraise. She wasn't above begging online if it meant her mother could die at home, in relative comfort.

The denial she'd been hoping for never came.

Instead, he grinned. "It's what you've been wanting, isn't it? The reason you keep coming back here to see me?"

She was appalled. How could he have misread her so badly? "You're a boy!"

"I'm sixteen years old," he said, moving closer. She backed away, and the wooden shelves pressed into her, their contents jingling ominously. If any one of those jars broke.... "That is hardly a child."

"Niles, I'm – I'm sorry if I gave you the wrong idea, but my interest lies in helping you find justice. I wanted to solve the mystery of what happened to you. That's all." *You're dead*, she wanted to scream, much like Terri Foxworth had done at the séance, but she didn't dare. He'd always been touchy about that.

He made an odd snorting sound.

Every cell in her body screamed at her to run, but he blocked her exit. Still, as solid as he appeared, he *was* a ghost. She could run through him. "Who did this, Niles?" she asked, indicating the horrors behind her. As frightened as she was, she couldn't leave without learning the answer at last. "Was it Henrietta?"

"Pardon? No, of course not. This is all mine. Isn't it beautiful?" He opened his arms wide to encompass his grisly collection. "Henrietta has never been interested in science."

She'd known. Deep down, she'd known the truth. Henrietta had not done this. This was not the work of a woman, and certainly not the prim and proper woman who was her former employer. *I'm sorry.* She sent her thoughts to Henrietta, hoping the woman would hear them in her dreams, as Gertrude doubted she would get the chance to tell her face to face. *I was wrong. So terribly, terribly wrong.*

"My dear, whatever is the matter? Why do you look so sad?" Niles's expression belied his words. He was clearly delighting in what she was going through. He'd never cared about her, had never been her friend. It had all been a game. A sick, twisted game.

"But why? Why would you do something like this?"

"Something like what? Euthanize my sister's beloved pets? In the name of science, obviously. The medical community frowns upon experimenting on human specimens, no matter how enjoyable that may be." He flashed her that wicked grin again, and she shuddered. She had to get out of there, had to get away from him. If she yelled, would someone hear her? But what if Dallas came instead of Terri? Would he hurt her too? "Also, I despised her."

"Henrietta?"

"No, are you daft? Where is your brain?" He lunged toward her, as if to tap on her skull, but she flinched away from his touch. Now that she understood he *could* touch her, she didn't want those hands anywhere near her. Rather than appear offended, he laughed. "Emma. These are *her* pets. Or, at least, they *were* her pets. You should have seen her face as each one disappeared. She would mope around for weeks. It was something to see."

All this time, she'd believed Henrietta was the target of his loathing, and he'd let her believe it. "Why would you hate Emma?" She was curious, but mostly, she was stalling for time, trying to think of a way out.

"Who *wouldn't* hate Emma?" His face contorted into a sneer, and Gertrude suspected this was the Niles that Terri had seen before he attacked her. "Darling, perfect Emma. So good at everything, so capable. Never ill a day in her life. Ran the family business from atop her horse, while saving the world's homeless animals without a hair falling out of place. Who could help but loathe her?"

"She was your sister, Niles." She sought for his humanity, though it was like looking for light underground.

"Correct, she was my sister. If I could have fucked her, she would have had some value."

Gertrude's eyes widened as her breath caught in her throat.

"Is my language too rude for you, my love? I apologize. Forgive me, but she was a handsome woman, and I was trapped inside this dreadful house. A man has needs."

"You didn't—"

"Molest her? Sadly not. Her death was a tad messy for my taste. Difficult to ravage a woman whilst her brains are leaking from her skull."

She cringed at the image. *Poor Emma.* All his sister had done to inspire such hatred was to be exceptional, and kind. "What did you do to her?"

"I did not do a thing to her. Did you not hear? My darling sister perished in a horse-riding accident." He laid his hand on his forehead and sighed, lifting his gaze heavenward in a parody of grief. "It was a tragedy. This family shall never recover."

"Emma was an accomplished equestrian. I don't believe her death was an accident." She always *had* believed it, but not anymore. Not since she'd found the woman's brain in a jar in her twisted brother's version of a laboratory.

"Ah, now we're getting somewhere. Now you're using that pretty noggin of yours. But you don't have all the answers yet. I have revealed my great secret to you, and you believe that it's the solution to everything, but it's not. There is more to the Vandermere family than you could ever fathom."

"What are you saying, Niles?"

"I am saying *think*, you silly woman. *Think*. Do you truly believe that all the blood shed by this family is upon my hands? I was quite ill, remember. I did the best I could with the energy I had, but it was never enough. No, never quite enough."

"So you didn't kill Emma..." she said slowly, trying to process what he was saying. "If that's true, why do you have her brain?"

"Perhaps I should give it to you, so you could acquire some desperately needed intelligence." His fingers reached for her again, and she backed away, but she could feel his touch against her face. "I weary of this conversation. I thought you were bright enough to understand, but clearly you are not. I've spoken enough. It's time for other things."

The thought of what those 'other things' might be filled her with dread. Gertrude scanned the crawl space for a way out, but Niles blocked her only exit. She might be able to squeeze into the nook under the stairs, but then she would be completely trapped. And Lord only knows what was hidden there.

"You're not the type of lady I'm attracted to, to be fair," he said, closing the distance between them. "However, in my current situation, it doesn't pay to be too selective. Other ladies do not tend to last long."

Gertrude's mind whirled, remembering all the times female employees had abandoned them, failing to show up for work soon after they were hired. They didn't return phone calls and changed their email addresses. It had become such a problem that Henrietta had insisted on hiring men as much as possible. Men were the only ones who had stayed, aside from her, of course. Gertrude the fool. "What did you do to them, Niles?"

"You'll soon find out, my lady." Baring his teeth, he lunged at her. She dodged him, shoving him away with all her strength, but her hands pushed through air. "You amuse me," he said, laughing. "This is good sport."

"You're disgusting."

"In a delightful way."

When he went for her again, she closed her eyes and willed all her hatred for him into her right hand. She felt his touch on her breast and without looking, she put everything she had into a single punch and let it fly. This time, her hand made contact with something, and the feeling of his fingers on her vanished.

She dared to look. He held his nose, glaring at her. "How did you do that?"

Keeping her voice steady, she said, "If you can touch me, I can touch you."

"Oh, I will do more than touch you, my love." His hand shot out, and she dodged again, but it wasn't her he was after this time. He grabbed a shelf, and Gertrude understood what he meant to do too late.

With a single tug, he brought the entire thing down upon her, all his carefully constructed shelving, all the glass jars with their ghastly contents. The thought of their slimy, long-dead bodies sparked new panic in her. She tried her best to run, but she tripped on the edge of the raised threshold and went down, the shelves trapping her underneath them.

No....

A silent scream was the most she could manage before the sharp, acrid tang of formaldehyde assaulted her senses. One of the largest glass jars, which contained a skinless dog that had once answered to the name of Rex, crashed against her skull.

All was silent.

CHAPTER SIXTEEN

It was just a dream.

A dream brought on by reading the journal before bed. Emma's fear, so perfectly expressed, had become her own.

But she knew it wasn't that simple.

Somehow, the spirit of Emma Vandermere had shown Terri the truth of her death, and it had been more terrible than she could have imagined.

What now? What does one do when the nightmares are real? Who was ever going to believe her?

At that moment, she felt an unexpected kinship with Gertrude. Gertrude would believe her. Even though she'd hoped never to lay eyes on the woman again, or so much as hear her name, perhaps they could figure out what to do together. She had to do something. She couldn't go on, quietly restoring this house, knowing what she knew.

Then Terri heard something that made her give up on the idea of sleeping that night for good.

A tremendous crash, echoing through the house, sounding far away.

The scream was a lot closer.

Dallas.

Tossing the duvet aside, Terri sucked in her breath as the freezing air hit her bare legs. The room was like an icebox. She grabbed her robe from the bed and pulled it on, tying the belt tightly around her waist as she ran for her daughter's room.

"Dallas?"

"Mom?" She sounded as if she'd been crying. "Hurry!"

The white porcelain doorknob was slick with frost. Terri's hand slipped when she tried to turn it. Her fingers burned from the cold. Covering her hand with fabric from her robe, she tried again, gritting her teeth. The terry cloth provided the friction she needed to open it.

Terri stopped short, gaping at the ghoulish scene in her daughter's room.

"Who would do this, Mom?" Dallas cried, her small face streaked with tears. "Why would anyone do this?"

"I don't know, honey."

But she *did* know. Of course she did.

Rufus, her daughter's beloved teddy bear, hung suspended from the ceiling, a noose around his neck. His button eyes stared back at her, looking confused about how he'd found himself in this situation. The prank, if that's what it was intended to be, was cruel and heartless and had Niles written all over it.

She hoped it wasn't intended as a warning.

She removed the little bear from the noose and handed him to her daughter, who crushed him to her chest, sobbing. Dallas had cherished Rufus from infancy, and his symbolic murder had affected her like few things could. Terri cursed Niles under her breath, craning her neck to see how the noose had been attached to the light fixture. She'd need a ladder to get it down, and she didn't have it in her at the moment. But there was no way in hell she was leaving her daughter in a room with a noose hanging from the ceiling.

Terri held out her hand. "You're staying with me, at least for tonight. Come on."

Scrambling to her side, Dallas clung to her, weeping. There was no argument this time, no concerns about establishing her independence. Her little girl needed her again.

Once they were safely in her room, Terri barred the door with a chair. Noticing Dallas staring at the cross-stitched aphorism on the wall, Terri took it down and tossed it in a closet. *Prepare to meet thy god*, indeed.

"See? We'll be fine in here for what's left of the night," she said with a cheerfulness she didn't feel. "It's perfectly safe."

"I don't think anywhere in this house is safe." Dallas shivered, and her teeth chattered so loudly Terri could hear them.

"No, you're probably right, but this is as good as it gets." She ushered her daughter into bed, pulling the duvet and then an afghan over her and Rufus. Checking her phone, she saw that it was half past one. Too late to call Henrietta and tell her they were leaving; too late to call Gertrude and let her know what happened to Emma.

She shuddered, recalling how the woman had felt at the moment of her death. What had it been like to be Emma in that house? Beautiful, accomplished, intelligent. Sane and compassionate. A flower in a yard of weeds. If only she'd moved, left the country for study or some other adventure. If she had, she'd probably have enjoyed a long life. Married, most likely, and had children of her own. In those days, any children would have carried Emma's husband's name, and that was all right. The more she learned about the Vandermere family, the more she was convinced it was a name that needed to die out.

"We're not staying, are we?"

"No, we're not staying." That she was sure of. After her dream – *vision* – of Emma's murder, she couldn't imagine spending another day in that house.

"But what about the money? We need it, right?"

Terri patted her daughter's hand under the covers. "We do, but we'll figure something out."

"Are we going to be homeless?" Dallas's face looked so concerned that it would have been comical if she hadn't been so close to the truth.

"Of course not. That's nothing you have to worry about." *I hope.*

"Niles is evil, isn't he?" Dallas lowered her voice to a near-whisper. Thankfully, since they were in a servant's room, there was no speaking tube. That didn't mean he wasn't eavesdropping, but it made her feel more secure all the same.

"Yes, I believe so." Her scratches were faint enough now that no one would notice them unless they knew to look for them, but she'd never forget the snarl on his face when he'd attacked her. Or how he'd smirked when he'd thrown the snake at Emma's horse. There was no question who had hanged Rufus, either.

"I thought he was my friend. I can't believe I trusted him." Her daughter's lower lip trembled, and Terri put an arm around her.

"It's not a bad thing to trust people. Thankfully, you'll meet very few people like Niles in your life. He's a special case."

If he was this bad as a ghost, what had he been like when he was alive? It was a disturbing thought. The diabetes had probably been the only thing that prevented him from racking up a large body count.

Holding her daughter, Terri remembered the crash that had shook the house and startled her from her non-sleep. "Dallas, did you hear anything strange tonight? It was loud, sounded like a lot of glass breaking. It happened right before you screamed."

She shook her head. "No, but maybe that's what woke me up. I'm not sure *why* I woke up. My eyes just opened, and I saw this weird shape in the dark, and—"

"It's okay. Don't think about it. It's not important."

But it was. Terri was sure of it. The urge to go downstairs and investigate, to see what had caused that thunderous crash, was strong.

However, it would have to wait. There was no way in hell she was going down there until morning.

*　　*　　*

Her eyes fluttered open. Shades of gray and pink blurred in front of her.

Don't look, a voice in her mind said, so she didn't.

Then the smell hit her. It was the worst stench she'd ever smelled, so foul it made her gag. Every choking cough made her head hurt terribly.

Where was she? What had happened to her?

The longer she was aware, the more parts of her hurt. Her back ached something awful, and her legs burned like they were on fire.

She tried to move, tried to pull away from whatever was hurting her, but an inch or two was the most she could manage. It felt like a boulder was on her legs and back, pinning her in place.

Closing her eyes and breathing from her mouth, Gertrude slowly stretched out her arms, relieved they still worked. She reached as far as she could, and then lowered them until her fingers touched the ground. One of her hands hit something cold and slimy, and she jerked away, gasping.

Don't look, the voice reminded her, so she didn't.

She tried again, and this time, touched only dirt. It was packed down hard enough to feel like stone, but under the other awful odors, she could smell its earthiness. She pressed her nose to it and inhaled deeply.

Hooking her fingers into the ground, she attempted to pull herself forward, away from whatever was holding her in that dreadful place. All she wanted to do was rest, but her instincts were shrieking at her that, wherever this was, it wasn't safe. She needed to get away.

The smell alone told her that.

Using just her arms would not work. Whatever held her lower body was too strong. Gritting her teeth to keep from screaming, she wiggled like a snake, moving her hips back and forth as she strained her fingers, fighting to get purchase on the packed earth.

She couldn't do it the first time. Or the second. Or even the third. Sweat dotted her forehead even though she was freezing, and many times she was tempted to give up, lay her cheek against the ground and rest. But she understood that if she did, she might never raise her head again. Slowly, she began to move forward.

*   *   *

A loud pounding from downstairs startled Terri awake. For a second, she forgot where she was, and then she saw Dallas snuggled into the crook of her arm, fast asleep and cuddling Rufus.

There were no windows in the room, so it was impossible to

tell what time it was. Stretching as much as she could without moving her body, she felt for her phone, trying her best not to wake her daughter.

Six a.m.

The pounding noise started up again, making her jump. It was definitely coming from the front door, and from the sound of it, whoever it was wanted to break it down. Who would be at the door at this hour of the morning?

Bang-bang-bang. "Open up," an angry male voice bellowed. "Police!"

Police? For a second, she wondered if they were there about Emma, but that was ridiculous. It's not like they could have read her mind. Or the diary.

Reluctantly disentangling herself from Dallas, she put on her robe.

"What's going on, Mom?"

Bang-bang-bang.

"I'm not sure. Stay here, I'll be right back."

Her uninvited guests continued to sound like they were going to bust the door in as she raced down the hallway toward them, trying her best not to trip and break her neck. Thankfully, she had taken care to clear her tools and supplies away from the entrance each evening, so it remained unobstructed, no matter what stage of the restoration she was in.

Cursing the lack of a peephole or chain, Terri opened the door to find two large, visibly irritated men glaring down at her. "Is Miss Vandermere here?" one demanded. He edged a foot towards the entrance, which unnerved her. What the heck was going on? Why were they acting like she'd committed a crime?

"No, I'm Terri. Terri Foxworth. Miss Vandermere owns this house, but she doesn't live here. She's hired me to do some restoration work."

The same cop stared pointedly at her. "But you *are* living here?"

"Only temporarily." *And not for much longer.*

"Ms. Foxworth, do you recognize this woman?"

The other cop handed her a photograph, which Terri squinted at, wishing she had her glasses. Her vision was never up to par in the morning these days. The photograph was terribly out of date, and she suspected it had been taken when the woman was in high school. Still, there was no question who it was.

"Yes, that's Gertrude."

The officers glanced at each other. Great, now knowing Gertrude was a crime. Not that she actually *knew* her, of course. Just enough to fight with her and throw her out of the house and—

Oh shit.

"What's this about? Is she okay?"

"That's what we're hoping you could tell us," the gruff cop – the one who succeeded in making her feel naked in her nightgown and robe – said. "She didn't come home from work this morning."

"I'm sorry to hear that, but I'm not sure how that has anything to do with me." God, had Gertrude told someone about their fight? It had gotten ugly at the end. What if she'd decided to charge Terri with assault? She didn't have the money to hire a lawyer.

"Can we come in?" asked the cop with the picture. "Relax. We just want to ask you a few questions You're not in any trouble."

"Yet," added the other one. Okay, she was beginning to really not like this guy.

She led the way to the parlor, bypassing the kitchen. The parlor was a mess, but it had a clear advantage: no speaking tube.

"Beautiful house," Photograph Cop said, and she couldn't help smiling. Terri had always felt a connection with those who appreciated heritage homes.

"It is, isn't it? Glenvale is the finest example of Queen Anne Revival-style architecture in the state."

"I'm sure it's going to be more beautiful when you're finished." He had a nice smile, a genuine smile, one that made his blue eyes crinkle at the corners. "What kind of work are you doing here?"

"Well, I—"

Gruff Cop interrupted. "This isn't *Better Homes and Gardens*. Let's move on with this, shall we? We don't have all day."

"Don't mind him. He hasn't had his coffee yet. Bit of a bear before his caffeine."

"Screw you, Molloy." Gruff Cop glowered.

"You can sit anywhere you like, but the furniture is antique, so the drop cloths have to stay on, I'm afraid." Terri gestured at the covered chairs and settees, gratified to see how uncomfortable Gruff Cop looked.

"I think I'll stand," he said.

"Suit yourself." Photograph Cop took the chair opposite her and balanced a notebook on his knee. "My name is Officer Molloy, and this ray of sunshine is Sergeant Gates. Can you tell us when you last saw Ms. Phillips? Gertrude?"

Terri hesitated, noticing that Sergeant Gates was leaning on her every word. She had to tell the truth, even if it got her in trouble. Cops were way better at spotting liars than she was at lying. "Yes, I saw her yesterday."

Officer Molloy nodded, jotting the information down on his pad. "What time, do you recall?"

"Um...." When had Dallas come into Emma's room? "I'm not a hundred percent sure, but I think it was around three."

"Three a.m.?" he asked.

She started at the question. "No, three *p.m.*"

The two men exchanged another meaningful glance. Enough, already. So she'd had an argument with Gertrude. That was hardly a crime. And they weren't here to charge her with assault. They'd have done that already. The knowledge made her bold. "What exactly is this about?"

Officer Molloy looked at his partner, who tilted his head the slightest bit. "She told her mother she was coming here to do some work around midnight. She was supposed to be home hours ago, but she never showed up."

"Ordinarily we wouldn't bother checking into this until more time has passed," Sergeant Gates added. "Ms. Phillips is an adult, she can come and go as she pleases. But, in this case, her mother's nurse said Ms. Phillips has never once been late to relieve her. She told the nurse that she was going to visit a friend, but the nurse thought Ms. Phillips acted suspicious when she left, as if she were trying to hide something."

Terri felt like she'd been doused with freezing water. "She didn't come here."

"No?" Molloy asked. "Are you sure?"

"As sure as I can be. Gertrude had ways of getting in the house without my being aware of it. I don't know how she did it, because she never showed me. So I guess it's possible she came in while we were asleep."

"We?" Gates scowled as if she'd said something offensive.

"My ten-year-old daughter, Dallas. She's staying with me."

"My daughter is nine," Molloy said with another megawatt smile. "It's a great age, isn't it?"

"Most of the time. When she's not acting like she's thirty."

He laughed. "True that."

"Look, can we stay on track here? I'm not sure I get why Ms. Phillips would have to sneak in if she worked here. That doesn't make any sense." Gates stared at her with an intensity that was unnerving. Terri bet he was the type of cop that scared false confessions out of people.

"That's the thing – she doesn't work here. Not anymore. Miss Vandermere fired her before I was hired, so she'd be the best person to talk to about that. I don't know all the details."

"If she was fired, why would she tell her mother she was coming here last night?" Coming from Gates, it sounded more like a demand than a question.

What a mess. Why couldn't Gertrude have left well enough alone? However, truth be told, she'd expected something like this. The woman's obsession with the house – and Niles – had been too strong for her to let it be.

"Listen, I don't know if this is true or not. She wasn't around long enough for me to learn anything about her personal life, but she told my daughter that her mother is quite ill, and that she's the only one who can care for her. Maybe she doesn't want her mother to find out she's been fired. It could be pride, or because she doesn't want her mom to worry."

"Why was she fired?" Officer Molloy asked.

"I'm really not sure. Henrietta Vandermere would be the one to ask about that. I can get you her contact info, if you like."

He smiled. "Great, thanks. That will save us a little digging."

"You know *something* about this," Gates said. "I can see it on your face. What is it?"

Damn him. "It's just a hunch. I don't even know for sure that it's true. Vandermere is the one who could tell you why she was fired, not me. I only met Gertrude twice."

"Let's hear it. Cops understand about hunches. We go by our guts all the time…right, Gates?" Officer Molloy said. His partner grunted.

Terri mentally crossed her fingers. "Gertrude was obsessed with this house. She has this theory that Henrietta killed Niles."

"Niles?" Molloy lifted an eyebrow.

"Sorry, sometimes I forget that not everyone is embroiled in this mess. Niles Vandermere, Henrietta's brother."

He made a note of it. "How long ago did Niles die?"

"I'm not sure of the exact date, but it would have had to have been over eighty years ago. I can look that up for you."

Both cops looked startled. Gates recovered first. "How old is Miss Vandermere? She'd have to be…."

"She's a hundred years old. But she certainly doesn't look it."

"Do you share this theory, Ms. Foxworth?"

There it was – the million-dollar question. Recalling her nightmare, she shifted on her seat. A dream wasn't proof, and neither were suspicions in a journal. She met Molloy's eyes, trying her best to be as honest as possible. "As far as I'm aware, Niles died from complications of his diabetes. He was sixteen years old. Miss

Vandermere was a child. I have no reason to believe otherwise. I was hired to restore this house, not play detective."

"This is curious. I wonder where she would have gotten this idea," Molloy said. "So you think this is why Vandermere fired her?"

"I don't know for sure, but I believe so, yes. When Henrietta first showed me around the house, she told me I might run into Gertrude, that Gertrude was an overly enthusiastic employee. Gertrude came by the house not long after that, and she was the one who told me she had been fired." Terri had a sick feeling in the pit of her stomach. Why did she feel like she was ratting Gertrude out? The woman had been no friend of hers. And there was no way she was telling two police officers Glenvale was haunted and blaming the whole thing on ghosts.

"Do you believe she came here last night?" Seeing her hesitation, Molloy added, "Give us your best hunch."

"She could have, yes. At around one a.m., I heard a loud crash. It shook the house and woke me up. I didn't think of it at the time, but it could have been Gertrude."

"Did you investigate this sound?" Gates asked.

Terri shook her head. "No, my daughter had a nightmare at around the same time, and I was busy comforting her. I'd forgotten all about it until now. Plus, old houses make strange noises. You get used to it after a while."

Things shift. Radiators clank. There are drafts.

Gates stood, his beady eyes surveying the room. At least he'd stopped studying her for the moment. "If she is here, it sounds like she could be trespassing. Do you mind if we take a look around?"

"It's fine by me, though I should tell Miss Vandermere you're here. And yes, Gertrude is definitely trespassing if she's in this house. Henrietta told me that she doesn't want her around."

Another betrayal. But Gertrude had tried to drive a wedge between her and her daughter. Surely she didn't owe her anything.

If that was true, why did she feel so guilty?

"That's fine. Ask her to come by. We'll need to talk to her too," Molloy said.

"This house has over twenty rooms. Gertrude knew this place as well as anyone, aside from Henrietta. If she doesn't want to be found, you won't find her." Terri remembered how furious the woman had looked when she'd ordered her to leave. The thought of her hiding somewhere in the house was distressing. Why hadn't she thought of Gertrude when she'd heard the crash? It was a good thing they'd be leaving today. If she stayed much longer, she might become as obsessed as Gertrude.

"If she's here, we'll find her." Gates gave her a look that felt like it went right through her. "Whether she wants to be found or not."

CHAPTER SEVENTEEN

"You're alive. Now *this* is a surprise."

Cowering from his voice, she tried to scream, but the sound that escaped was a strangled croak. She wriggled her hips faster, pulled harder with her fingers, but it was hopeless. There was no getting away from him, never had been.

"I must be losing my touch. It's a shame I can't have more fun with you. We could have done a few experiments, if only my hands worked the way they used to. I would *love* to see what you look like on the inside, but I'm afraid you would not be around for that. People tend to die when I cut them open. It's the strangest thing."

He touched her hair and she recoiled, a squeal emitting from her throat. It felt like her mouth was full of broken teeth. There was no use in yelling, even if she could. Terri would never hear her, never come down here. Gertrude had seen Henrietta's plans – the cellar was not part of the restoration. If she were going to get out of this alive, it would have to be her own doing. She was going to have to rescue herself.

She focused on her mother's face. Imagining what would become of Esther if something happened to her kept her going despite the pain and fear. If she didn't come home, her mother would give up. Or worse, she'd believe Gertrude had abandoned her.

She couldn't let that happen.

"What do you think you're doing, exactly?" Niles sounded amused as he watched her flail, trying her best to escape. "You're gravely injured. So injured, in fact, that you might find death a relief. Until you end up here with me. *Then* we will have some fun."

Gertrude summoned her will. She spit out a tooth, tasting the copper tang of her own blood. *He* had done this to her, along with other appalling things she dared not think about right now. Niles, who she had tried so hard to help. She put all her anger, betrayal, and pain into finding the energy to speak.

"Fuck…you."

Rather than have the effect she'd hoped, her words made her tormenter laugh. "Why, Miss Phillips, to hear such language from a lady. I am shocked, honestly shocked. Unless…could that be a request? Have you not had enough of me yet?"

She whimpered, the threat inspiring her to wiggle faster. She struggled to move her legs, to kick his hands away from her, but her lower body was still pinned. Though it had taken every last ounce of strength she had, she hadn't made much progress.

"It's too bad you can't clean yourself up. You are a tad foul, even for my liking. However, I've never minded getting dirty."

As his hands ran over her body, the revulsion made her voice return to her, and she *did* scream. It sounded garbled, like she was screaming underwater.

"Silly woman. Who do you think is going to hear you? These walls are solid stone. Besides, the Foxworths are hardly on your side. You've burned that bridge, don't you think? They would be delighted to see you like this, absolutely delighted."

It wasn't true. They'd had their differences, but Terri and Dallas were good people. They wouldn't be happy to see this happening to her.

"They…*hate*…you."

"Do they? Perhaps they do. I haven't given it much thought, to tell you the truth. What other people think of me has never been a great concern." Niles spoke the next words into her ear, and she quailed at his nearness. "It's what *I* think of them that matters."

This time, her scream got a response.

"Ms. Phillips? Gertrude Phillips?"

She felt Niles leave, and that was enough to rekindle her strength.

She screamed again, her throat burning, her voice hoarse. She didn't care. She would scream until she died.

"Hang in there, Ms. Phillips. We hear you."

The tinkling of broken glass. "Can we get some light down here? It's blacker than a cat's asshole."

Gertrude wiggled as fast as she could, using her fingers to finally pull herself forward over the threshold. If she remained trapped in the crawl space, they'd never find her. She couldn't be there when Niles returned. She had to escape.

Finally, she felt a release as her legs pulled free of whatever had been holding them. More glass broke behind her as she moved, and it was much louder than the noise her rescuers were making. It was better than a scream.

"Christ, what's that smell? Did something die in here?"

Yes, she wanted to yell. Many things had died in here, but she wouldn't be one of them. Not anymore.

When she saw the lights of her rescuers, she began to cry. It was over now, almost over. She had no more screams left, but she made as much noise as she could, managing to wave one of her arms in the air. It was weak, as far as waves went, but thankfully, it was enough.

"Jesus Christ. Ms. Phillips?"

Yes. It was getting impossible to speak, but the man seemed to understand her. She felt a gentle touch on her head. "Molloy, call for an ambulance. And tell them to hurry."

$$\star \quad \star \quad \star$$

Light rain fell as their sad little group waited on the veranda, watching as the paramedics rushed Gertrude to an ambulance. There had been so much medical equipment and people around her that it was impossible to tell what state she was in, but Terri had seen a lot of blood. Gertrude's hair appeared to be soaked with it.

Dallas clung to her, and when Gertrude was wheeled past, she buried her face in Terri's side. "Is she going to be okay, Mom?"

"I hope so." Why hadn't she investigated that crash? Why hadn't she called the police then? She should have suspected there was someone in the house, should have figured it would be Gertrude. She'd never forgive herself if the woman didn't make it.

Seeing Molloy, she left her daughter long enough to go over to him. "Is she going to be all right? What happened to her?"

The cop grimaced, and she saw the truth of Gertrude's condition in his eyes. "I can't tell you for certain. It looks like she was involved in an accident in the cellar. Some shelving fell on her, and the... contents hit her pretty hard. She's also suffering from hypothermia. I'm not going to lie to you, Ms. Foxworth. She's in bad shape. If she'd been down there too much longer...."

"Will you – will you be the one notifying her mother?"

"I believe so." Molloy shook his head. "Worst part of the job."

"Please don't tell her Gertrude was fired. You don't have to tell her that, do you?"

"I suppose not. It's not relevant at the moment. But why?"

"Gertrude had her reasons. Maybe it was pride, or not wanting her mom to worry. Whatever the cause, she didn't want her mother to find out. Let's do that for her, at least."

"Okay, you have my word."

"Thank you, Officer." Terri turned to walk back to her daughter when Molloy called after her. "Yes?"

"I notice Miss Vandermere has arrived." He gestured at the elderly woman, who was hurrying in their direction. "Please ask her to hang around for a bit. We have a few questions for her."

Terri shivered. She'd been hoping to be far from Glenvale before Henrietta showed up.

Vandermere appeared to be in far better shape than the rest of them, which was surprising, considering her relationship with the victim. But, then again, perhaps not so much, given their contentious history.

"I warned her," Henrietta said. "I always told her that her obsession with this house would be the death of her."

It was an unfortunate expression for the old woman to use. Terri couldn't think of a thing to say in response. She had a hard time imagining anyone could be that insensitive. From what Molloy had told her, Gertrude might actually die.

"I can't imagine what she was doing in the cellar, but I've been told it's a godawful mess down there." Her face contorted. "I suppose I'll have to pay for someone to undo whatever damage she did. I rue the day I hired that girl."

"With all due respect, Miss Vandermere, Gertrude may not make it. Whatever mess she made, whatever grief she caused you, she doesn't deserve to die."

Henrietta waved a hand, dismissing her. "Of course she doesn't deserve to die. Who would suggest such a preposterous thing?"

"Officer Molloy has asked that you stay around. They want to ask you some questions."

"Which one is Molloy?" She squinted at the small crowd of cops, paramedics, and media that lingered on the front lawn. Terri pointed him out. "I suppose they'll make this out to be my fault."

Terri was disgusted by the woman's priorities, but it didn't matter. She wouldn't have to deal with them much longer. "I can't see how. You fired Gertrude. You told her not to come back to the house. If she broke into the cellar, it's hardly your fault."

The woman lifted her bony shoulders in a gesture of defeat. "I suppose not, but you know how police officers are. They rarely let facts get in the way of making an arrest."

"You'll be fine. You *did* fire Gertrude, right?"

"I don't care to use that word. I find it rather harsh. I prefer the word 'dismissed', but I suppose there's no point in quibbling over semantics, especially now. Yes, I told her she was no longer an employee of Glenvale. Why do you ask?"

"It's just — like you say, it doesn't matter now, but when you took me on the tour of the estate, you told me she was laid off for financial reasons. Gertrude is the one who told me she'd been fired."

"Well, that's her business, isn't it? It's hardly my place to go around blabbing about what happened to potential employees. What are you getting at, Ms. Foxworth? Do you feel I deceived you?"

"No, but what *did* happen? Why did you let Gertrude go?"

"I'm not sure I understand why you're asking me this. It's between me and Gertie."

"I'm asking because I want to know if she was telling me the truth."

Henrietta sighed. "I wish you would let this go. I thought it was the police who were supposed to be interrogating me."

"Please. It's important."

"I can't see why. As you've said, poor Gertie might not make it. But if you must know, I could hardly employ someone who kept accusing me of murder."

So Gertrude had been telling the truth. Terri had new admiration for the woman's bravery. She couldn't imagine confronting this steely-eyed dowager.

"I can tell from your face that she let you in on her outlandish theories. But of course she would. She's been attempting to cast doubt on me for a long time now. Me, or my father – she seems to change her mind with the weather. Tell me, Ms. Foxworth – what do you believe?"

Facing the woman who employed her, the person who could hold the key to Terri's future and reputation in her hands, Terri said the only thing she could. "I believe your brother died from complications of his diabetes."

Henrietta clicked her tongue. "Yes, a sad, sad thing that was. If he'd been diagnosed earlier, he would most likely have enjoyed a long life, but back then, so much was still misunderstood. I loved my brother. When he wasn't ill, we did everything together. We were two peas in a pod, our father liked to say."

"Your sister's death was stranger. It's odd that a woman who was such an accomplished rider, who spent so much of her time with horses, would die in a horseback-riding accident."

She watched the woman's face carefully, but didn't detect the slightest flicker.

"Not so strange, really. The creatures are unpredictable. By spending so much time with them, my sister increased her odds of something unfortunate happening." Henrietta leaned closer then, and Terri took a step back. "Whatever happened to your face?"

She raised her hand to feel the scratches she'd forgotten were there. "I'm not sure. It must have happened during the restoration work."

"Looks like a cat got to you." Henrietta returned her attention to the officers, who lingered around their patrol cars, deep in conversation. Her eyes acquired a far-off look, as if she was seeing something occur in the past. "My sister loved cats. When I was a child, one of her pets – Smoky, its name was – got spooked about something and scratched me." She smiled at Terri. "It only happened once."

CHAPTER EIGHTEEN

If Henrietta Vandermere had thought firing Gertrude would stop the rumors from swirling about her family, she was disappointed. Eventide was a small town, and people talked. Once word got out about the gruesome discovery in Glenvale's cellar, the gossip mill worked overtime. Henrietta refused to speak about it publicly, or would have refused, if anyone had dared ask her. When it came to the police interrogations, Terri was fairly sure the heiress had blamed her brother.

The situation troubled Officer Molloy, who wasn't convinced that what had happened to Gertrude was an accident. He had kept the lines of communication open, and he was the one who'd told Terri about the most disturbing thing they'd found in the cellar: a portion of a human brain.

"The jar it was in was smashed when the shelving collapsed on Ms. Phillips, so we can't be sure who it belonged to. It might have been a medical specimen. It was so poorly preserved, it's hard to say. We're hoping the DNA test will tell us more."

Terri had a hunch she knew who the brain belonged to, but said nothing. She'd grown to like Officer Malloy quite a bit, and trusted him to an extent, but there were some things she could never say. Once Gertrude had finally regained consciousness, she'd been ranting and raving about ghosts to anyone who would listen, and now people were speculating that a mental institution would undoubtedly be her next destination.

Molloy had also told her Gertrude wanted to see her. She was surprised. Given their last exchange, the women were hardly friends. However, considering the link they shared, perhaps it wasn't so surprising after all.

She had the time. Once the police began going through the Glenvale cellar with a fine-tooth comb, Henrietta had put her and Dallas up in the hotel down the road 'until this entire mess blows over'. There hadn't been a good opportunity to quit yet, but she would. As soon as she got a chance. It was difficult to admit, even to herself, but the paid accommodations gave her time to figure out what was next for her and Dallas. Terri realized it wasn't ethical to let Henrietta pay for the room when she was planning to leave, but she didn't see any choice. They had nowhere else to go.

The hospital room was dim, the shades drawn, when she arrived. Someone had paid for Gertrude to convalesce in a private room, and Terri guessed that someone was Henrietta Vandermere. Keep your friends close and your enemies closer, after all.

Since Gertrude was sleeping, Terri had time to survey the damage close up. The woman's head was bandaged, and her face was a rainbow of cuts and bruises. Her left leg was in a cast, and her mouth was swollen. Molloy had mentioned she'd lost quite a few of her teeth. Terri had braced herself for the worst, but it was impossible not to be shocked at Gertrude's condition. What had happened to her? It looked like a hell of a lot more than being trapped underneath a set of shelves.

Her stomach churning, she turned to leave.

"Don't go."

The raspy whisper, loud in the stillness of the room, made her jump.

Gertrude's eyes were open now, and something in them had changed. She wasn't the woman Terri had met — she saw that instantly. There was an awareness to her that was both understandable and frightening.

"I'm glad you came." She attempted a smile, but Terri looked away, unable to bear the thought of seeing an empty mouth.

"How are you feeling?"

"I've been better. But I'm glad to be alive." Gertrude reached for her hand, and Terri gave it to her, feeling uncomfortable. "Thanks to you. If you hadn't let those men search for me, I would have died. You have no idea what was about to happen to me when they found me."

She didn't, and she didn't want to. Molloy had hinted around the subject enough for her to get the gist. "Please don't thank me. It's my fault you were down there as long as you were. If I'd called the cops as soon as I'd heard that crash—"

Gertrude squeezed her hand. "Don't blame yourself, Terri. Please. You did the right thing, the only thing. You and I both understand what it's like in that house. Hearing strange noises in the night is the tip of the iceberg."

"It was Niles, wasn't it?" She wasn't sure why she asked. The last thing she wanted was to have her suspicions confirmed, and yet, it wasn't safe for her to remain ignorant. Some of their belongings were in that house, and eventually, she'd have to go retrieve them. She couldn't shy away from any information that might protect her daughter.

Gertrude's eyes darkened. "Yes. It was Niles."

"Did he lure you there?" Terri felt anger boiling a hole in her insides. The little creep. She'd known he was evil. He'd shown her that the night he'd attacked her. She'd never fallen for his 'sweet young man' crap.

"Not in the way you mean. I wish I could say he did. That would mean I wasn't quite so stupid."

"You aren't stupid. I'm sure you had your reasons for going back to the house." *Oh, how I wish you hadn't.*

"I was so close, Terri. *So* close. Or so I'd thought. Niles told me the truth was in the cellar. He promised he'd show me where to go if I came back one more time. And he did, but the truth wasn't anything I'd thought it would be."

She finally understood how Gertrude had found the crawl space. It was so hidden that even if the cellar *had* been included in the restoration plans, she might not have found it.

"He was proud of it, you know? Proud of all the horrible things he'd done, and proud that he'd fooled me for so long." Tears shone in her eyes. "He's a monster. I can't believe I listened to his lies. I am such an idiot."

"No, you're not. Most people can't communicate with spirits. They don't even believe they exist. You had no reason to suspect he was lying to you. A young man appears, says he was murdered, and asks you for help. What else could you have done? I think anyone in your position would have done the same."

"It wasn't quite like that. Niles never told me he was murdered, not directly. You saw how sensitive he was about being dead. He didn't like to talk about it, or even admit it. But he certainly dropped enough hints and let me think that he was murdered."

"So you don't think Henrietta killed him anymore?"

She snorted. "If she did, she did the world a favor. No, my fixation on Henrietta is over. Maybe you were right. Maybe it was more about wanting to get back at her for firing me than it was about finding justice for Niles."

"I don't really believe that. You were trying to find justice for Niles before Henrietta fired you."

"That's true." Gertrude sighed. "Well, that's over with, and Henrietta actually did me a favor when she dismissed me. All I want to do now is get out of this hospital and figure out what's next. I'll never go in that house, ever again."

"That makes two of us. I do have to go back to get our stuff, but I'm not planning on sticking around." She actually didn't *have* a plan at all, but she didn't intend to tell Gertrude that.

Gertrude's eyebrows shot up so high they were hidden by the thick bandage that covered most of her head. "What do you mean? You're still doing the restoration, aren't you?"

"Not currently, no. The cops can't decide if the cellar is the scene of an accident or the scene of a crime, and until they do, Henrietta has me staying at a hotel. There hasn't been a great time to tell her that I mean to quit. She's been a little preoccupied, as you can imagine. Everyone is acting like her brother was a twisted psychopath. But once I get the chance to talk to her, I'll tell her me and Dallas are leaving. I'm just not sure where to yet."

Gertrude tightened her grip so much that she crushed Terri's fingers, causing her to yelp. "You can't leave. You have to keep working in the house. The evidence is still there."

"After what happened to you? Are you crazy?" Immediately after she said the words, she regretted them. There was, after all, a lot of speculation that Gertrude was mentally ill. "I'm scared to go back there for a few minutes to get our things. It's not safe."

"Terri, I don't think he's going to hurt you *or* Dallas, not anymore. I was his target – for whatever reason, he wanted me to suffer. I see that now. But he won't do that to either of you, and besides, he has nothing to hide now. His little lair of horrors is gone. He made sure of that when he pushed it over on me."

"I'm sorry, but I can't take that chance. With me *or* my daughter. Why would you want us to stay? I thought you'd be happy we were leaving."

"I don't care how Niles died now. Maybe it was natural causes, or maybe Henrietta purposely fed him candy until he burst. It doesn't matter to me, not anymore."

"But...?" The fierceness in the other woman's eyes unnerved her. Maybe she *was* insane. She had to be, if she thought there was any way Terri would go back to stay in that evil house.

"You know what he wanted to show me most, Terri? Emma's brain. He had his fucking sister's brain in a jar. She didn't die in an accident. He was *there*."

"Couldn't she have died in an accident, and he saw the opportunity to...take a piece of her?" she finished lamely, thinking uncomfortably of her dream, the vision she'd had of Emma's death. *But was it a vision?* She'd been reading Emma's journal, with all those horrible stories, right before she went to sleep. "I get how awful it sounds, and clearly there was something very wrong with him, but that isn't a crime. Not as serious a crime as murder, anyway."

"Look me in the eye. If you can look at me and tell me you

honestly believe Emma Vandermere died in an accident, I won't say another word about it. You and Dallas can leave Glenvale and move hundreds of miles away from Eventide and never hear another peep from me."

Terri tried, she really did. She even opened her mouth, but no words came out. Gertrude's intensity was too unnerving. And besides, she'd always been a terrible liar. Triumphant, the other woman settled back against the pillows, releasing Terri's hand.

"I knew it. You have to solve this, Terri. Put an end to this mystery, once and for all. You're in the best position to do it."

"Honestly, what does it matter? Emma Vandermere is dead. Niles Vandermere is dead. Henrietta has more than one foot in the grave. You're alive, but it could have easily turned out differently. Why should we risk our lives trying to solve a murder that everyone else believes is an accident?"

"Because it's the right thing to do," Gertrude said quietly.

"That's worth risking your own life, and mine, and Dallas's? Gertrude, because of what you found, everyone in Eventide already knows Niles was a monster. Why isn't that good enough for you?"

"Because that's not the end of the story, and you know it."

Terri pictured her nightmare again, and what she'd seen through Emma's eyes. What if it had been real? Could she go to her grave keeping that secret?

"There were dozens of animals in that cellar. Animals that Emma loved, that had been killed because she loved them. It was awful."

This time, the tears fell. She took Terri's hand again, and Terri found herself crying with her. She'd never been able to tolerate the abuse of animals, who were the only creatures truly capable of unconditional love. People who hurt animals were the lowest of the low.

"Do it for Emma," Gertrude whispered. "Please, Terri. Do it for me."

*　　*　　*

"What are we doing, Mom?" Dallas looked puzzled, and Terri couldn't blame her. She'd knew been acting weird since she'd returned from the hospital. Seeing Gertrude, along with the promise the woman had coerced from her, had Terri spooking at shadows. Glenvale was like a spider who'd caught them in its web. No matter what she did to escape, it pulled them back in again. "We're not religious."

Terri waited a moment, looking up at the church with its imposing steeple. It didn't appear friendly *or* welcoming. "Maybe we will be after this. Come on."

Her shoulder bag contained a number of empty jam jars and a small travel mug, every container she could find. The jars clinked when she walked, and the sound made her feel a little braver. If she were going to return to the belly of the beast, at least she'd be well armed.

The church's heavy wooden doors opened silently, emitting them into the sanctuary. She was relieved to see it was empty. After setting her bag on the floor, she opened it and handed Dallas two of the jam jars. "Fill these from that font over there, and close them tight. Be careful not to drop them."

Awed by their surroundings, her daughter nodded and did what she was told without arguing or questioning. Come to think of it, it had been some time since Dallas had argued with her. They were in uncharted territory, and Terri figured her response to it had been as good as anyone else's.

Filling her own containers from the other font, she felt like she was stealing. She'd watched so many movies where the heroes burst into a church and filled all manner of things with holy water, but she didn't know if what they were doing was allowed in real life or not. Dallas was right; they weren't religious. Terri's mother, a lapsed Catholic, had raised her without what she'd referred to as 'the unreasonable restrictions of the church and its culture of guilt', and, not knowing anything different, she'd done the same with her own daughter. But a little faith would be a good thing right now. Faith, and the feeling that something all-powerful and benevolent was looking out for them.

"Hello," said a soft voice from behind her, and Terri nearly jumped out of her skin. She whirled to see a diminutive woman with short gray hair curled like her own grandmother's. The woman smiled, revealing deep dimples. "I'm sorry, I didn't mean to startle you. I'm Sister Grace. I don't recall seeing you here before."

Sister Grace. Could there be a more perfect name for a nun?

"Hello, Sister. I hope we're not doing anything wrong." Her cheeks burned, and the jam jar in her hand, dripping with holy water, felt ridiculous. What had she been thinking, coming here to stock up? Niles wasn't a vampire. "My name is Terri, and this is my daughter, Dallas."

"Not at all. Our blessed water is free for anyone who needs it." She nodded at Dallas, who stared at her, jam jar forgotten in her hands. "Hello. Nice to meet you, Dallas. Terri." Terri's tongue-tied daughter barely managed to return the greeting. "Do you mind if I ask why you need so much of it? Are you holding a service of your own?"

She knew the nun was kidding, even before she winked, and it was a relief to confide in someone who might understand. In the movies, churches were always full of experts who rushed into the haunted house and made all the evil spirits disappear. And Niles *was* evil, of that she had no doubt. What he'd done to Gertrude had confirmed that without question.

"Can I speak to you for a moment?"

"Certainly. That's what I'm here for. Why don't we sit down and chat?" Sister Grace indicated the last pew in the church. "After you're finished. Please, fill any container you like."

Face burning so hot Terri was surprised it didn't catch fire, she took a travel mug from her bag. Its bright pink exterior, with its irreverent *Vacation Bound!* motto and flamingos, looked like a bad joke in the solemn atmosphere of the church. Glancing at the nun, who waited for them at the pew, Terri could have sworn Sister Grace was trying not to laugh. She covered her mouth and coughed daintily when she noticed she was being watched.

It doesn't matter if people laugh. Let the entire town of Eventide line up and make fun of you. If they haven't stayed in that house, they don't understand. If they haven't been attacked by Niles, they *can't* understand. She thought of Gertrude's ravaged face and closed the travel mug with a defiant snap. Dallas was already at her side, waiting. Once the mug had joined the other containers in her bag, she took her daughter's hand and walked over to Sister Grace.

"Please, sit down. Would you like something to drink? I have water, and some juice in our little fridge. I'd be happy to share it with you."

"I think we're okay. Thank you, Sister. We appreciate your kindness."

"I can see something troubles you. Do you feel comfortable talking about it with me?"

Terri looked over at Dallas. Her eyes were as wide as saucers as she took in their surroundings: the vaulted ceilings, the stained-glass windows in many shades of blue, the life-sized Christ figure dying on the cross. Other than her obvious awe, her daughter looked like any other ten-year-old girl. Her coloring was fine; her hair was neatly brushed and confined in her standard ponytail. "How did you know we're troubled?"

"It's my job to know," Sister Grace said. "But most people who come to a church for the first time seeking holy water are in some sort of trouble. I'd like to help you if I can."

"You're a nun, right?" Dallas blurted. Terri squeezed her daughter's hand, hoping it conveyed the *Be seen and not heard* signal well enough, before Dallas said something really embarrassing.

"Yes, child. I am a sister in the Order of Marguerite. We look after the sick and the dying. It's a good job when you love helping people as much as I do. This has been my calling since I was younger than you are now."

"But why aren't you wearing—"

Another squeeze. Now was not the time for Dallas to gain a

religious education or ask invasive questions. Terri wanted to melt into the floor.

"A habit? The black-and-white outfit you've probably seen on TV, or in the movies?" Sister Grace asked, and Dallas nodded. "My order doesn't wear habits. A lot of orders don't these days. Habits are considered to be fairly old-fashioned. We're allowed to wear our own clothes." She smoothed her long skirt as she spoke. "Within reason, of course. No miniskirts or blue jeans for me."

This was too much for Dallas to handle. "You've never worn *jeans*?"

Next she would be asking Sister Grace about her sex life. Terri had to nip this in the bud. "Dallas...."

"A few times. When I was about your age. But not since I became a nun and joined the church."

"Wow." Dallas touched her own worn jeans with their patches and embroidery. They'd cost a fortune and it was clear her daughter couldn't fathom life without them. "Are jeans unholy?"

"Dallas, I think Sister Grace has better things to do than answer these kinds of questions."

But the nun smiled again. The expression was so permanent Terri would have suspected it was painted on if it hadn't been so natural. "Actually, I was bored before you two showed up, and I love children's questions. Children are the only truly honest people in the world. They mean what they say, and they say what they mean."

Her daughter shot her a triumphant look. *See?*

Although she was impatient, she couldn't blame Dallas for her fascination with Sister Grace. Her daughter had no religious education to speak of, no exposure. Of *course* she was fascinated. And what was she in such a hurry for, anyway? Glenvale wasn't going anywhere, and unfortunately, neither were its ghosts.

"No, Dallas, jeans aren't unholy. Nuns wear more formal clothing as a sign of respect, for our duties to Christ and to the church."

Dallas frowned. "Are my clothes disrespectful?"

Sister Grace patted her arm. "Not at all. Church isn't in session right now. But if you were to come for a service, you may want to dress up a little."

"Can we come for a service, Mom?"

What was with her and the tough questions today? "We'll see. I don't know if we'll still be in Eventide by the end of the week."

The nun's smile deepened. "You're not from here?"

"No, I'm here for work. I've been hired to do the restoration on the Glenvale estate."

For the first time, Sister Grace's smile vanished. Terri saw a shadow cross the nun's features. "What is it? Did I say something wrong?"

"No...." The nun cleared her throat. "You're working for Henrietta Vandermere." It wasn't a question. Her hands strayed to her rosary.

"Yes. I am. Do you know Henrietta?"

"I've never spoken to her, I'm afraid, but I'm aware of her family, and of the house. I hope it doesn't frighten you to learn that you are not the first people with an association to Glenvale to come here for assistance."

Terri felt uncomfortably warm all of a sudden. A droplet of sweat trickled down her back. "Gertrude Phillips?"

"Ms. Phillips is one of our parishioners, yes. Or at least, she was. I'm afraid I haven't seen her in a while, not since her mother's condition worsened."

"She's in the hospital. She survived a terrible...." She hesitated, about to say 'accident', but it didn't feel right, lying in a church, whether she was religious or not. "Attack."

Sister Grace sucked in a breath. "I had no idea. Is she all right?"

Terri was surprised the nun didn't know. The town seemed unable to talk about anything else these days. She glanced at Dallas. She hadn't told her daughter the details. Despite their issues, Dallas had been fond of Gertrude. "Not yet, but I hope she will be."

Fortunately, the nun appeared to interpret her silent signals correctly. That was probably part of her job too. "Thank you for letting me know. I'll look in on her myself, see if I can offer any comfort. Is her mother still…."

"I believe so, yes. I think she has a nurse looking after her."

Dallas nodded, the authority on all things Gertrude. "Her name is Maria."

"Maria, that's right. I do see her now and then. I can ask after them both."

"Thank you, Sister. So…Gertrude – and others – have come here about the house?"

The nun looked reluctant to pick up that line of conversation. Talking about Gertrude and her mother, however unfortunate their circumstances, had clearly been a welcome reprieve. "Yes. Glenvale is a dark place. But I suspect you know that already."

"Yes." Terri turned her cheek to the light, displaying the faded scratches. "Something in the house attacked me as well."

Sister Grace's face went slack. "Wait…Gertrude was attacked *at* Glenvale?"

"Yes." Dallas snuggled closer to her, and Terri put an arm around her daughter, hoping to provide some security, though both of them were well aware that there was little she could do against Niles. They had to put their trust in Gertrude's convictions that the spirit wouldn't harm them, as long as they continued to feign ignorance about its true nature.

Not exactly comforting.

"Forgive me if this is an invasion of your privacy, but…do you *need* to keep working there? Some things are much more important than money."

"I made Gertrude a promise. It's hard to explain, but for the time being, I need to go back there, yes."

"Well, you're going to need more than holy water. Let me see what I can find for you."

Before the nun could leave them, Terri touched her hand. "Please, Sister. Tell me what you know about the house."

"I'm afraid I don't know much. Nothing that will be of value to you. It's a dark place, full of evil. I pleaded with Gertrude not to take the position with Henrietta Vandermere, but she was adamant. She said she'd already fallen in love with the place." The nun crinkled her nose. "I told her that she was hearing the siren song of the Devil."

"Have you been to Glenvale?"

"No, but Father Donovan has. Henrietta has asked him to bless the house more than once. It never does a bit of good."

Terri felt a sinking sensation in the pit of her stomach. "Then the holy water isn't going to help."

Sister Grace patted her hand, but there was a sadness in her eyes that was concerning. She hadn't smiled since they'd begun talking about the house. "It's better than going back there with nothing – if you're certain you have to go back."

"I am. At least for now. Depending on what happens, I might re-evaluate." Here in a church, in the company of a visibly worried nun, her decision to go through with this seemed worse than insane. Why was she putting their lives on the line for the sake of a woman who had died before she'd been born? And for another woman, whom she barely knew, who had caused her nothing but grief?

She saw the face of Emma's killer again, recalled the terror the woman had experienced right before she died.

Because it was the right thing to do.

She just hoped this altruism didn't get them killed.

"Give me a moment," the nun said. "I'll see what else I can give you."

Once she'd left, Dallas turned to her, her eyes still unnaturally wide. "Are we doing the right thing, Mom?"

"Yes, I think so. But if you ever feel you're in danger, tell me and we'll leave. I'm hoping Niles will leave us alone, and that we won't have to stay long." Maybe the atrocities he'd inflicted on Gertrude would be enough to satisfy him for a while. She shuddered to think what would happen if he came after her – or her daughter.

Sister Grace returned with her arms full. Laying the objects on the pew beside them, she explained, "Everything you see here has been blessed. It will help protect you, as much as it can."

She handed a rosary to Terri, and put another around Dallas's neck, gently lifting her ponytail so the beads wouldn't get tangled. There were several crucifixes and an icon of Mary as well. "Hang one in the room you choose to stay in, and try to keep a couple near you as you work. Avoid sleeping in a room that belonged to Niles or any of the Vandermere children."

The statement alarmed her. What did Sister Grace know about the family? There must be something she could tell them. "What have you heard about Niles?" she asked.

"Not much, but my mother used to tell us stories." She frowned. "He was an awful child, cruel and sadistic. It wasn't safe to let animals or younger children anywhere near him. No one could prove it, of course, but everyone in town knew, at least back then. It's terrible to say, but it was a blessing when he fell ill. Many children breathed a sigh of relief that they didn't have to worry about running into him anymore."

"What about Henrietta?"

"My mother didn't care much for her, either. To hear her tell it, she was her brother's partner in crime, encouraging his cruel acts and urging him on. Perhaps she wasn't as directly responsible, but she played a role in it, all the same." She paused. "But I shouldn't speak ill of your employer. With God's grace, anyone can change. Most of us learn and grow as we reach adulthood, and I hope that is true of Henrietta as well...for your sake. She is an elderly woman now, nearing the end of her life. It's a good time to make peace with her Lord and Savior."

Terri doubted Henrietta would ever be saved. "And Emma?"

"Emma was older, too far ahead of my mother in school for her to know Emma well, but I've never heard a bad word about her. She may have been the one Vandermere to take after their father. It's a shame she died so young."

Picturing the rock that had crushed Emma's neck and ended her life, Terri shivered. "Yes, it is." At least her instincts had been correct about Emma. No sense risking her life for another monster. "Thank you so much for your help, Sister, but I don't feel right about taking all of this and giving you nothing in return. Can I at least make a donation to the church?"

The nun closed Terri's hand around the rosary. "Keep yourself and Dallas safe. Trust your instincts, and leave the moment you feel either of you are in jeopardy. Visit me again before you leave Eventide. Seeing you safe and alive...that will be thanks enough."

CHAPTER NINETEEN

The sight that met her when she pulled up to Glenvale was one she dreaded more than any ghost.

Derek, otherwise known as her ex-husband. In some ways, it *was* like seeing a ghost. "What's your father doing here?"

He'd been aware of the Glenvale project, of course. As her daughter's other parent and guardian, he had every right to know where she was, and where to find her. But he'd never intruded on her time with Dallas before. The possibilities overwhelmed her. Had something happened to his parents? Or to Trudy, the long-suffering woman who now had the joy of cleaning up after him?

"Uh, Mom." Dallas caught her sleeve before she could open the door, staring up at her with a beseeching expression. "There's something I should tell you first."

This 'something' wasn't a good thing. That much was obvious. Terri mentally braced herself, but tried her best to sound unconcerned. "What's that?"

"Well, you know I text Dad, right?"

"Yes." Every night, shortly after they'd finished dinner. Initially, it had amused Terri, and then it began to irritate her, though she hoped she'd never let that show. It was great Derek wanted to be so involved in his daughter's life, but why now? Why only after their marriage ended? It seemed fake, like keeping up appearances, and if there was one thing Terri couldn't stand, it was phonies.

"He kept asking how things were going here. You know, how I spent my time, if I was left by myself while you worked, if the house felt unsafe."

Heat built in Terri's chest until it reached her throat. A fishing expedition. But why? Did he plan to use the information to get her in trouble with the judge? To renege on his payments again? What was the point of it all? "Yes? Go on." *Stay calm, stay calm, stay calm.*

"And...." Her daughter bit her lip, looking incredibly guilty. "I might have told him."

Terri groaned, sinking in her seat. "Dallas...."

"I'm *sorry*, okay? He kept asking, and I didn't want to lie. I didn't expect him to actually come here." Tears glimmered in her eyes, and Terri immediately felt terrible. It wasn't her daughter's fault that she'd made a mess of this, and that the entire summer had been a fiasco. Dallas shouldn't have to lie to her dad. This was *her* fault, not her child's.

"Hey, that's okay. I don't want you to lie to anyone. Lying is never the answer." Though she'd lie her face off to Derek if she needed to. "But I can't go into this meeting unarmed. What exactly did you tell him?"

"Not much. Just about the séance and how Gertrude was staying with us and that your face got scratched."

That's it? Jesus, Dallas. She was screwed.

"I didn't tell him about being left alone with your tools, though."

"That's great," she said, trying to unclench her teeth. Why was Derek asking her daughter that, anyway? Dallas wasn't a toddler. She was smart enough to stay safe around Terri's equipment. What was she going to do, go running through the house with a nail gun? "What did he say when you told him that stuff?"

"He asked if I was okay, and I told him I was, and then he said that it didn't sound safe."

"But he believed you? About the séance, and the scratches?" She couldn't imagine Derek having the patience to sit through a ghost story, let alone believe it. She'd never met a more pragmatic man. Her ex-husband was a card-carrying member of the *if I don't see it, it doesn't exist* school of thought.

"He seemed to. Why wouldn't he? I don't lie."

"No, but sometimes children…imagine things. He didn't tell you he was coming?"

"No!" Dallas's shock was genuine. Whatever she had told her dad in innocence, she'd never expected it to lead to this. "I have no idea why he's here. Unless it's because he misses me. He did say that a lot. He said Trudy misses me too, and that summers aren't the same for her without me. That's nice, right?"

"Of course it is." Terri forced a smile, though she didn't give a flying fuck what Trudy missed. "Let's go get this over with."

The dark cloud hovering above her daughter disappeared as Dallas left the car and ran into her dad's arms. "Dad! What are you doing here?"

Terri felt a twinge at seeing the easy affection between them, even though Dallas was much more demonstrative with her now. Maybe Derek was reaping the benefits of the Glenvale experience too. It was impossible to say, and Lord knows he'd never tell her. God forbid he ever intimated that she'd done something right.

He nodded at her as she approached. "Terri."

"Derek." She was cool with playing cool, if that was what he wanted. "To what do we owe this pleasure?"

"I came to see my girl," he said, his face softening as he regarded Dallas, which in turn softened Terri. Maybe he *was* interested in their daughter now, for real. Maybe he'd changed. Don't know what you've got until it's gone, and all that. "And to talk to you. Got a minute?"

"A couple. It's been a long day, and we're ready for dinner."

"I could take you girls out somewhere. How would that be?"

"That would be awesome," Dallas chimed in immediately. Eating in restaurants was a rare treat, one Terri could seldom afford. "Please, Mom, can we?"

"You go on ahead with your dad, hun. I'll grab something around here."

"No, Mom, you have to come. I'm not going to leave you here alone. Puhleeeeeeeze?"

Derek's forehead creased as he attempted to gauge her reaction, and she noticed how much more gray hair he had now. Perhaps life with Trudy wasn't so blissful after all. Maybe she didn't pick up his newspapers fast enough. "Surely we can handle having a meal together. One meal. It'll give us a chance to talk."

Yes, in a public restaurant. Great place to hold what was guaranteed to be an intensely private conversation. "It's not that I *can't* handle it. It's that I don't want to. You two go ahead. I'll be fine." She directed her last statement to her daughter. Derek wouldn't care if she was fine or not. He hadn't cared during their marriage, so why would he start now?

"It looks like it would mean a lot to Dallas. Right, honey?"

She glared at him. The nerve of him, using their child against her. It was a new low, but thankfully, their daughter didn't fall for it.

"It's okay. If Mom doesn't want to go, she doesn't have to. Sorry, Mom."

"Can you give us a few minutes alone then, sweetheart? Maybe go wash up and get ready? I need to say a few things to your mother in private."

Terri winced inwardly. This was going to be bad. Derek had said all manner of insensitive, spiteful things in front of Dallas before. How much more awful could he possibly be?

"Okay...." Dallas hesitated, studying her face. The maturity in her ten-year-old features, still rounded with childhood, made Terri sad. "Are you going to be all right, Mom?"

"Your mother will be fine. I'm just going to talk to her, that's all."

'Just' talk. As if words weren't some of the wickedest weapons available. "Do you want the key?" she asked Dallas, and was gratified when their child shook her head. For obvious reasons, but also because she was annoyed with Derek for showing up out of the blue and thinking he could order Dallas around. This was *their* summer.

"No, it's okay. I'll wait in the garden."

As soon as she was out of earshot, Terri exhaled. Best to rip off the Band-Aid. "Dallas told me she filled you in on some of the more…*interesting* parts of our summer, and I can understand your concern. But, as you can see, she's fine. And this is still my time with her. So I hope you'll get back in your truck and return to Montana after dinner."

She held her breath, hoping for the best, but this was Derek, after all. She should have known better.

He shook his head. "This isn't about that, Terri. Or, not just about that. This is more like a last straw."

Terri bristled at the expression. Why did she have the feeling that the only back broken around here was going to be hers? "Then what is it about? I don't intrude on your time, Derek, and I certainly don't come to your work. I'd like to say it's good to see you, but this feels invasive."

"No disrespect, but we're talking about what's right for our daughter, not what's right for you. I don't much care what you feel right now. I care about Dallas."

"And you don't think I do?"

"I'm sure you tell yourself you do, and you might even believe yourself, but look at this place." He gestured to Glenvale looming above them. "There's gotta be black mold, asbestos, and who knows what else in there. That's no place for a child."

She glowered at him, folding her arms across her chest. "The same could be said of any older home. Not everyone can afford to live in a place that's been built from scratch."

"The house would be bad enough, but then you go let some crazy woman fill her head up with all these strange ideas."

"What strange ideas would those be?" Terri wondered if she could fill his head up with the strange idea of driving off a cliff.

"You know, ghosts and silly stuff like that."

She sighed heavily, but she'd asked for it. She'd known exactly what Derek was referring to. Dallas had told him about the séance, the scratches — she could hardly deny it now. "It's an old house. You know how it is. They make strange noises. Things shift. Radiators clank. There are drafts."

"Don't tell me you're okay with this?" he asked, pushing his cowboy hat back so he could wipe his forehead. She crossed her fingers that he'd been waiting all day in the heat for them.

"Dallas is happier here than she was in Montana. We're getting our relationship back on track. I think that bothers you a hell of a lot more than black mold or asbestos."

"I'd hoped to have a civil conversation with you, but that seems to be impossible."

Terri refused to let him get to her. He'd played that old, woe-is-me act one too many times. "What do you want, Derek? If you wanted to see her, you've seen her. If you wanted to make sure she was okay, you've checked on her. The only thing you haven't done is bring Trudy over to see her too, and that's why you're still standing."

"There's no need to get nasty. Talk like that isn't going to help you in court."

"In *court*?" Was she hearing him right? "What are you talking about?"

"Trudy and I have talked about it, and—" He scratched his head, looking around to make sure Dallas wasn't nearby. "We've decided to go for full custody."

"Full custody? You already have her most of the year anyway." This was unbelievable. "What more could you possibly want?"

"We want full custody. With supervised visitation."

"*What?*" Was he for real? This kept getting worse and worse.

"You're not acting responsible, Terri. It's not that I think you're a bad mother, but you never should have brought Dallas into this situation and exposed her to this."

"Into what situation? I restore old homes, Derek. It's what I do. What's so bad about our child learning about history? Or how to build and repair things?"

It was as if he hadn't heard a word she'd said. "It isn't safe."

"Is this coming from you, or from Trudy? Funny how you didn't give a shit about spending time with Dallas when we were still together."

He pressed his lips together. "That's not true."

"If she wants a child so damn badly, she should get one of her own, and keep her grubby hands off mine."

"Trudy can't have children of her own, Terri. You should be happy she loves Dallas as much as she does. She's a good woman, and a great mother. She's a positive influence on Dallas."

"She's not a mother," Terri snapped, loathing the thought of that simpering fool around her daughter. But she realized her anger was misdirected. It was Derek she should be angry with, not the poor unfortunate who'd taken up with him. Still, it was Trudy's words she was hearing come from her ex-husband's mouth. If it had been up to Derek, he would have happily spent the summer watching television, can of beer in hand. No, Trudy had put him up to this. "She's a stepmother at best, and that's all she'll ever be."

"Cruelty doesn't become you. These unkind words are proving what I suspected all along. You don't care about what's best for Dallas. You only care about yourself."

"I *do* care about what's best for Dallas. I just happen to think that's being with her mother, not some woman she barely knows."

"She knows Trudy better than she knows you. Hell, she knows your mother better than she knows you."

It was all she could do to keep from throttling him. But an assault charge wouldn't help her case. "That's unfair. I went a long time without work, you know that. But as soon as I could afford to have her back with me, I came and got her." Part of her wondered if she should let Dallas go with her father. Could she trust Gertrude that they'd really be safe in the house? But if she let Derek take Dallas, the courts might hold that against her. She might never get her daughter back.

The idea of being limited to supervised visitation while Trudy, a woman she barely knew, raised Dallas was more than she could bear.

He shook his head again. "I've come for Dallas. She's going back to Montana with me."

"Like hell she is."

"The custody situation can play out in the courts, but I'm not leaving her in a dangerous situation. She's coming with me."

"You can't take her from me. This is *my* summer." Terri caught what she'd said, and how Derek would twist it. "*Our* summer," she corrected. "She wants to stay with me."

"We'll see about that." He made a gesture over her head, and she turned and saw Dallas watching them, looking worried. Had Dallas asked him to come get her? No, she would have warned her. She would have told her the truth. "Sweetheart? Can you come over here, please?"

Sweetheart again? Don't make me puke. Since when had Derek been a terms-of-endearment kind of guy? Why was he acting so fake?

Their daughter hesitated, looking like she'd prefer to face a firing squad than join her parents on the veranda. "See?" Terri said, gratified at the doubtful expression on her daughter's face, even though it hurt her heart. The joyful hugs of a moment before were long gone. "She doesn't want anything to do with you."

"Oh, hush. We need to ask you a question, hun. Please come on up here."

"What is it?" Dallas asked when she was a few steps away. She was like a skittish foal. One wrong move, and she'd bolt.

"Trudy and I want you to come back home for the summer. What do you think of that?" He gestured at Glenvale, his lips curling in a sneer. "No more old houses falling apart around your ears, no more ghosts."

Terri waited, scarcely daring to breathe. She couldn't imagine surviving another night at Glenvale without Dallas. Dallas had kept her sane. But then again, if she went with her dad, Terri wouldn't have to worry about Niles so much. She didn't care what Niles did to *her* at this point. She only cared about Dallas.

"But...I am home. I'm with Mom. I always spend the summers with Mom." Dallas bit her lip, and looked at Terri. "Do you want me to go?"

"Of course not. This is all your father's doing. He's convinced you're not safe with me." She could feel Derek scowling at her, but she didn't give a shit. It was wrong to make your child choose between her parents, and that's exactly what he was doing. Fuck him.

"You told me you don't feel safe here, sweetie. I thought this was what you wanted."

Right. As if this had anything to do with what *Dallas* wanted. This was all about what Trudy wanted, and he knew it.

"The house scares me," Dallas admitted, "but I feel safe with Mom. I want to stay with her. Besides, we'll be leaving here soon, right, Mom?"

"Right." She felt like she'd run a marathon, or won some big award. She wanted to dance off the veranda. *Suck it, Derek.* "We're nearly done here."

"Nearly done?" He sneered at the house again. "This place looks like it's about to fall down."

"Like you know *so* much about heritage houses. Really, Derek. You said it was up to Dallas, and she's made her choice. Please go."

She watched as her ex-husband evaluated the situation. He'd never been the fastest thinker, which was more reason to believe Trudy had put him up to this. Derek looked at his daughter, and Terri wondered what she would do if he picked up Dallas, threw her in the truck, and drove to Montana. Call the police? Charge him with kidnapping?

"You don't have to stay to protect your mother's feelings," he said. "We both want you to do what makes you happy."

"But I *want* to stay with Mom. I'm sorry if I made you worry, but I'm okay."

"All right, then. If you're sure." He tipped his hat at Terri, scowling at her from under the brim. "My lawyers will be in touch."

"So will mine."

He snorted. "You don't have a lawyer. You don't have two nickels to rub together."

"And whose fault is that, Derek? Who decided child support was optional?"

"Why should I pay you support? She's with us most of the year."

"Yeah, well, I think that's about to change."

His right eye twitched. "Over my dead body."

"Trust me, nothing would please me more."

"You're a classy lady, Terri. Always have been. Glad to see that hasn't changed."

She finally spoke the words she'd long wanted to say. "Suck it, Derek."

He stalked back to his truck, cheeks flushed, and climbed inside without giving Dallas so much as a wave. Her daughter joined her on the veranda, and together they watched him go.

"I'm sorry you had to see that," Terri said, and she was. Dallas didn't need to be embroiled in the misery of their failed marriage. Damn Derek. And damn Trudy too. She could adopt if she wanted a child around twenty-four seven.

"What was that about? What did Dad want?"

"He wanted you to come home for the summer. Apparently Trudy really misses you." As soon as the words were out of her mouth, she regretted them. She shouldn't be snide in front of her daughter, or make Dallas feel like she had to choose between them. It was a good thing she got along so well with her father's new wife. Better than the alternative.

Dallas rolled her eyes. "Whatever. Trudy is nice, but she acts like I'm a doll to play dress up with, rather than a kid."

It was a remarkably astute observation for a ten-year-old to make, but Dallas had been forced to grow up fast after their divorce. Terri hated what they'd put her through. And if Derek made good on his threats to seek full custody, it would get even worse. "I'm sorry I said that. I don't want you to feel like you have to choose between us. You can love Trudy, and your dad, and me too. Love isn't limited. There's always enough to go around."

"I know. But it isn't a choice. You're my mom. I only have one mom."

Terri released the breath she hadn't known she'd been holding. "Do you want to go out for dinner?"

Dallas's eyes lit up briefly, but just as quickly, the spark faded. "We can't afford it."

"Sure we can. Your dad promised you a night out on the town, and there's no reason why you shouldn't have one."

"But...where will we find the money?"

She hugged her, beyond grateful that Dallas was still there. "I'll figure it out. You leave that up to me."

"Honestly, I'd rather eat here. If anything scary happens, we can leave, right?"

"Of course, but are you sure? I thought you were excited about going out."

"I was, but now I'm more excited about staying in. We have a lot of work to do, Mom."

Terri laughed and hugged her again. "That's right. We certainly do."

CHAPTER TWENTY

The house was quiet. *Too* quiet. None of the explainable strange noises Henrietta was so fond of. No air in the pipes, or clanking radiators, or doors creaking open on their own.

Terri didn't trust it, not for a second. It felt like Glenvale was listening, *waiting*.

For all her bravado in front of Derek, Dallas wasn't thrilled at the prospect of being back in the house, or going to bed before her mother. They'd surrounded her with enough crucifixes and holy water to fight off a legion of vampires. Terri had spread a line of salt across the entrance of the cook's room for good measure.

"What's that for?" Dallas asked.

"It's supposed to keep evil spirits from entering."

"Where did you learn that?" Her daughter was visibly impressed.

Terri smiled. "Saw it in a movie." She put the figure of Mary on the dresser, overlooking the room and her daughter. "Do you feel safer now?"

"A bit. I'm still scared, though. Where are you going to be?"

Where was she going to be…that was a damn good question. Not in the cellar, that's for sure. She had enough faith in Molloy to feel confident his team had found everything there was to find.

She'd promised Gertrude she'd find proof that Emma had been murdered, but what that proof would be and where it was located was beyond her. "I guess I'll search in Henrietta's room for now, see if I get any bright ideas." She hoped it wouldn't take a full night to find what they needed. The place gave her the creeps.

"You could be waiting a long time for those," Dallas said, sticking her tongue out.

"Good night, smart ass. Call if you need me. Got your phone?"
Her daughter held it up. "Right here."

"Seriously, if you feel scared and can't sleep, call me. It doesn't
have to be a big reason." She hoped there wouldn't be any more big
anythings. They'd been through more than enough for one summer.
"Promise you'll call."

"I will. Get to work, Mom. Find what you need to find so we
can get out of here."

Find what you need to find. Good advice. But what was she looking
for? Unfortunately, Emma's journal had contained no more answers.
Her last entry had been the one about suspecting her brother of
messing with the horses. Soon after she'd written it – maybe that
same day – she'd gone out for a ride and never come back.

Unlike many of the other rooms, Henrietta's had been stripped
bare. There was no furniture to search, and the walls were blank.
After running her hands along the windowsill and checking for loose
floorboards, she gave up. There was nothing to find. Frustrated, she
returned to Emma's room.

She'd spread salt across the entrance to Emma's room too, and
would do the same no matter where she was in the house. Her hand
strayed to her cheek, remembering.

How could she prove Emma had been murdered? The heiress's
death had looked enough like an accident to fool the police. It's not
like those who killed her would have been stupid enough to write
it down, and if they'd spoken about it to anyone, that person would
be long gone by now.

Every now and then, she felt someone watching her, but when
she turned, no one was there. Her hands trembled as she ran her
hands over the walls and searched under the mattress. One thing
was certain – they needed to get the hell out of there as soon as she
found any proof of what had happened to Emma. The house had a
heaviness to it now, as if the walls themselves had soaked up the evil
energy from the family that had once lived there.

Unlike Niles's belongings, which had been carefully stowed in a closet, Emma's things – her guns, her swords, her musical instruments and fine clothes – were all gone. Terri hadn't been able to find a thing of Emma's aside from what had been hidden in the window seat. Everything else had been given away, perhaps, or maybe sold. The thought made her sad, but then again, Emma Vandermere might have preferred that. The woman struck her as the practical type. She probably would want someone using her things, rather than having them rotting away in a closet.

After quite a few hours, Terri still hadn't the faintest clue where to look for her evidence. Disheartened and exhausted, she decided to make herself some tea before cleaning up the mess she'd made.

Bracing herself for whatever lay beyond the door, she closed her eyes briefly and attempted to pray. She knew the Lord's Prayer, but that was about it. Oh well. That would have to do.

Clutching the rosary Sister Grace had given her, she said the words under her breath.

"Our Father, who art in Heaven…."

Creak.

Her mouth went dry. Someone had just walked past Emma's door, she would swear it. She'd heard their footsteps.

Taking the crucifix from her back pocket, she gripped it in her clammy hands, holding it toward the door. "Who's there?" she asked, although she desperately didn't want to know.

Silence.

"Hallowed be thy name."

Creak.

She rested her hand on the doorknob. Emma's was filigree silver on both sides. It was cool to the touch, but not freezing, as everything had been the other night. Didn't rooms get colder in the presence of a ghost? Maybe all she was hearing was the normal sounds of an old house settling.

But no, that was bullshit. She knew what footsteps sounded like. Someone was on the other side of this door, someone who was either trying to keep quiet and failing, or who wanted to be heard.

"Dallas?"

Perhaps her daughter was scared and had come to find her instead of phoning.

Silence.

It wasn't Dallas. Her daughter was too smart to leave her sanctuary at night, and for a moment, Terri wished more than anything that she was with her. Now she could *feel* someone on the other side of the door, almost hear them breathing. Their presence bore down on her, exhausting her. She bowed her head.

"Thy kingdom come, thy will be done...."

Creak.

Terri raised her voice, extending the crucifix toward the door. "On earth as it is in Heaven. Give us this day our daily bread, and forgive us our trespasses, as we forgive those who have trespassed against us."

She heard laughter now – chilling, evil laughter. It raised the hair on the back of her neck and made her arms prickle. Though tears of fright stung her eyes, she wiped them away with her sleeve and kept going.

"And lead us not into temptation, but *deliver us from evil*." Terri spoke louder now, nearly yelling the last words. She pictured Niles backing away from the door and slinking away to his hole in the cellar. "For thine is the kingdom, the power and the glory, forever and ever, amen."

The house was quiet, and the atmosphere felt lighter. Whatever had been lurking outside the room was gone. Holding the crucifix toward the entrance, she slowly opened the door with her other hand, half expecting Niles to leap out at her. That was exactly the sort of thing the psychopath would find funny.

The hallway was dark, but as she waited, eyes straining to see any shadow, the lights flickered and came on. She'd left them on – she *knew* she'd left them on. Continuing to hold the crucifix in front of her as if it were a weapon, she shut the door behind her and made her way to the kitchen.

As she crossed the parlor, she noticed a light glowing in Howard Vandermere's study. It was the one room in the house where she hadn't spent much time, but the one that had been kept most intact. The man's shelves of books, his pipe, and his ram's-head snuff mull were still there, as if he had left the room briefly, intending to return. Terri knew full well that *she* hadn't turned the light on in the study. Was someone else in the house? *Ghosts don't need light.*

She was startled to see a man in a suit sitting at the desk, writing in a book with a fountain pen. He looked up when she entered, but his face remained expressionless, as if he wasn't the least bit surprised to see her.

"Hello," he said.

"Hello?" From the old photographs she'd seen, she recognized the man as Howard Vandermere, but he looked so real. She really had to get over this notion that spirits were transparent.

"I assure you, I am quite dead, and unlike my son, I am not the slightest bit hesitant about admitting it." He gestured at her hand, which continued to clutch the crucifix as if to ward him off. "You can put that down, if you like. I am – *was* – a man of God, and I have no wish to harm you."

Terri lowered her arm, feeling foolish.

"That's better. Would you like to have a seat?" he asked, indicating the chair across from his desk. "We have much to talk about, but I am afraid I do not have much time."

On wobbly legs, she crossed the room and collapsed in the chair, unable to keep from staring. She couldn't believe this man was a ghost. It was easier to believe she'd traveled back in time, to when Howard Vandermere had been in his prime.

But not quite. The man's spirit didn't look well. There were shadows under his eyes, and his suit jacket didn't fit properly, as if he'd lost a considerable amount of weight.

"My son did that to you," he said, gesturing to her cheek. "I apologize on his behalf. I assure you, my wife and I did everything we could to rid the world of his evil, but unfortunately, forces such as that are stronger than human will."

"Your wife…?" She found his meaning hard to follow.

He sighed. "One of the greatest mistakes I made was involving Elizabeth. I should have taken care of it myself, and left her none the wiser. Let her believe that our malevolent progeny slipped away in his sleep. How simple would that have been? However, for all my faults, I have always been an honest man. It was one of my greatest qualities, as well as my greatest curse."

Terri had a hard time believing what she was hearing. She'd never, not for a second, suspected Howard, in spite of Gertrude's suspicions. "*You* killed Niles?"

"My son would have died in any case. Terrible disease he had, and the promised cure wasn't working. Perhaps that was what destroyed his mind as well. What my beloved wife and I did was ensure no one else would meet an untimely death by his hands."

He lowered his head, as if ashamed to look at her. "I should have taken care of it myself. That was my great failing. But it took the two of us to hold the pillow over his head. Despite his illness, our son had the strength of the Devil.

"She never recovered, my darling Elizabeth. Though she understood it had to be done, the weight of that terrible secret haunted her for the rest of her days. It destroyed her. I will never forgive myself for that."

Terri leaned forward, clutching her head with both hands. Against her will, she saw Niles's parents pressing a pillow over his face, the teenager's arms and legs flailing as he fought to survive. As disturbed as Niles had been, had he deserved that? It was an appalling death.

"I can see you're horrified by what we did, that you believe we were monstrous, taking the life of our own son. I don't blame you, but we truly felt we had no choice. When animals were his victims, we could turn a blind eye, pretend we were not aware. But once he directed his wrath toward people, we had a responsibility we could no longer ignore."

"Emma."

The man blanched, looking pained. "Yes, Emma. If we had taken action sooner, we might have saved her. That is yet another great regret. We could not let her death go unanswered.

"Her spirit is unquiet. She has visited you, and showed you the truth of her murder."

It was not a question, but Terri nodded. She'd always suspected her vision of the day Emma died hadn't been a dream.

"So you understand our son did not act alone." Howard Vandermere paused, looking at what he had written, and then set his pen aside. "I could not find it in me to cause harm to a girl, even a girl capable of such a foul act. Her mother and I prayed that, without Niles's influence, the darkness in her own soul would retreat. For the most part, I believe that it has."

Terri wasn't so sure. There had been too much joy on young Henrietta's face when she'd brought the rock down on her sister's neck. That kind of bloodlust didn't just vanish. The Vandermeres had plenty of money and power, two things that could cause questions to remain unanswered, and problems to go away.

"I need your assistance to bring this sad chapter of our history to a close," he said. "There is a compartment in that corner." Vandermere pointed over her shoulder. "Within it, you shall find the proof you are seeking. Once you have found it, I ask that you do one final thing for me, and for the others who have needlessly suffered because of my family."

"What is it?"

He stared at her, making her squirm. "Burn it. Burn Glenvale to the ground."

Her jaw dropped. "I-I can't do that."

"You must. It is the only way to free all of us, and to ensure Niles does no further harm. Do you want what happened to Miss Phillips to happen to another woman? For more contractors to go missing? You are living on borrowed time yourself, Miss Foxworth. Once you have restored this house to its former glory, do you truly think my daughter will let you leave? You already know too much." He held up his hands, and she could see the light shining through them.

"I would do it myself, but these old things do not work so well these days."

With her mind reeling over what he'd revealed — that perhaps the other contractors' absence wasn't as straightforward as Henrietta had led her to believe — Terri forced herself to focus on his deranged request. "That's arson, Mr. Vandermere. You're talking about arson, which is a crime, a crime that carries a lot of jail time. I *restore* old homes; I don't destroy them."

"Don't think of it as destroying anything. You would be protecting others from this evil. You have doubtlessly felt it yourself."

"Yes, I have, but I can't burn down this house. That would go against everything I believe in."

"I can't guarantee you would not face trouble with the law," he said as if she hadn't spoken. "Nevertheless, I will do everything in my power to protect you, and I am certain the other benevolent spirits in this house will as well."

"I'm sorry, I can't. If I go to prison, I might never see my daughter again. My ex is already trying to take her away from me."

"*Please*, Miss. Foxworth. I don't know if I'll be able to make this appeal again, or speak to another soul in this house. Glenvale is evil. It has become his source of power and her playground. As long as it stands, more people will suffer and more people will die. Do not let their deaths be on your conscience."

Before she could argue, he held up a hand again. "Find the compartment and look at the evidence before you make your decision. Will you do that much for me?"

Terri nodded. "Okay—"

But he was gone. The aroma of cherrywood tobacco lingering in the air was the only tangible proof he hadn't been a dream.

The last thing she wanted was to have anything more to do with the Vandermeres. What despicable people, what a loathsome family. The son and daughter had murdered their own sister, and then the parents had murdered the son. How sick was it possible to get? Only Emma remained blameless, and God forbid Terri dug too deeply into *her* life.

She remained in the chair for a moment, head spinning, but the sensation of heaviness had returned to the house. She suspected she didn't have much time. Whatever Howard Vandermere had wanted her to find, she needed to get it and then get the hell out.

Terri hurried to the far corner of the office where the ghost had indicated, and started her search for a compartment. She looked behind books, going so far as to remove some of the shelves, but nothing.

"Where is it, Howard?" she whispered. "Where did you put it?"

Though the books could conceal a hiding spot, it wasn't where the spirit had pointed. He'd appeared to be pointing at a blank wall, but that didn't make much sense. Could Vandermere have gone to all this trouble for a joke, a joke on her? She didn't think so. Did ghosts lie? Niles had definitely misrepresented himself.

I have always been an honest man. It was one of my greatest qualities, as well as my greatest curse.

She could hear his voice as if he were still in the room, speaking to her.

"Okay, Howard. If you're so honest, where is it?" In desperation, Terri ran her palms over the wall, with no clue what she was looking for.

One of her hands sunk slightly into the plaster. Her heart picking up speed, she used her fingertips to feel along the wall. There was an indentation! She kept feeling until she came to what she thought was a corner. Then, moving her hands farther down, she pressed on it, hard.

Nothing happened.

Taking a deep breath, she tried again, but this time light and quick. She heard a soft popping sound, and a compartment in the wall opened.

"Holy shit. I apologize, Howard. You *were* honest."

Hands shaking, she opened the little door wide enough to see what was inside. If she'd expected a smoking gun, she was disappointed. Instead, the contents were a bundle of cloth about the size of a small pumpkin, and a sheaf of folded paper.

She removed the cloth-wrapped parcel first. It was surprisingly heavy. After setting it on the man's desk, she scurried back for the papers.

Tempted to carry both items back to the room she shared with Dallas, she again felt that sense of urgency. Was it Howard Vandermere's influence, or her own instincts? Whatever the cause, she decided to examine them right there in the study, but didn't feel right using his chair. Instead, she opted for the same one as before.

The bundle first. It was an effort to lift it from a sitting position. Within the cloth, the object was solid and unyielding. She began to unwrap it, feeling uneasily as if she were removing the bandages from a mummy. This object, whatever it was, had belonged to the Vandermeres. For all she knew, it was Niles's skull she held in her hands. She wouldn't have put it past them to keep something ghoulish.

The last bit of cloth fell away to reveal a seemingly ordinary stone. It was jagged in places and spotted liberally with what looked like brownish-red paint. But Terri knew instantly that it wasn't paint. It wasn't an ordinary rock, either.

Emma.

With her hands shaking so violently she could barely control them, she laid the rock on Vandermere's desk and unfolded the papers.

To whom it may concern,

If you are reading this, it may be assumed that I am dead, and that my fair wife Elizabeth has also passed. I trust that this document has fallen into honest hands, and that the person who learns my truth will make sure that justice is done, as if justice will ever be possible.

We were overjoyed when we were blessed with a son, a male heir to carry on the family name, but we soon learned that what we had initially thought was a blessing was, in fact, a dreadful curse. When he was an infant, our son refused to give us a moment's peace, forever wailing and shrieking at the top of his lungs. Elizabeth took him to physician after physician, but not a one could find any cause for his distress, or any method to relieve it. The opium-

laced sleeping aid, which had come highly recommended and worked so well with our other children, had no effect.

While my dear Elizabeth tried to shoulder the burden bravely, I would catch her looking at me with fear in her eyes as our son screamed. If he is such a trial now, her countenance appeared to say, what will become of us once he is older?

If we had known what awaited us, this story would have ended much sooner.

His screaming subsided once he became a toddler, but any relief was short-lived. Our son revealed an alarming knack for cruelty. He had some uncommon ability to detect which objects were most precious to a person, and systematically undertook the task of destroying them all. His mother and eldest sister Emma were favorite targets, and both ladies lost many cherished possessions before I ordered locks for their rooms. Even so, this only worked for a time; as he grew older, he taught himself how to dismantle any lock. Instead of the heir we had longed for, our son had the makings of a gifted thief.

When he was five or six, his desire to cause destruction and grief became fixated on the family pets. He killed the first canary in front of my wife, and it was the first time she punished him severely. In response, he soiled her bed, and ever after, each bird died of an 'accident' we could never prove. Once the last had expired, we resigned ourselves to a house without song, and decided not to subject any more feathered creatures to his torture.

With his easy prey now out of reach, he turned his attention to our daughter Emma's pets. All manner of creatures – kittens, pups, rabbits, even a foundling squirrel she had rescued and nursed back to health – began to vanish. Emma confided her suspicions to me, but dared not confront her brother. There were already troubling indicators that he was capable of so much worse. The sole being in this house who had no fear of him was his other sister, Henrietta, and the implications of that were troubling, to say the least. The two of them grew ever closer, often laughing and whispering, as if they shared some private joke the rest of us weren't a party to. When Niles disappeared for hours, Henrietta could not be found either, and they would invariably traipse in together, hours late for dinner and not caring the slightest bit how they had inconvenienced us.

You may think we were fools to not foretell what was to come, but I beg you, dear stranger, to understand that, however hateful and monstrous he might have been, Niles was our son. Henrietta, though her character is as yet a mystery, is our daughter. Denial is a powerful thing, and that is the one defense I can offer for our blindness. We were two parents trying our best to love an unlovable child.

To this day, I am not certain why Emma was their favorite target. Perhaps it was her good nature that they despised, or her great love for animals that made her the perfect prey. In time, she began to come to me with all manner of complaints: they had removed a sizeable chunk of her hair while she was sleeping, they had stolen her grandmother's ring, they had broken every string on her violin and snapped the tip from her epee. No lock could stop them. She often awoke in the night, crying in pain from a nasty pinch, and eventually the bruises ran up and down her arms. No matter what punishments we devised, they had no effect. Niles (and Henrietta with him, I wonder?) continued to torture his sister.

Emma's plight, though bad enough, began to worsen, as all situations did with Niles. She told me of waking up and finding him in her room, watching her. She was concerned, as was I, that he may do something immoral. She was a handsome woman, and he would not have been the first male to feel lustful toward her. She also expressed concern for her horses; they had been uncommonly spooked and difficult to control. While she could not prove it, she suspected her brother was behind it, and I saw no cause to doubt her. While I could not imagine what he would be doing with her horses, I was ill-equipped when it came to deciphering or predicting the actions of my son. He was willing to sink to depths I had not known existed.

The day we lost Emma, arguably the very best of all of us, Niles and Henrietta had disappeared once again. Emma was not present either, but her absence was not a mystery; she always went riding at the same time each morning. When Niles returned with Henrietta, they were in pleasant spirits, smiling and laughing. This continued as the day wore on and the expected time for Emma to return came and went. Finally, as my darling Elizabeth grew beset with worry, I saddled my own mount and set off to retrace my daughter's path.

I found her not far from the house. One of our long-time servants had discovered her before me, and was cradling her poor, shattered head in his lap, sobbing. I knew immediately that this had not been an accident, and my convictions were confirmed when the servant, so overcome with grief he could scarcely speak, told me what he had seen.

The strange behavior of my other children now made terrible sense. The one shock, if one could rightly call it that, was who had struck the killing blows. Not Niles, as I would have suspected, but Henrietta. My beloved Emma had perished at the hands of her own sister. Even so, I was convinced Niles's influence had been behind it. Henrietta had been a normal child before Niles began to reveal his madness. Any darkness in her heart had arrived with the awakening of her brother's.

I elicited the poor man's silence, promising him in return that I would ensure no other creature suffered at the hands of my children. Then I returned home to my worried Elizabeth, and confided in her the dreadful news, and held her as she wept. For a time, I let her believe that Emma's demise had, in fact, been an unfortunate accident. My wife's ignorance was blissful but all too brief, for I understood full well what was required of us.

She did not need as much convincing as expected. This gentle woman, who had rarely raised a hand to anyone or uttered an unkind word in her life, had been especially fond of Emma, the one child who had inherited her nature. She was devastated when I told her what I had learned from the servant, who had temporarily been sent away for his own protection, but not shocked. Our dearest Emma was not able to have a viewing, her lovely face and neck had been so destroyed. My wife was not a fool. She was well aware that such gruesome injuries did not occur from a fall off a horse. The creature would have been required to return, and kick her face repeatedly, deliberately, to approximate this destruction.

My quick-thinking wife asked the cook to prepare an especially sugary meal that night, praying it would put Niles into a diabetic stupor, and make our repulsive task easier, but such was not to be. Much like the sleeping aid when he was a child, the additional sugar seemed to have no effect, and he fought like a tiger when we laid the pillow over his face. It took all of our combined strength, but we were determined to protect others from suffering Emma's fate. God forgive me; I did not regret what we had done. I felt in my heart it was the correct and sole possible course of action. My wife, however, suffered greatly. I fear that she will end her own life before long, but every day I selfishly plead for her to stay by my side for a little longer. I cannot abide the thought of living in this ghastly house without her.

As for my remaining daughter, she was so young that I admit we could not bear to lose her as well. We have agreed to keep a close watch, and see if her behavior improves now that she is free from her brother's influence. If we see any indication that she embraces the same darkness, then we will do what has to be done. I pray that will not be the case.

For you who have found this letter, please destroy it if my surviving child, Henrietta Vandermere (assuming she has survived me), has proven worthy of the second chance we gave her. However, if she has followed in the path of her brother, Niles, you have my express permission to take this account, along with the stone that was used to kill my daughter Emma, to the appropriate authorities.

Do not delay. Like her brother, Henrietta has an uncanny ability to decipher thoughts before they are spoken. If you have suspected her of ill doing at any time, I can promise you one thing with complete assurance....

She knows.

CHAPTER TWENTY-ONE

"Ah, so you've found it. I've been searching for that for years."

Terri froze at the sound of her voice, but there was nothing she could do. There was nowhere to hide, and no time to conceal what she'd discovered. Why hadn't she followed her first instincts and taken everything to the servants' quarters?

Henrietta strode to the desk on silent feet, and hefted the rock in her hands, turning it over almost lovingly. "I'll never forget the expression on her face. She suspected Niles, but never me. *No one* suspected me. The sweet, dutiful daughter. The helpless female. Why should anyone be worried about me?" As Terri stared at her in horror, Henrietta smiled and replaced the rock on the desk. "This was quite heavy for a child, you know, but even then, I was strong for my age. Being female, everyone underestimated me from day one. It grew tiresome, but it also came in handy. I was above suspicion."

"Your father suspected you."

She laughed, eying the pages in Terri's hands. "Did he really? Good for him. I'd certainly given him enough hints. I'd wanted him to truly know me, to see me for who I am, but he always turned a blind eye. As did Mother."

"But I–I don't understand why you killed her. She was your sister."

"I wish you wouldn't remind me. That simpering, do–gooder fool. I was mortified to share the family name with her. Precious Emma, talented Emma." She scowled, remembering. "It was such a relief when she was gone. Niles was the one person in this house I could stomach."

She plucked the pages from Terri's nerveless fingers. "He killed Niles, didn't he?" She scanned her father's letter while Terri sat as if paralyzed, wondering what to do. Henrietta Vandermere was a murderer, but she was also a hundred years old. She couldn't honestly expect to restrain Terri, strong for her age or not. "Oh, Mother did too. Now *that* is a shock. I wouldn't have thought she had it in her.

"Ah, Niles. Such a delightfully twisted little thing he was. He made life interesting, but he didn't do a very good job of hiding his...tendencies. Not like me."

As Henrietta continued to scan the pages, Terri slowly rose from the chair. The elderly woman gave her a bemused look. "Now, where do you think you're going, dear? You know I can't let you leave."

"I'm afraid I can't finish this job, Miss Vandermere. I–I was going to tell you in the morning. I'll just get Dallas and we'll go. You don't have to worry about me saying anything."

"You're right, I don't," she said, pulling a pistol from her purse, "because no one is going to see you again. It'll be as if you were never here."

Cold dread seeped through Terri's body, paralyzing her once more. She'd never been on the wrong end of a gun before. *Dallas.* If she'd let her go with Derek, her child would have been safe. But who could have imagined this would happen? As Henrietta had said, she'd been underestimated – or misunderstood – her entire life. "My ex-husband, Derek, knows we're here. He's serving me with court papers. If I disappear, an alarm will be raised. He'll scour the country searching for Dallas. He'll never let it go."

"Hmm...." She pretended to look concerned. "I'm terribly sorry to be the bearer of bad news, but Derek met with a little accident this evening. If he survives, I don't believe he'll be in much shape to be searching for anyone."

"Derek?" Terri's knees weakened, and she clutched the desk for support, mind whirling. She'd wanted more than anything for something to erase him from her life, for a lightning bolt to shoot from the sky and release her from her misery. But now that he might be gone.... "But how? That's impossible."

"See? You're no different from the others. You underestimated me as well. No one expects a woman, especially a woman of my age, to be mechanically inclined, but I know *lots* of things I'm not supposed to. And, before you think of taking this gun from me, I can pull the trigger before you take more than a step."

Terri didn't doubt it. She wondered about all the other restorers who had abandoned the project. That curious comment Howard Vandermere had made. Had they really abandoned it, or were their bodies buried on the property? In the garden, where her daughter had been spending so much time? "Please let us go, Henrietta. I promise you, I won't breathe a word of any of it. No one would believe it anyway."

She smirked. "How dumb do you think I am? The second I let you go, you'd be phoning your charming little cop friend, bringing him here to arrest me."

"No one's going to put you in jail. I promise."

"Why, because I'm old? Because I'm a *lady*? I'm a murderer, Ms. Foxworth. They don't tend to let murderers walk free in this country." She laid her father's letter back on the desk, and then used both hands to hold the pistol steady. She cocked the gun, and at that ominous *click*, Terri's mouth went dry. "Not with such wonderful evidence. My father was too smart for his own good. I knew he'd hidden something somewhere, especially with Gertie tearing this place apart with all the subtlety of a deranged mountain lion."

Was this it? Was her life going to end here, in this hateful house? And what of Dallas? She could scream, yell, try to warn her, but the chances of her daughter hearing her were next to nil.

"I wasn't that worried, of course. I knew she would fail, as *I* had failed. No one knows this house better than me, and I couldn't find it…but a restorer, an expert in old houses like Glenvale…well, they might have a chance."

"If you weren't worried, why did you fire her?" Terri stalled for time, but she wasn't sure why. This wasn't one of her beloved movies. Officer Molloy wasn't going to burst through the door to rescue her. All she could do was postpone her own death, and for a matter of minutes at most.

Henrietta wrinkled her nose. "She irritated me. Always acting like she knew more than anyone else, always sneaking around thinking no one noticed what she was doing. Please. She knew nothing."

"She thought you killed Niles. And you know why? *Niles* told her so. He was the one pushing her to keep looking for proof. He was the one who told her about the cellar."

"Oh, so *that's* how she found my little hiding spot. I was wondering about that. I didn't suppose she was smart enough on her own. Pretty little thing, but she was standing behind the door when God handed out brains."

"*Your* hiding spot?" This kept getting worse and worse. Terri didn't want to hear anymore, couldn't hear anymore. The thought of this genteel woman, this woman with her pleasant smile, doing all those atrocious things....

"Yes, mine. You're doing it again — underestimating me. I told you, all the best ideas were mine. Niles tried to match my wickedness, but he didn't have it in him."

"I guess that's why he thought *you* killed him."

Something flickered across Henrietta's face, something Terri couldn't identify, but that gave her a spark of hope. If she could get to her, distract her long enough to disable her. Maintaining eye contact, she slowly felt the surface of the desk. Wasn't there a letter opener somewhere close by? She was sure there was. Or the Stanhope pen. That was sharp enough to do some damage.

"That was a ruse to lure Gertie to the cellar. He never believed that."

"If you loved him so much, why did you keep giving him candy? That easily could have killed him."

Henrietta smiled at the memory. It was a terrible sight. "I was a child, Ms. Foxworth. My brother loved sweets, and I loved my brother. Of course I brought him anything he wanted. How was I to know?

"Anyway, stop baiting me. I know what you're trying to do, and it won't work. Niles had to know it was Mother and Father who murdered him. He had to have seen them when they came into his room."

"Not necessarily. Not if he was asleep, and they put the pillow over his face quickly enough. He thought it was you."

Henrietta shook her head. "No, that can't be true. Why would I kill Niles? Niles was the one person I loved in this entire family."

But Terri could tell that wasn't true, either. She'd seen the woman's face as she'd read her father's letter. Henrietta had loved her father, and her realization that he'd known exactly what kind of person she was had pained her. For all her boasting, she hadn't wanted him to see the monster she was. "What about your father? You loved him."

"Loved him? I love him still. He should not have killed Niles for the things I'd done. That was foolish. But he was a good man."

"Maybe that's why Niles would never believe Howard killed him. He thought it was you. *You* were the murderer in the family."

Terri wasn't sure why, but hearing Niles had suspected her was the one thing that appeared to aggravate Henrietta. The gun lowered slightly. "It isn't true. He would never have believed that. We were thick as thieves. Two peas in a pod. I would never have hurt him. He *had* to know it was them. They were the ones who confined him to his room day and night. They were the ones who starved him. They were the ones who put the white knobs on his doors to let him know his place in the family, as if he were no better than a servant. They treated him as if he were less than human."

The woman made a strange face, and at first Terri thought it was in reaction to the thought of her brother blaming her for his death, but then she smelled it too.

Smoke.

"Do you smell that?"

"Henrietta...." Terri's eyes widened as she saw smoke, drifting like mist toward them from the hallway. It appeared like fog, and in seconds it had grown so thick that she could no longer see more than a foot or two outside the door. "The house is on fire! We have to get out."

"But how—" Squaring her shoulders, Henrietta raised the pistol. "It doesn't matter. This will make it easier to get rid of you."

This is it. Terri closed her eyes, waiting for the sound of gunfire, the last sound she would hear in her life. *I love you, Dallas. I wish I'd been a better mom.*

Instead, she heard coughing. She risked a look. Henrietta was doubled over, gasping and hacking. Smoke poured into the room, stinging Terri's eyes.

"Mom? Mom! Where are you?"

Dallas.

She could hear sirens in the distance, and that spark of hope returned. Perhaps she wasn't going to die here. Maybe she'd get a second chance.

As her coughing fit continued, Henrietta fought to hold the gun steady, but it was impossible. Her hands shook. Terri took a chance and dropped to the floor.

The gun went off, deafening her. Glass shattered, but she was still alive. She crawled toward the door, tears streaming from her eyes. Strong hands grasped her wrists, and she cried out. They yanked her from the room so fast she had no chance to look for Henrietta.

The unseen hands pulled her to the door, her sweater riding up around her breasts, the friction of the floor tugging painfully at her skin. Through the smoke, she could see the emaciated face of Niles. "Get out," he said. "Your daughter is already outside."

She didn't trust him, would never trust him, but what choice did she have? The door creaked open before she could touch it, and the cooler air was a benediction against her sweaty, burning face. The sirens were louder now.

"Mom!"

"Dallas?" Her eyes were too blurred with tears to see.

Arms lifted her, and a familiar voice spoke into her ear. "I've got you, Terri. Don't worry. You're safe now."

Safe.

"H-Henrietta Vandermere is in there. In her father's study." As Officer Molloy set her gently on the grass, and Dallas flung her arms around Terri's neck, she explained where the study was. He nodded, and left them.

"Mom, you're alive! I was so scared."

"W-what happened? Are you okay?"

Dallas bit her lip. Her beautiful face was streaked with soot. "Please don't be angry with me. It was an accident."

"*What* was an accident?"

"I swear I didn't mean to, Mom. I didn't mean to knock over the lamp."

"What lamp?" None of this made sense. Knocking over a lamp wouldn't have started this fire. Terri stared at the house, that gorgeous house. The entire first floor was engulfed in flames, and smoke billowed out of the second-floor windows. There was no way to save it now, even though firefighters had arrived and rushed toward the house, hoses in hand.

Glenvale would never be restored.

Her daughter clung to her neck, and Terri reached up to hold her hands. *Dallas.* She'd thought she'd never see her daughter again. And yet....

"Dallas, what's that smell?"

Her daughter drew back, widening her eyes in a pantomime of innocence. "What smell?"

"You reek of kerosene."

The feeling of cold dread returned. *Oh no...Dallas, what did you do?*

"I told Officer Molloy – it was an accident. I didn't mean to knock over the lamp. I swear I didn't."

But there hadn't been any kerosene lamps in the house. Had there?

"He told me I wouldn't go to jail. He *promised*. Not for an accident. They won't send me to jail, will they, Mom?"

"No, they won't send you to jail. It was an accident," Terri repeated, knowing it wasn't.

Together, they watched Glenvale burn.

EPILOGUE

She was grateful when the nice cop stopped coming around.

She liked him, and she wanted her mother to be happy, but in the end, it was for the best.

It was his eyes – the eyes that seemed to look through her, that saw through all her lies. The longer he looked at her, the closer he was to the truth. It had been a relief when her mom broke up with him. He was a great guy, but having him around brought up too many bad memories, she'd said.

That was truer than she realized.

How could Dallas ever tell him the truth? That a grandfatherly man had woken her up that night and shown her how to start the fire? He'd told her it was the only way to save her mother, the only way to stop Niles from hurting anyone else.

He'd been wrong about that.

The night after the fire, Dallas began having nightmares. Except she understood they weren't *really* nightmares. They were real.

Her mother kept begging her to tell her what was wrong. "Was it the fire?" she asked. "You can't keep blaming yourself for the fire. It was an accident."

But they both knew it hadn't been. Her mother wasn't dumb. She'd known there was no kerosene anywhere near Dallas's room. But for whatever reason, she'd let it go, and Dallas was grateful for that too. Maybe her mom didn't want to know the truth. If she let herself believe the fire had been an accident, she could look that nice cop in the eyes and let him take her out for dinner. Her mom was better off that way.

The truth haunted Dallas. She couldn't sleep, couldn't close her eyes without the nightmares finding her again. She had destroyed a beautiful old house, and killed a lady. Henrietta Vandermere had never made it out alive.

But someone else had.

Niles smiled at her, the skin pulling taut against his cheekbones. His head looked even more like a skull than usual. The horror of it made her want to scream, but she bit her lip and kept quiet. What else could she do? That sweet old man had been wrong, but that wasn't his fault. Everyone had been wrong about Niles.

He tapped her cheek playfully, the feel of his fingers like spiders crawling over her skin. "Wakey-wakey. You weren't sleeping, were you?"

Her mom had tried, really tried. Dallas knew she was desperate to do whatever she could to help. There had been a long line of psychologists, therapists she was well aware her mother couldn't afford. She'd had to leave the restoration business and work two jobs, just to pay for all those people who'd patted Dallas on the head and made her draw pictures and do puzzles and asked her about her feelings.

They treated her like a child.

Dallas may be eleven, but she wasn't a child. Not anymore.

The diagnosis, when it finally came, would have made her cry if it hadn't been so damn funny. *Post-traumatic stress disorder.*

She was eleven, but she understood what 'post' meant. Post meant it was over. Why didn't anyone see it? *None* of it was over.

It was only the beginning.

She'd known that from the moment Niles had appeared in her bedroom at her grandmother's house, thanking her for setting him free. Burning Glenvale hadn't stopped his evil, as the old man had promised. The house had kept Niles trapped like a giant cage, protecting everyone on the outside.

But now Glenvale was gone. All because of her.

If she hadn't set the fire, her mother would have died. Henrietta would have killed her for sure. She clung to that thought during those long, dark nights when she waited for Niles to visit her, but a part of her wondered if she'd been selfish. If she'd let her mother go, let Henrietta kill her too, would more people have lived? Would it have been worth it to keep the world safe from Niles?

She sighed. "No, Niles, you know I wasn't."

"Good. Perhaps we can go have some fun then."

Her eyes focused on his face. There were dark streaks on his cheeks and around his mouth. His teeth looked black when he smiled. She sat bolt upright in bed.

"You didn't go visit Gertrude again, did you?"

He smirked, curling a lock of her hair around his fingers, but she slapped his hand away, marveling at how it could feel so solid. "Maaaaayyybe."

"Niles! You promised you'd leave her alone." Dallas wanted to weep at the thought of what that poor woman had gone through, was still going through. Her mom had told her that Gertrude had been put away in some place for the mentally ill, that everyone thought she was crazy. Who would believe a deranged spirit was attacking her? Better to believe she was doing it to herself.

Dallas knew Gertrude wasn't crazy, but she was just a kid. Who was going to listen to her?

"I had my fingers crossed behind my back," he said, laughing. "Fooled you!"

"You *have* to leave her alone, Niles. You have to. Or I won't talk to you anymore."

His lower lip protruded. "Spoilsport."

Sometimes she thought of ending her own life. It was so tempting she'd thrown out the tie to her bathrobe, along with anything else in her room she could use to hang herself. She'd come too close too many times, felt the fabric cutting into her neck, her breath stopping.

But she couldn't do that to her mom. Terri needed her. Especially now that the nice cop was gone. It was the two of them again. They were a team. Thanks to Henrietta, even her dad wasn't around anymore.

There was another, bigger reason she didn't kill herself. A reason she didn't like to think about.

If Niles was this bad while she was alive, what would happen if she was dead? What if death wasn't an escape, but another trap, another nightmare she couldn't wake up from? Committing suicide was a sin, and she'd already committed the ultimate sin when she'd burned the house down and killed the old woman. She wouldn't be welcome in Heaven.

Best not to risk it. While she was alive, he listened to her. She was able to control him, to some extent.

Niles would stay young forever, while she'd get old and would eventually die anyway. But it was better not to think about that too much. Maybe by the time she was as old as Henrietta Vandermere, he'd lose interest in her. Or, maybe when she got older, she'd figure out a way to defeat him for good. Maybe someday that nice grandfatherly man would return and help her.

She could only hope.

"Do you want to play a game?"

"Sure, Niles. Let's play a game. Which one do you want, *The Game of Life*?"

He stuck his tongue out. "Nah, that's boring. I'm weary of that game. Let's go and hurt someone."

She folded her arms across her chest, fixing him with a stern look. "I've told you a hundred times. I'm *not* going to hurt anyone. Hurting people is bad."

"That is what you keep saying." He winked at her. "But eventually I'll wear you down and get what I want." His grin broadened, displaying teeth that were stained with poor Gertrude's blood.

"I always do."

AUTHOR'S NOTE

On September 13, 2019, I was one of four dark-fiction authors invited to spend the night at Dalnavert House, a heritage home in Winnipeg, Manitoba, Canada. Now operating as a museum, this extraordinary mansion is rumored to be haunted. We were allowed to roam freely through the house without supervision all night, and explore as much as we wished, in order to write stories inspired by our experience. These four stories were then published in a limited-edition chapbook.

During my stay, I opted to spend most of my time in Jack Macdonald's room. Jack had died in the room from complications of diabetes when he was still a young man, so I figured that if anything ghostly were to happen, it would happen there. I wasn't wrong, and I wrote about that eerie experience on my blog, www.jhmoncrieff.com/blog (search for the post "Overnight in a Haunted House"). Dalnavert House also has a wonderful virtual tour, if you'd like to 'visit' the real-life Glenvale. www.friendsofdalnavert.ca/virtual-tour.

While this is a work of fiction (the Macdonald family was *nothing* like the Vandermeres, and no slander is intended), this novel would not exist without the kindness of Thomas McLeod, former Executive Director of the Friends of Dalnavert Museum Inc., the Winnipeg International Writers Festival, the magnificent Dalnavert House, and the spirit of Jack Macdonald himself.

ACKNOWLEDGMENTS

Special thanks to the Friends of the Dalnavert Museum, notably former executive director Thomas McLeod and former curator Alexandra Kroeger. Your generosity with your time and allowing me so much access to the house made this novel possible.

Thank you to writer Jess Landry, who talked me into applying to the Winnipeg International Writers Festival's Fantasmagoriana program. This novel would not exist without her. A shout-out to the two writers we shared the experience with: Adam Petrash and Dave Demchuk.

I cannot fully express how grateful I am for my editor, Don D'Auria, who has championed my work from the beginning. I'm so happy to be working with him again, and to be published alongside many of the wonderful writers I began my career with. The title of editor doesn't do him justice – there are so many great writers who broke into the industry because of Don.

Thanks to the amazing team at Flame Tree Press, including Don, Nick Wells, Maria Tissot, Sarah Miniaci, Carole Rogers, and Jessica White. To all the readers and friends who continue to encourage my crazy writing dreams, especially Christine Brandt, Simon Fuller, Kimberly Yerina, Nikki Burch, Catherine Cavendish, Tara Clark, Kelli Lea, Lee Murray, R.J. Crowther Jr. from Mysterious Galaxy, John Toews from McNally Robinson Booksellers, Dana Krawchuk, Steve Stredulinsky, Erik Smith, Hunter Shea, Janine Pipe, JG Faherty, Russell R. James, Teel James Glenn, Jim Edwards, Lisa Saunders, Alex Cavanaugh, Toinette Thomas, Mary Aalgaard, and the phenomenal Insecure Writer's Support Group.

Thanks also to my parents, Gary and Shirley Moncrieff. And to my agent, Rosie Jonker, for talking me off the ledge and keeping me sane.

FLAME TREE PRESS
FICTION WITHOUT FRONTIERS
Award-Winning Authors & Original Voices

Flame Tree Press is the trade fiction imprint of Flame Tree Publishing, focusing on excellent writing in horror and the supernatural, crime and mystery, science fiction and fantasy. Our aim is to explore beyond the boundaries of the everyday, with tales from both award-winning authors and original voices.

•

Other titles available by J.H. Moncrieff:
Those Who Came Before

Other horror and suspense titles available include:
Snowball by Gregory Bastianelli
Thirteen Days by Sunset Beach by Ramsey Campbell
Think Yourself Lucky by Ramsey Campbell
The Hungry Moon by Ramsey Campbell
The Influence by Ramsey Campbell
The Wise Friend by Ramsey Campbell
Somebody's Voice by Ramsey Campbell
The Haunting of Henderson Close by Catherine Cavendish
The Garden of Bewitchment by Catherine Cavendish
The House by the Cemetery by John Everson
The Devil's Equinox by John Everson
Hellrider by JG Faherty
The Toy Thief by D.W. Gillespie
One By One by D.W. Gillespie
Black Wings by Megan Hart
The Playing Card Killer by Russell James
The Sorrows by Jonathan Janz
Will Haunt You by Brian Kirk
We Are Monsters by Brian Kirk
Hearthstone Cottage by Frazer Lee
Stoker's Wilde by Steven Hopstaken & Melissa Prusi
Creature by Hunter Shea
Slash by Hunter Shea
Ghost Mine by Hunter Shea
Misfits by Hunter Shea

•

Join our mailing list for free short stories, new release details, news about our authors and special promotions:

flametreepress.com